By Moonlight

By Moonlight

BY MOONLIGHT SERIES BOOK 1

CHELSEA BURTON DUNN

4 Horsemen
Publications, Inc.

DEDICATION

To my Mom and my Aunt Kay; I hope your reunion in the beyond was joyous. Save some margaritas for the rest of us when we get there. We miss you. We love you.

TABLE OF CONTENTS

 BY MOONLIGHT

CHAPTER I

It was a warm June day in Kansas City. Not so hot that it was unbearable, but the kind of perfect weather that had everyone opening their windows and doors. Door propping weather, which was exactly what most of the little shops on the Roanoke strip of Westport Road were doing including the little locksmith shop called, "The Missing Key."

Inside, thoroughly enjoying the breeze wafting through was the owner of that shop, Vee, fixing a safe for a client. She was secretly hoping a house call came through so she could put all the windows down in her lemon, a 1990 Chevy Lumina, and have a reason to get out of the shop. She was still in her twenties, nearing thirty, and she loved the simplicity of her little life. She had owned her own shop, manned it alone, lived alone, and liked it that way.

National talk radio was on in the background, giving the latest update on the deaths that had been seen popping up from New York all the way down and across to Illinois. Brutal killings that initially investigators had suspected were the work of some sort of rabid animal, but now that they had continued in a straight trajectory they were concerned it could be a human. Vee wasn't usually a fan of true crime, but something about this made her skin crawl more than normal.

Between the talk on the newest victim and the broken safe before her, she was zoning out. She pulled out parts and replaced them when suddenly there was a shadow over her work and a block to her breeze.

"Hello, Vee. It's nearly noon," came the familiar deep tone of her friend, Durran. She was her only friend, having met her when she first got back to the city as a customer in the restaurant she worked at. Like clockwork, Durran was there on Friday to take her… well, more like drag her, out to lunch. Vee looked up at her through the curtain of bangs that often obscured her large emerald eyes, her magnifiers down on the end of her nose.

"Just… let me…"

"It will be there at 12:30 when you come back," Durran said, raising one of her black, unruly eyebrows at her.

Vee rolled her eyes, putting down her tools and feigning irritation. She turned her answering machine to the lunch recording, switched off the radio, and grabbed her messenger bag, heading to the open door to lock up. Despite the nice weather, she still dressed in overly large clothes, mostly in grey. She didn't like getting attention, and though she never put much thought into her petite body, she was also female. She, unfortunately, knew more about what went on in the heads of men than the average person, causing not-so-unfounded doubts. Not that those doubts weren't justified. Hence why she tried to cover up. If it was hard to see, it was hard to fantasize about, right?

There were so many restaurants in the Westport neighborhood, so it wasn't a far walk to any of them, but like usual, they settled for one of the Mexican restaurants just down the street from her shop. She often felt paranoid about leaving longer than the thirty-minute interval she set on her door sign and voice message. She didn't want to scare off any potential customers.

"So, what's the schedule like for today?" Durran asked while she held the door open to the restaurant she had selected. Over the years, Durran had stopped letting Vee have input on the lunch decision, since she could never make up her mind.

"Repairing that old safe and I have some padlocks that I need to finish up. The heart-shaped ones seem to be the best sellers for some reason," Vee told her, glancing over the menu, even though she knew exactly what she was going to order.

"Yes, for some reason people gravitate toward heart-shaped locks and keys… I wonder why," Durran said sarcastically, rolling her eyes as dramatically as possible.

Vee narrowed her eyes at her friend from across the table, but was momentarily saved from their conversation as their server happened to come by to set down chips and salsa before them.

"You know, you could make it a full hour since you own the place… or even hire a part-time employee?" Durran suggested, as she had many times before. Vee knew she was just looking out for her well-being, Durran thought she was overworked, but Vee didn't want to miss the business. Honestly, she felt like she was barely holding on financially. She couldn't afford to take time off or have extended lunch hours, let alone pay another employee.

"Employee means money. Did I miss the line of customers and overly filled voicemail back at the shop?" she asked sarcastically, munching loudly on a chip.

"You shouldn't work yourself so hard. It's okay to have a life too."

To that she scoffed. Saying things like "it's okay to have a life" suggested that she didn't already have one. She was comfortable with her little routine and, quite frankly, so was Durran. She would stop by at least once a day and on Fridays for lunch. What would she do if Vee wasn't available whenever she wanted to drop in?

"So, you're keeping up with that story?" Durran asked, changing the subject abruptly and lacing her fingers together before her. She looked questioningly at Vee as she referred to the radio program that had been on in the shop.

"It's just a little strange. Figured I should stay in the know," Vee said, shrugging.

The overly cheerful server came back to take their orders, before Durran could ask any more questions about Vee's sudden true crime interest, and Vee cringed a little when the poor girl talked. Just a little cringe that only someone who knew Vee could spot, but Durran certainly knew her.

"People put on fake emotions all the time, Vee. I feel like you should be used to that," she said once the server left, watching Vee's shoulders rise with tension ever so slightly.

"Not usually this bad," she murmured, snapping a chip that she had been scooping salsa with, and mournfully watched the chip piece get consumed by the spicy red goodness.

"It is the first full moon tonight," Durran said, trying to be nonchalant, but it wasn't really working. The three nights surrounding the full moon, brought out a lot of, let's say, interesting behavior.

"Well, crap… late night at the shop isn't going to work tonight then," she grumbled, managing to scoop the drown piece with another chip.

"No, it's best you get home before sundown. I have a bad feeling."

Unfortunately, Durran's bad feelings usually turned out to be true. Vee did have quite a few orders to finish up for tomorrow, but they would have to wait. It would have to be an early morning at the shop instead of a late night.

As they walked back, her work cell buzzed in her pocket, and Durran grabbed it before Vee could, making her narrow her eyes as she tried to swipe it back out of Durran's grip.

"It's not 12:30 yet," Durran said, chuckling at her frustration.

"House call!" Vee snapped, snatching the phone from her hand and swiping hastily to answer. "The Missing Key, locksmith and repairs. How can I help you?" she said, her voice strictly professional, but not that high-pitched-fake-happy tone some people take on when talking to customers, like their server for example. Vee never understood why any customer would take that as genuine.

She did have a slight advantage to seeing through these social lies, however.

She was an Empath, capable of feeling others' emotions.

So, while the server had put on a very fake tone of voice and smile, Vee could also feel how much she had hated doing it. The resentment seeped from the girl like poisonous gas, and since the three nights of the full moon were starting, Vee was a little more sensitive than usual.

The customer on the phone didn't seem to care that Vee made no attempts at being overly friendly though. They were clearly more concerned about the fact that they were locked out of their house and their car.

Rushing inside her shop, Durran in tow, she scribbled the name of the customer and the address and gave an approximate time of arrival before hanging up and switching the voicemail message from the "lunch" to the "house call" recording.

"I have work to do, otherwise I'd watch the shop for you," Durran said, half joking as they both walked out the door, Vee quickly locking it behind them.

"Don't you have wards that need watching instead of my tiny lock shop?" Vee asked, playing into the joke as she walked to her car.

"The only reason I can't!" Durran hollered back to her, waving from the sidewalk.

Along with being an empath, Vee could *sense* the presence of *others*, beings that were not human. They had a different feel in her brain. When she was a teenager, she learned about what different types of preternatural beings were and how they felt inside her head.

Durran was no human. She was a Watcher. It's hard to describe what a Watcher is exactly. They were some of the most powerful and oldest beings that walked this plane. Watchers had a ward, sometimes two, that they oversaw and assured no harm came to them. Usually, the ward was chosen because they were thought to be of some importance in the future. They were not only incredibly powerful beings but also extremely secretive. The little information that Vee knew about them was more than many others had. From what she had gleaned, even some other types of preternaturals didn't know if Watchers were real.

As Vee drove to the house on Morningside Drive, she considered what Durran must do every day. Obviously, she would take breaks from whomever she was charged with watching to come by and see her. She wondered if she was Durran's only friend like she was hers.

Morningside was one of those strange streets in the city that decided to be different. Most streets and neighborhoods were a carefully planned grid of blocks, but no, not Morningside. A very rich man by the name

JC Nichols owned the property formally known as Brookside and had his friend, Fletcher Cowhert create the exceptionally wide luxurious street. The homes were large, not mansions, but quite massive from Vee's modest view. Her entire one-bedroom apartment would fit inside one of the kitchens of these houses.

She pulled up to the address and found a distraught woman pacing outside her house. She was dressed nicely, a blue, silk top that accentuated her bright, blue eyes, tucked into linen pants, as if she had just come from her office job for lunch and when the mistake had been made.

"Hello, I'm Vee, your locksmith," Vee said in greeting as she got out of the car. She had helped this woman, Cora Byers, many times, but she always felt the need to reintroduce herself. In her opinion, she wasn't a particularly memorable person, or she certainly tried not to be, so it shocked her a little when Cora's face turned to a familiar smile.

"Oh my god! Thank you so much! I feel like we call you all the time, and you're always so quick. I just moved too fast for my brain to keep up. Our back door has a knob lock that I usually use when I'm trying to leave in a hurry. Well, I hurried out so fast I left my keys on the counter of the kitchen. And this is *really* not the day for this," she said, speaking very quickly, her curtain of blond hair whipping around as she walked toward the back of the house to show Vee the door in question.

The house was, as most of them were in that neighborhood, a center hall-style colonial. The basic plan of a colonial was a two- or three-story rectangle with the rooms flanking a centralized hallway. Vee couldn't help but marvel at the perfection of the side of the house. It was one thing to have your front yard manicured, but it was quite another to have the side of your house also beautifully landscaped with plants edging the driveway. Even the paint was immaculate.

"This one," Cora said, gesturing to the back door.

Now that she was in front of it, looking at the knob and lock, Vee felt that this particular lock was very familiar. Not that there weren't plenty of locks that looked similar, but this one she knew like she had repaired it once before. She felt bad when she didn't always remember the exact situation she had dealt with when helping a repeat client.

"Not a problem. I'll pick it quickly, if you'll show me your ID, so I can assure you aren't trying to rob the place," Vee said with a wink.

"Oh! Of course!" Cora said, rummaging through her purse for her wallet and pulling out her driver's license. Vee was not surprised that the driver's license photo was one to envy. Cora happened to be one of the few people who actually looked good in hers.

"Perfect. Just give me a few minutes..." Vee said, pulling her tools from her bag and looking the lock over.

Yes, this was definitely the same lock she had repaired, and this was definitely a house with something *other* living here. Not Cora, though. That woman was completely human. She tried to recall which kind lived here. Werewolves? Had to be. This whole neighborhood had them dotted here and there. The pack leader must live nearby to have so many in such a small radius.

She made quick work of it, picking the lock and making a few tightening adjustments as Cora ran in and grabbed her keys from the very lovely kitchen counter. It was all quartz counters and delicate white tiles, clean as a whistle and shining. It could have been ripped right out of a magazine. Vee felt dirty just standing in that room.

"Oh, thank you so much! I don't know what I would have done. The run is tonight… I have so many things to get for the pa—" Cora nearly choked on her words. Vee felt the anxiety burst out of the woman in waves. She messed up, and any other person would probably question what she stopped short of saying, but luckily, she had Vee. She knew Cora was going to say "pack," but Vee didn't need to be asking questions she already knew the answers to. That would only bring unwanted attention her way.

"Not to worry. I was looking for an excuse to get out of my shop and into this beautiful weather," Vee said quickly, making it as if there were no secrets almost revealed or awkward, anxiety-filled pauses. Vee didn't want to be revealed herself let alone get tangled in something with werewolves.

Cora paid Vee via check, thanked her again profusely, and hastily pulled out of the driveway and out of sight, southward bound for the grocery store, Vee imagined.

She sat in front of the house, looking around the street for a moment. When she had made other house calls on this street, and in this neighborhood before, she had realized several of them were werewolves at the time and kept her head down. No one had ever suspected that she was something *other* save for Durran. Anyone else who had ever known was because she revealed it to them.

They say it's a small world, and Kansas City was certainly an incestuous city. There were connections everywhere. She knew that when she came back. Sometimes that knowledge worried her, that she would be found out, with all the preternaturals in the area. There were territories, nests, and districts of all kinds hidden right before the human's very eyes. It was a wonder that the humans seemed blinded to it all.

At that thought, she shook her head and smiled, momentarily considering herself not human. She was human, or human enough, for other preternaturals to not give her a second thought.

As she started her car, she noticed a man come out of one of the houses across the street. He had clearly come out to greet the person in the car that had just pulled into his driveway. He was tall, broad, olive-skinned, and dressed in slacks and a button-down shirt. She could tell he was well-muscled underneath the clothes, which seemed to be tailored specifically for him. His hair was slightly salt and pepper by his temples, but mostly a deep, dark brown that was nearly black.

She had never seen him at that house before, but she knew she had also worked on those locks before. This pack, she decided, seemed to need replacements and repairs on both house and car parts on a regular basis. But it was usually someone else that called on her; she had never seen him, but she felt his power. Just the way he stood there, talking to the equally large man who had gotten out of the car, he owned that home. It was his property.

She rolled her eyes at him, and her own reaction to seeing him as she drove away. Yes, he was attractive. Yes, she had been to that home. But she didn't need to be ogling the man or wondering about him. He was clearly out of her league for many reasons. One being, he was very much a werewolf.

She already got close to them often enough with their regular need of her services.

She was just lonely.

No need to be looking him up and down.

She sighed as she pulled back up to her shop. It was the first full moon of the summer in Westport. Unless she had walk-ins for custom pieces or a key duplication, she doubted she would get much business for the last few hours of the day. Although, she would most likely have plenty of house calls tomorrow when people realized they lost their keys at the bar that night.

She walked back in after unlocking, switching the sign to "Open" from "Be Back Soon - On a House Call." She glanced at the little mail drop to see if anyone had left anything before changing the shop voicemail back to ring.

After setting her bag down, she looked again at the projects she had been working on prior to her lunch with Durran. She was nearly done with the safe repair. Of course, she had more of those heart locks to complete, and the other was a restoration of a lock from one of the historic homes in the area. These were some of her favorites to work on. Restoring old locks from hundred-year-old homes so they could go back where they belonged and be used for a hundred years more. There was something magical about that.

Many locksmiths only replaced, not really repaired or restored. The number of people who would go out of their way to insure they could keep an original lock was always surprising to her.

Donning her magnifiers, she settled in to finish the safe. The last of the afternoon flew by, only a few window shoppers came in to peek at some of the things she had on display. Since she was planning on making a few more, she had recently put out her display heart padlocks again. They looked old and weathered. The perfect size for locking a chest, like from a fairy tale.

As she cleaned up for the night and balanced her register, she somehow got lost in the thought of fairy tales. It amused her that so many of them actually held truth. She would have never known when she was small and her mother read them to her that the fairies, witches, and other monsters in those books actually lived amongst them.

Vee had started her life fairly normally. She had two loving parents and a sister, Eliza, but she always felt like something was not right, something was different. Her sister would tease her that she was adopted or tell her she was too weird to ever be accepted into normal society. Despite her sister's obvious mixed feelings toward her, when tragedy struck their home, Eliza did the right thing.

Vee was not quite ten when her parents died. The nature of their deaths was kept from her, but from what she gathered, it was horrific. Eliza had just graduated high school and took the responsibility of raising Vee herself. While the sacrifice was great, and Vee appreciated it, there were obvious problems. Eliza clearly blamed Vee for their misfortunes, whether warranted or not.

"Eliza, the lights don't work," a little Vee said, wandering into living room where her sister usually fell asleep.

"Yes, because you needed to get new shoes; that's why the lights don't work!" Eliza would snap, malice thick in her voice as she used a flashlight to look over bills.

"But they wouldn't let me wear them to school anymore! The sole was falling off!" Vee said, trying to fight back tears.

"You shouldn't run around so much and wear them down, then" was all Eliza said.

It was those moments and the overwhelming emotions she felt from her sister that finally built up enough guilt to force Vee to leave. She knew that if she was gone her sister would move on to something better for herself and maybe Vee could too.

She left Kansas City and managed to get to St. Louis. She stayed hidden with a small, unlikely group of friends she made there. They finished school together, watched out for each other, and taught her more about herself and the world than she had ever known before. Unfortunately, that time became a black mark in her heart too when her new, little family fell apart as well.

She escaped back to Kansas City and tried to make something out of herself. Her first job had been a little breakfast restaurant in Westport, just a few blocks from where her shop was now. She didn't make much money there, but she scrimped and saved enough to get training on becoming a locksmith. Her frugality paid off when she eventually got to open her own business.

She accomplished a lot, with no upsetting mishaps, in the ten years she spent alone than she had ever been able to do before. So, she decided she was just a person who needed to be that way. She needed solitude to survive.

She supposed she was thankful for the first ten years she had with her parents. Even for the short time she had and remembered them, her mother ignited her imagination and encouraged her empathetic gifts, even if she scared them a little. Her mother, Sarah, had been a far cry from Eliza's parenting since Vee was only ever admonished at the mere mention of her abilities.

It made Vee wonder about Eliza's daughter. Very rarely did Vee see her sister, let alone her little family. When Vee moved back to Kansas City, Eliza was already married and wanted nothing to do with her. She could respect that, having felt like she was a burden to her sister despite not meaning to be. Vee stayed away. She stayed in her lonesome existence since she felt like every relationship she touched turned to ashes. Just her presence destroyed the people around her.

The only times she ever saw Eliza were when she would randomly stop by the shop. It was usually for something dumb. She needed a spare key for her car. She "found" something in storage that was Vee's from her teenage years and didn't want it taking up space in her home anymore. The visits always seemed strange and unnecessary, especially considering it was a bit out of Eliza's way to get to her shop.

Vee continued thinking about her sister as she walked to her car. She patted the hood as she climbed in, babying it as much as she could, hoping that would keep it going for a little while longer. She was saving to replace it with something that was a bit more practical and reliable for work, and she was very nearly there. She estimated, given no unforeseen mishaps, she'd have enough for a decent vehicle by August.

She drove through the side streets, avoiding the main thoroughfares of Midtown, as they were already overcrowded with the Friday night traffic. Everyone wanted to drink away their problems after a week at work. She couldn't sympathize, mostly because her work was her life.

She shook her head as she arrived back at her apartment, shooing away the thoughts of her sister and the little, intrusive thoughts of the werewolf she had seen earlier in the day from her mind. She had to get back to her own reality. She was meant to be alone.

CHAPTER 2

S hane crossed the street, heading to Thomas's house. It was customary that the pack meet at the leader of the run's house prior to heading out. There weren't any newly turned Weres to worry about, so they could leave a little later and start the three-day run whenever they wanted. This weekend, however, Shane would not be joining, hence why he wasn't hosting. Normally, being the leader of the pack, he would have them all over to his house, and they would go from there onto the Ozark wilderness, but he had to begin the process of changing his job. It was important to start "fresh" with a new company. It had to be done every so often when you simply do not age like the humans around you.

As he went through the back door and into the kitchen he got a familiar scent. Clearly a woman, she smelled like a human… mostly. There was something a little extra there, but he couldn't quite put his finger on it. Somehow she smelled more appealing than any human woman he had ever smelled. He had noticed the scent many times before, at the other pack members' homes as well as his own, yet he could never place the smell with a person. Something always ended up distracting him from really investigating where it came from. He had never met a person with a scent like this.

Cora, Thomas's human wife, was still in the kitchen with several of the pack members getting serving platters ready and sending people out with them to set out at the dining room table for everyone to munch on. Lori, her daughter, was by her side not exactly helping since she had clearly just been complaining to her mother.

"No, Lori! I'm sorry. I understand you want to go over to Morgan's house this weekend, but I already told my sister we would be staying with her."

"Why do I have to go with you to Aunt Ava's? I'm in high school now, Mom! I should be able to hang out with my friends!" Lori whined, crossing her arms with disdain. Shane smiled as he moved a little further into the room, so they noticed him.

"Oh! Shane! I'm so sorry…" Cora started, shooting a glare toward her daughter.

"Never mind me; I also have a teenager. I understand," he said, smirking as he moved to grab a glass from the cabinet.

Lori rolled her eyes at them and decided to make a not-so-subtle exit, he assumed, back to her room. Normally he wouldn't interject in the more human side of his pack members' lives, but having a son only a year older than Lori, he couldn't help himself.

"What's the harm in letting her stay at her friend's this weekend? It's not like she's going to change. She gets to be human. Let her have that," he said quietly, making Cora turn and look at him. His eyes were sincere, and there was a little pain there too. She could tell he wished he could send his son, Patrick, off to a friend's house instead of going on the run with the rest of the pack. As with most males born from a werewolf… he didn't have the luxuries of living a normal human life.

"Maybe I will. I just don't want her getting into trouble," Cora whispered as she continued to stack sandwiches onto the plate in front of her.

He nodded, taking a moment to listen to his pack in the other rooms, chatting and laughing. Plenty of stories from other runs to reminisce about. He glanced over at the door that he apparently hadn't closed all the way. A breeze blew it open a little more and the smell of the unknown woman again wafted his way.

"Cora… was someone here earlier today?" he asked, keeping his eyes firmly planted on the door. She turned to set the platter on the buffet ledge for someone else to take into the dining room but followed where he was watching.

"Oh… yes. That locksmith came by again. I locked my keys in the house right before I was heading to the grocery store. She saved me from losing my mind today."

Shane's eyes narrowed.

"Locksmith?"

"Yes, um… what's it called… *The Missing Key*? I think the whole pack started using her a few months ago," she said, now taking an empty dish that had been set down as the sandwich plate was swiftly taken away.

"And she's trustworthy?" he asked. There was always the worry about the preternatural world being exposed to the humans, especially as time and technology advanced. More precautions had to be made. Often that meant not using the same service more than once, if it could be helped, and knowing now that he had most certainly smelled this individual before, in fact many times over, he didn't need anyone catching on. He didn't need their secrets exposed. It wasn't just about him, or even his pack. It was about the whole of the community.

"I don't think she knows a thing, like most people, Shane. From what she's told me before, she owns the shop and works alone. The bigger corporate locksmiths track things. I think Margaret and I found her and have been using her ever since."

"You all know we can't do that. We can't be using the same person or same service too much…" he said very quietly, his voice filled with warning. Cora hung her head a little, sheepishly.

"I really don't think…"

"No. No more. Use someone else next time," he said, his words not harsh or cruel, but definitely a demand. Cora wasn't a werewolf, but as the wife of a member, she was part of the pack, and that meant following Shane's orders.

"Of course," she said, not meeting his eye.

Patrick came in at that moment, sheer excitement oozing from every ounce of him. Patrick looked so much like his father; the only hint they were not the same person was his youthful appearance of a teenager. Since his change last year, he had never been on a run without his father, and although it caused his heart to twinge a little to miss any moment like this with his son, Shane knew it was good for him to get out from under his shadow.

"Dad, Tommy said he'd take me to the caves." Patrick grinned eagerly. Each time they had gone out Shane had made it a point that they would not be going to the caves. It was too easy to get lost, and with Patrick having only ever changed with the moon up until recently, he hadn't been using enough of his human brain to be permitted to explore.

"You're lucky you've finally gotten control of your wolf; otherwise, with talk like that, I wouldn't even let you go," Shane said seriously, raising his eyebrow at his young son, whose expression turned chagrined.

"We won't go far, just enough for him to get a little worried," Tommy said, entering the kitchen with a playful grin and kissing his mom on the cheek. Tommy was Thomas and Cora's oldest. He, like his little sister, took much more after his father. He was tall and broad, with light brown skin, only a few shades lighter than his father's. The only hint of his mother in his features was the more Anglo look to his nose. He had just moved out on his own, and was, by far, the goofiest of the pack. It had taken him quite a while to gain control of his own wolf, but it could have been because he, himself, was a wild and playful spirit. His wolf followed suit.

Along with Shane's main job as a financial advisor, he also ran a security company. Almost all the members of the pack where under his employ, mostly to give them freedom when he needed them to watch someone or patrol the territory. It was hard to explain to a human boss that you had to take a week off on a regular basis because it was your turn for patrols, or another pack leader was coming into town, and you had to be present at a meeting on short notice.

They also worked human events depending on the duration. They never held contracts that lasted more than a few days. Long-term contracts almost always interfered with pack business. Tommy was probably his most used employee. Thomas and his son were some of the most physically intimidating in the pack in their human forms based on size alone, and Shane liked to use that when the need arose. Tommy's playfulness didn't often get in the way of his duty.

"Are you sure you can't come, Dad?" Patrick said, his voice bringing Shane back to the strange feeling he had toward the beginning of the day. He felt like something had shifted. That a change was coming, but he couldn't quite place his finger on it. Obviously, the actual moon change was upon them, and they all felt that familiar vibration in the air, as their wolves were called to it. This feeling of change was something greater than that though.

He only had this sort of feeling a few times before, and it usually was followed with some huge upset that turned everything on its head. He was hoping staying in the city wasn't a mistake, but he had to take care of his job situation, and he just… *knew,* somehow, he wasn't meant to be going on the run.

"I have to get that changed over today, son. We don't need the people at the company to catch on to anything different about me."

When one starts getting comments like, "You seem so young for your age!" or "You don't look a day over 30." When you are, on paper, supposed to be closer to your fifties, it's time to head to another company. His plan was to start his own financial company to avoid having to do this whole process again for quite a while, but like most things, it takes time to get that groundwork laid out. Unfortunately, he only had the course of a weekend to get the finishing touches done.

"I'm going to grab a few things to eat before I head back over to the house. Cora, thank you so much for hosting. I know it's not ideal to have them all over here at once," Shane said, smiling in the hope that he would put her more at ease since their previous conversation. She smiled back, though clearly still feeling guilty about potentially putting the pack, and by extension her family, at risk by using the same locksmith too many times. It was difficult being a human companion to a wolf in a pack. Shane tried to be respectful of that.

He moved into the dining room and was completely horrified at the scene before him. As if they were, in fact, wild animals, the pack was standing everywhere, food and dishes strewn about and placed precariously atop surfaces.

"What is this?" he growled, causing them all to quiet down and look over at him. Apparently, most of the lower ranks didn't expect him to be showing up, since they decided to treat this like a party, instead of a dinner before departing. "You can all act like animals when you get to the woods, but you better start cleaning up after yourselves. You aren't leaving this mess for Cora to clean up after she spent all day getting this ready for all of you!" he yelled.

Without another sound they, seemingly in unison, moved to clean up after themselves. Patrick even went to grab a broom and began to sweep up the remnants of a plastic chip bowl that had toppled off the table. Nothing had been broken, but Shane never failed to feel like he had to be everyone's father, not just their leader.

Thomas caught his eye from the living room and gestured for him to come over. Earlier in the day, they had met to discuss the murders that had been steadily breadcrumbed to the most western part of Illinois. It was nearly to Missouri, whatever the creature was. These killings could not have been human. They were brutal and animalistic.

Shane had asked Thomas to look into it, to reach out to other packs, and to see what they had discovered. It was clearly heading toward them, whatever it was.

"Dante's second said it smelled of a Were when he sent scouts to investigate the latest victim," Thomas told him, his voice low to not attract attention from the rest of the pack. Dante was the St. Louis's pack leader, though his territory stretched into the lower half of Illinois instead of into Missouri where Shane's territory was. Dante was an old, brutish wolf that ran his pack more like a mob syndicate and less like a family, the way Shane liked to.

"So, it's a rogue, lone wolf then," Shane said as confirmation. He took a deep breath. This would have to be dealt with soon. He hoped that Dante's pack would be able to track it down before it crossed into his state, but he wasn't counting on it.

They had been quite fortunate for the last decade. Very little preternatural upheaval had been happening. As the years had gone on it had almost made Shane more nervous. Long periods of quiet made for long periods of chaos. He wasn't looking forward to whatever was to come.

"How long do you think we have? It's only four and a half hours from the last attack to our city," Thomas asked, glancing at the room full of pack members eager for their rendezvous through the woods. Shane followed his gaze, looking at Patrick and Tommy laughing. That excitement was soon to be dashed when they realized there was a threat.

"Whoever it is, they have lulls between killings… I imagine the full moon will keep them there for a few days," Shane murmured. He was worried of course. He'd be the only pack member in the city over the weekend, and while he was strong, he would want the backup if the wolf made its way there.

"I'll go tonight and leave Margaret in charge after," Thomas said, having watched his leader's face change.

"That might be for the best," Shane admitted, clapping Thomas on the shoulder and giving him a weak smile.

"I heard my name," Margaret said, as she leaned against the archway. "Changing the plans as usual?" Both men laughed a little.

"Of course, we are," Thomas said, eyes sparkling with amusement.

"The killer is a Were," Shane said, letting the realization settle over Margaret for a moment. "It's right outside St. Louis now. Thomas will be coming back tomorrow night just in case we run into problems."

Margaret nodded, taking this information in. She would be in charge of the run for the final day. Margaret was unusually dominant for a female wolf, and her human appearance showed it. She wasn't tall, quite average height, but she was sturdy; her muscles could have rivaled Shane's. Her hair was a curly mass that hung past her shoulders, but she usually tied it back. Her blue eyes tightened with the information, but she kept the rest of her face stoic.

"Of course, you leave me with the hardest day of the run, Thomas. Getting them to come home," she joked, shoving his shoulder a little, but the edge to her voice wasn't as humorous as she had wanted it to sound. The threat was very real.

"Whoever the killer is may be passing somewhat close to the Ozarks on their way, so you'll have to be vigilant on that last day," Shane said, obliterating the minuscule amount of lightheartedness that Margaret had been trying to keep alive.

"Absolutely," she said, hanging her head. "Do we tell them?" she asked, looking out over at the pack.

"Only when it's necessary, but you two should make sure the patrolling members are in pairs this time," Shane told them, continuing to watch his son. His heart ached a little at the thought that his young son, just barely in control of his wolf, might have his first run without his father be ruined by the likes of a rogue. Patrick wasn't helpless, he was a werewolf, but he was also his father's son, having been trained to defend himself, if not fight, when necessary. But he was still a boy.

"Tommy won't leave his side, Shane," Thomas said quietly, watching Shane's gaze. Shane nodded to Thomas in appreciation.

He bid them all farewell after making sure they had actually cleaned up to his satisfaction and headed back to his house as the cars started pulling away to head down to the Ozarks.

That nagging feeling of change was still there, the unease of this rogue Were was increasingly worrisome, and the thoughts of that locksmith lingered in the back of his head, especially after he considered how many times he had smelled her in his own home before. But he had to put that out of his mind. He had to complete his paperwork.

Once it was done, he could go back to worrying about all the things he couldn't control.

CHAPTER 3

Vee pulled up to her apartment building. It was going to be a sauna in there, especially given how humid it had become over the course of the day. She took in the clear sky that was just barely starting to turn for the sunset. The summer sun was always taking its time to rest. As she got closer to her building, she felt the familiar hum of her neighbors. It seemed like many of them were choosing to stay in tonight as well.

She didn't mind her neighbors most of the time. She had gotten used to their presence, and for whatever reason, she had been fortunate to have picked the most subdued building in the area. No one who lived there had particularly interesting lives. That wasn't to say they weren't happy, but they all went to work, came home, and occasionally, had depression or were lonely, but then again, so was Vee. She appreciated that she wasn't overwhelmed by them and that she could go on living her life, however boring it might be.

She was getting into her building when her neighbor's cat trotted up beside her.

"Well, hello," Vee said, bending down to pet the sweet girl. Una lived down a floor and across the hall from Vee, but she was probably the only person in the building that Vee ever actually interacted with. Mostly because of the cat.

Midi, the cat, was an escape artist. She would find her way outside more often than not and somehow, she always showed back up when Vee was coming home. It wasn't every day, but usually on days when Vee was feeling particularly strange. She actively tried not to read into things, but she had always felt that cats were very sensitive to emotions, like her. Perhaps Midi felt that connection and was waiting for Vee to come home for the night, to keep her safe.

"Let's get you back to your mama," Vee said, scooping her up with one hand as she unlocked the door and went inside.

She walked up the stairs, stopping on the second floor and knocking lightly on Una's door. She knew Una was home, of course, but had learned over the years that she had to be more subtle, and hesitant, to make it appear she wasn't aware of their presence beforehand. People got uncomfortable when she didn't pretend to be like them.

"Una? You home?" Vee said to the door, listening as she heard her neighbor's footfalls crossing the apartment.

"Vee?" Una asked, as she started unlocking her door.

Vee grinned holding Midi up as Una's face appeared.

"I guess I should have known," Una said, giving an exasperated look to her cat as she took her from Vee's arms. Midi didn't fight the exchange, she simply happily snuggled into her human mom's arms. "She seems to find you on the most interesting nights, doesn't she?"

"The full moon will do that," Vee chuckled, giving Midi a final scratch on the top of her ears. "Hopefully she doesn't wander out again tomorrow!"

"Thanks, Vee!" Una said, closing the door as Vee went back to the stairs.

As she walked through her door, she couldn't help but wonder about what was so interesting about this day. Nothing really of note happened. Vee had the house call to Cora's house, but nothing was strange about it. She had been there many times before for similar circumstances. Cora and Vee had both played off the little verbal stumble and simply moved on. There was no big upset, no clear moment to change things, to set things in motion from that.

But now that she started on that thought path, she couldn't help but feel that something *was* shifting. Something was changing. She furrowed her brow and tried to reason away the feeling as she dumped her bag on one of the futons in her front room and headed toward the kitchen to see about making something to eat.

Well, one thing she had forgotten about was how absolutely little food she had left in her house. She had exactly one tortilla, a few slices of cheese, a tiny bit of yogurt and granola left, and a dribble of milk.

She looked at her counter and remembered the "list" she had started that morning. It was nothing more than a scrap of paper with the word "Groceries" written on the top. She had abandoned the idea when she felt like she was taking too long to get to her shop. Sometimes her hastiness to get to work did not work in her favor. She hated to admit that Durran was right. Vee did tend to overwork herself, even forgetting basic things, like going to the grocery store. Durran had clearly won that particular argument, even if she didn't know it.

Vee started writing out all the groceries she would need while she made herself a crude quesadilla for dinner. If it hadn't been past 6 p.m. already, she would have ordered something to be delivered, but it was far too late on a Friday to expect any food before midnight at this point.

She abandoned her list again when her quesadilla was ready, trying to distract herself from the now nagging feeling she had. She had felt it before, a few different times: once when her parents died and once when her little group of friends were about to go their separate ways in St. Louis.

Change.

It was as if fate itself was putting it into the air. It made goosebumps rise over her skin. She didn't want changes. She didn't need changes. She thought about what her life was and decided she was perfectly content to continue that way forever. She wanted to be safe, and that's what she had been for the last ten years. Safe and alone.

She turned on the television; the news was on, covering the murders that had been going across the country again.

"We're finally getting more intel about the most recent murder. As we mentioned this morning, just outside of Greenville, Illinois they discovered the body of a woman, between the ages of twenty-five and thirty years of age. She still has not been identified, but missing person reports are being reviewed. Like the others, she was found in a nearby wooded area. Police are still unsure if this is simply a rabid animal or a person with the help of a dog. The victims have all been about the same age, gender, and sex…"

Vee glanced up. The shiver down her spine felt more pronounced. That creature was crawling across the country murdering women in her age range by horrible violent means. There was so little information about the women that were the victims other than their age. Who were they? Where did they live? Who was missing them?

Was she safe in the city?

Her eyes glazed over thinking about it.

It had to be a Were of some kind. The modus operandi was too specific for it to be wild animal attacks, and the nature of the brutality was too animalistic and carnal to have been done by a mere human.

The news story changed to something else and did not even register as she became lost in thought. The idea of this being a Were of some kind was extremely concerning, especially given how much recent contact she had had with their kind.

What change was coming?

Why were the werewolves calling on her so often?

Why did Durran seem to be coming around more than usual?

What was happening?

She thought about the Were she had seen when she left Cora's house that afternoon, recalling that she just *felt* he was the owner of the house he was standing in front of. She had never quite had a feeling like that about anyone before. She felt their emotions, sometimes their intentions, and occasionally, she could see their imaginings. What she got from him was different, she could feel his power, which was strange. She had never been around a pack leader before, or at least not that she was aware of. She imagined that's what it must have been, that the magic that surrounded his abilities increased when he had become the leader of the werewolves in this city.

It wasn't just the feeling she could feel coming from him. He certainly looked powerful. He had been sleek and put together, but she could tell, somehow, that he could get rough around the edges every now and again.

She would like to see him rough around the edges.

Stop. She admonished herself internally.

There were many reasons to stop that train of thought, one being that a man of that status was so far out of her league it was laughable to even think otherwise. Two, he was a werewolf. That should speak for itself. Three, she wasn't meant for it. She was meant to be alone. And four, she shouldn't be switching between horrific anxiety to bizarrely lusty thoughts about a preternatural.

What was wrong with her?

She switched the channel and attempted to get engrossed in the movie that was on the television. It was a far cry from successful but better than dwelling on any of the things she was currently feeling. Disassociating, the key to blissful monotony. As she watched, she realized it was *Queen of the Damned* from 2002, and it just so happened to be the scene when Lestat revealed he was a vampire to the world.

Great.

Her unsettled feeling only got worse.

CHAPTER 4

Durran sat perched in a tree across the street from Vee's apartment. She had tested it before and made sure that Vee couldn't sense her presence from that distance. It allowed her to watch her ward but leave her to feel as if she was alone. The massive trees that dotted the older neighborhoods around the city really helped when doing this Durran had found, and she certainly didn't consider it creeping on Vee since that's what a watcher's whole job was, to watch, to protect.

She could see as Vee moved about her apartment, making herself a small dinner, watching a dumb program, and writing out, most likely, a list for groceries to gather. Vee certainly was a creature of habit, which made it much easier for Durran. Those habits didn't make it boring; in fact, they were even more endearing, at least to Durran.

Despite the fact that Vee was an exceptional person in her own right, she was also very much not human, or at least not completely human. The Elder Watchers had assigned Durran to Vee when she returned to Kansas City, mostly because of the waves she had made during her time in St. Louis. They, despite their thorough knowledge and time observing, had never seen anything quite like her before, and the fact that she could move through the human world fairly easily without being detected, without the humans sensing she was different from them, baffled them. So, they decided she needed to be protected.

And protect her, Durran did. The worst Durran had ever had to do was deter human threats from Vee. It seemed like she remained out of the preternatural eye. Just thinking about her being exposed to other preternaturals sent shivers down Durran's spine. She could think of nothing worse. If the Elders didn't know what Vee was… well, Durran could only imagine what sorts of tests other preternaturals would do to her to find out.

Vee was cleaning up and heading to bed now, Durran noticed, watching her move from the living room toward the tiny hall to her bedroom. How she wished she could be there, watching her sleep. How did she sleep, with all the emotions she could feel around her? Vee always managed to get some, at least. In truth, Durran didn't fully understand Vee's abilities since it wasn't something that she openly discussed.

As all the lights went out, Durran sighed, closing her eyes to envision how it must be in that room. How

Vee's rich, dark hair would be splayed over the pillow. A gentle breath as it escaped her relaxed lips. The flutter of her eyes as dreams danced behind her lids.

What did she dream of?

"Ah, I assumed this is where you'd be, Durran," came a voice from above. Durran opened her eyes to see Cormac, another Watcher. He was tall and lean like most Watchers. His pale skin seemed to glow in the moonlight, and his normally brilliant red hair was dampened by the dark hues of the night.

"Get down before you're spotted!" Durran hissed, frantically looking at the windows across the street and the street itself to be sure no human saw his expansive wings. It was quite dark, and the wings were, like most Watchers, black, but it still was rather conspicuous for him to be flying around the city with no apparent qualms.

Cormac laughed and landed next to her on the branch, sitting and happily kicking his dangling feet in the air.

"So, playing the usual game of watch the… well I was going to say human, but she's a little bit more than that isn't she?" he said, gesturing to the darkened bedroom window that Durran had been staring at previously.

"Yes… that's typically what a Watcher does, watches over their ward, is it not?" Durran said, giving a side eye to her friend. "Oh wait… I forgot. You don't have a ward. Why is that again, Cormac?" Durran braced her head on her hand, furrowing her brow in mock confusion.

Cormac grimaced and sucked through his teeth.

"Yes, yes… you don't have to remind me of my punishment. It's bad enough to be without purpose right now. What else are we good for?"

It was sadly true. Watchers, while powerful beings, had little more to do in life than to protect their wards until the day they died. The goal was that the ward's importance in the world be fulfilled, and they lived out their remaining life, hopefully, to peaceful completion. However, Cormac had gambled too many times with his wards. He had left them to their own devices. He failed to steer them away from dangers that awaited. He had lost too many, and because of that, he had a two-hundred-year punishment. A ward-less Watcher.

It had its benefits. He wasn't bound to anything really. He occasionally had to assist another Watcher when things got especially hairy, but for the most part, he could roam the world as he pleased, so long as he didn't expose the entire preternatural community while he was at it.

Durran and Cormac had been friends for centuries. They had two wards that were friends many years before, and they watched them together as a team. At that time, Durran had taken a male form to better suit the needs of their ward. It was rare that Durran would take a female form, but Cormac didn't mind the looks of it. It was certainly still Durran, even if the features were softer than he was used to.

"So, you still don't know what she is, huh?" he asked, his eyes narrowing as if he were trying to peer through the darkened glass and see her for himself.

"No, I did research recently and found out she was, in fact, adopted. She told me her sister used to tease her and say she was adopted for years, but she was never sure. It certainly wasn't something that her parents revealed to her before they died."

"Have you told her yet?" Cormac asked, turning to watch Durran's face change. It was almost pained at the mention of it.

"There isn't much to tell. It was a closed adoption, and I didn't have time or patience to dig any deeper. It would hurt her too much, anyway," she admitted.

A Watcher's job wasn't just to physically protect the ward, but emotionally as well. This was certainly a fine line that Durran had to walk down because her orders were not only to protect her but also to find out what she was. Telling her and helping her find out the truth behind her biological parentage would eventually have to be something they did together. While Vee was resourceful and intelligent, this would be unknown territory and the emotions of the whole endeavor could push her into a spiral. A risk Durran was, at present, unwilling to take.

"So what? You're just going to ignore the elephant in the room until you can't anymore?" Cormac asked, chuckling at his old friend and shaking his head.

"There's no need for it right now. She deserves to have a little peace before her life is upended."

"You grow too attached to this creature, I fear," Cormac grumbled, watching the way Durran's face softened at the thought of her. There was emotion there that Cormac had never seen on Durran's face. Feelings that he could tell she had never felt before glittering in her eyes. It made him… jealous. They spent centuries watching their wards and seeing them fall in and out of love all the time but never got involved. Cormac knew there was only one being on this Earth that was for him… She was sitting right beside him. No matter the form she took, it was Durran.

"What if I found out and told you?" Cormac whispered. The thought formed in his head and came out before he had a moment to think it fully through.

"What?" Durran asked, concern flooding her features.

"What else am I doing with my time? I can find out what she is and who she is and then tell you. You can think of an easy way to break it to her."

Durran mulled it over for a moment. It wasn't the worst idea. It would keep Vee from having to seek the information out herself, which undoubtedly would be tiresome and costly, not to mention emotionally taxing. Then Durran could just slowly present the information to her. She could help ease her into it, instead of it being a traumatic event. For Vee, it seemed like her life was either mundane and lonely or outright chaotic.

"I suppose that would be alright. But you must promise me, Cormac," she paused drawing his gaze to her eyes, "that you won't cause trouble. Just seek out the information and bring back what you have. You don't need any more for the Elders to punish you for, and I don't think I could forgive you if you brought your bad luck to Vee."

"I promise," Cormac said, his voice shaky. Those final words that came from Durran's mouth cut him deep. He knew she had feelings for Vee, but these beings they watched over came and went. They died. That was the nature of things. How could she *not forgive him* if something happened? Was losing that plain, uninteresting thing, worth losing *him* over?

It was that moment that he realized he would be much happier if Vee was not in the picture at all. That her mere existence was a menace. He would seek out the truth. Perhaps use that information to win Durran over, but Vee, unknowingly, had just become his enemy.

"We should go now. I'll know if anything is wrong with her. It's late enough, so few humans are out now. We should be able to fly for a little while before the sun comes up," Durran said, smoothly standing on the branch and extending her hand to her old friend. She noticed his playful demeanor was gone. She assumed it was because he finally had a purpose after so many years without one. Determination, maybe? That had to be it.

They flew effortlessly together, staying just above the clouds to avoid any late-night viewers. For a moment it felt like times gone by, when there were less people in the world, and they had much more freedom to be themselves. Being a preternatural meant you had to stay hidden. Humans were far too sensitive and fragile to fully grasp the magics that ruled this earth. Too much of humanity was polarized. At some point in human history, they deviated from coexisting with preternaturals to deciding they were evil.

In reality, like everything in nature, it was a spectrum. Someone with stronger abilities to harness or be harnessed by magics did not make them evil.

Or at least not usually.

CHAPTER 5

Vee woke to her screeching alarm at 6 a.m. She hit her old alarm clock, trying to find the stupid tiny button at the back. No, she didn't want to snooze, she would get up. She wanted that teeth-grating sound to *stop, please, for the love of god!*

As soon as she found it, she sat up, stretching a little to relieve the knots that had formed overnight from her terrible mattress. It was little better than a futon mattress, and she had two in her living room, so she knew what sleeping on those was like.

She shuffled out to the kitchen. Coffee was already in the carafe since she set the timer the night before, and she sleepily, but happily, poured herself a cup and added her sweetener and milk. She pulled her phone from the charger and saw no missed calls. Not bad for the first night of the full moon on a Friday.

She despised the types of calls she always received over the weekend. Drunks who locked their keys in the car or lost them somewhere partying, unable to get home. No, she was not a rescue service for intoxicated people. She made a point of only working half days on Saturdays. She would fix and replace all of their key and lock mistakes once they woke up a little later in the morning and still be home early before the Saturday night shenanigans began.

Vee continued about her normal routine, getting the last bit of yogurt and granola out for her breakfast. She sighed, adding it to the list of groceries she had started the night before. Her fridge and cabinets were practically barren at this point. She, admittedly, didn't take much time for herself, something Durran loved to point out to her on their lunch dates… not *dates*… just lunches…

She shook her head. No, no… Durran was just her Watcher friend, nothing more. Nothing good came with getting entangled or overly attached to anyone, preternatural or otherwise. She just needed to be happy with the fact that she had a friend at all, let alone someone she could actually share everything with. No need to hide her abilities away as to not make Durran uncomfortable. Durran accepted her exactly as she was.

Durran was subtly beautiful. Her dark hair and eyes were striking against her pale skin, and her lean body was more androgynous than feminine. She was protective and pushy sometimes, but Vee knew it was only because she cared. She cared enough to keep her distance and allow Vee her life. Vee determined that was more valuable than any sort of romance or feelings she may have ever felt towards the Watcher.

She admonished herself internally for continuing to let these thoughts creep into her mind. She was lonely, but not lonely enough to change her life. Could she even handle having to deal with the same person all the time? She would much rather deal only with herself.

Her first cup of coffee going cold signaled it was time for a shower. She started the water, since it took at least ten minutes for it to get remotely warm enough in the old apartment building she lived in. Most of these buildings had been around for nearly a hundred years, and their water-heaters where probably half that, but they may as well have been ancient for how poorly they worked.

As she moved to her bedroom to select her clothes for the day, she realized, much to her dismay, that her clean clothing selection was nearly as dire as her food stock. She would have to take care of both situations before the weekend rush began, which, unfortunately, meant opening the shop later than she would have liked. It was more about her wanting to be there early, to work on her own projects, and less about the foot traffic in the store. Her cell phone was always with her for calls, which was most of what the weekend business was anyway, and people didn't start their actual weekend shopping until 10 a.m. Despite her *wanting* to open early, the shop itself did not *have* to be open.

She pulled out her last pair of jeans, ones that fit a little more snuggly than she would like, and one of her more worn, but still comfortably loose t-shirts to lay on the bed. That was why you kept those odd pieces of clothing you didn't actually like to wear, for when you run out of clean clothes, right? With an internal grumble, she gathered the dirty clothes strewn over her floor and smashed them into a laundry bag, promptly throwing it into the living room to be dealt with once her shower was over.

She closed the door to the bathroom so that the room could fill with steam and stepped into the hot spray. As she began lathering her hair, she recalled the day before, thoughts of Eliza. Vee never had a good excuse to just pop into Eliza's life unannounced, like she seemed to. As it always was in their relationship, it was on Eliza's schedule. In fact, Vee's whole life seemed to be on other people's schedules. Yes, she had her morning and evening routine, but lunch was often determined by Durran. House calls dictated how much time she could dedicate to getting her projects done in the shop, and most recently, those house calls were almost all from the werewolves in the area.

She did enjoy being in the field, though. House calls were good money, even from werewolves. As long as she didn't get discovered by them somehow, she was saving all their contributions for her new work vehicle. She really needed to narrow down what she was going to be getting. She loved the idea of a spacious interior so she could keep supplies stashed in there. As it was, she had a road bag and tools in her Lumina, but she couldn't keep a large inventory like screws and standard locks in there.

Having more supplies in her work vehicle would also free her up from having to load up a bag every time she had a house call. She sighed, thinking about the possibilities a van brought with it. More time… If there were a way for her to live in her shop so she could work during closed hours and have all the comforts of home at the same time, she would. As it was, she would just have to continue on the way she had been doing things. She didn't prefer it, but she was used to it. It helped that she didn't have anything else in her life to get in her way.

She got out of the shower, hastily getting dressed and brushing her hair. She briefly glanced at herself in the mirror over her dresser. She was a little shorter than average, which helped when she needed to get down low to work on locks, but her height didn't take away from her strength. She didn't actively work out, but she had taken kickboxing lessons years ago and had learned some self-defense from her friend she lived with in St. Louis. She also regularly hauled heavy boxes of tools and supplies. She had always been naturally strong, not supernaturally so, but strong enough to hold her own.

Her hair was nearly black, thick, and straight as a pin. It hung down past her shoulders except for her curtain of bangs, which she noted were getting a little long. She made a mental note that she would have to trim them soon. Her skin was on the pale side of olive, but she tanned beautifully if she ever got out in the sun. What really stood out, and what she actively tried to hide, were her bright emerald eyes. So crisp and green, they looked unreal, unnatural… inhuman.

She closed her eyes and shook her head as she turned away. She couldn't become burdened with things she couldn't change. She hid what she could, and right now she wanted to get these pesky errands and chores out of the way so she could get back to the shop as soon as possible. With her phone shoved in her messenger bag, grocery list in her pocket, and the laundry over her shoulder, she made her way out to her car marveling at how quiet it was in the still, early morning of Saturday, when people were still sleeping off their hangovers.

She made it to the laundromat just in time before a gaggle of moms came in. She had the best washer and drier selection of the bunch at her disposal. She pulled her notebook out of her messenger bag and began to make a list of all the bills she had to pay soon. Rent and utilities for the shop were due. Thank goodness she didn't have any employees to pay. It would have really dug into what she was saving up for the car. Or truck? She still could not decide which would be better.

As she started daydreaming about what kind of car she would get once she felt like she had enough saved, she felt an odd sensation. It was a strange thumping at the back of her head, rhythmic like a heartbeat.

Humans gave off a sort of low hum, nothing that couldn't be ignored easily, but each type of preternatural gave off something different. That's how she could distinguish between them. Werewolves were like a buzz, more intense than humans, but when they were near a change though … it was extreme. Watchers, like Durran, gave off practically nothing. Emotions were still felt, but there was a void where there should be something. Vampires were like the shivers that ran down your spine uncomfortably when you were cold, but they filled her brain as well. Witches felt like a low humming throb. It was more intense than humans but less so than werewolves, but this… this feeling… this meant a fae was here.

She didn't react. Her eyes stayed firmly on her notebook, continuing to write out a pros and cons list for car, truck, and SUV.

"I think your things are finished," came a raspy voice. She looked up, noticing the old woman standing before her, face heavily wrinkled and white wispy curls atop her head. For Vee, she could see the glamor shimmering around her, catching a glimpse here and there of the true form underneath: blue-grey skin, not at all wrinkled but smooth as it stretched over the small frame. Huge, almond-shaped eyes, black as pitch, looked at her from behind the shimmering, swirling blue of the old woman. It was beautiful and terrifying at the same time. Again, keeping her composure, she stood.

"Oh! I'll get it, then," she said, being very careful to not thank the creature.

You cannot thank a fae, Vee chanted to herself internally.

Moving her wet clothes over to a dryer, she hoped, desperately, that it would sit somewhere else so that she could just continue with her list in peace.

No luck.

The fae sat right beside her. Oh, how she wished she had thought to bring her headphones. She scrounged through her messenger bag, hoping they were still in there, but it was to no avail. It did buy a little time, though. The fae sat quietly, watching her as she finished sifting through her bag, and let the silence hang between them a few minutes. It gave Vee a false sense of security, thinking maybe she would go unnoticed long enough to get out of this without offending or accidentally owing this fae something. It could certainly mean disaster, depending on what type she was.

"I don't think I usually see you here, are you new to the area?" the fae asked, glancing not so subtly at what Vee was writing on the page.

"Um… no. I just don't come here very often," Vee said, staying truthful.

"Ah, so you're single, then. Only the single ones pop in every now and again."

"Yes," Vee said, smiling insincerely at her. The silence was reestablished, and she tried to look absolutely engrossed in her list, but of course, the only things that were coming to mind were avoiding conflict. Her pen stilled just long enough for the fae-woman to continue the disjointed conversation.

"So, what do you do for a living?"

The dryer was not drying fast enough for her. She was trying so hard to remember all the rules when conversing with fae.

"I am a locksmith," Vee said honestly, and the fae seemed to visibly recoil. At first, Vee thought she may have said something insulting, but she ran over her small sentence again, and realized that wasn't it. Many keys were made with iron, especially old ones. Her fingers, despite her best efforts, probably still had little shards of it under her fingernails. Pieces of iron were probably dusted on and in her messenger bag as well.

"That's not a job for a woman, certainly not a single woman," the fae said, her grimace causing her wrinkles to deepen.

"It suits me fine," Vee said, smiling a little more genuine this time.

Ten minutes left.

"What's your name, girl?" the fae asked, Vee could feel the magic spilling from the creature's mouth and hanging in the air, waiting for the answer to hold until it became useful.

Do not say your name.

The door opened then, causing Vee's head to turn abruptly, hoping for a distraction from the conversation and she wasn't disappointed. In walked Durran, nothing in hand and perfectly out of place. No one seemed to notice, except Vee and the fae. The old woman narrowed her eyes, and Vee could feel her irritation.

"Looks like you're nearly done," Durran said, sitting in the spot on the other side of Vee. The fae's spell receded back into her mouth as she looked at the two of them, irritation and suspicion flowing to Vee.

"How did you know I would be here?" Vee asked, thanking Durran with her eyes profusely. Durran nodded very slightly with a smirk.

"Happened to walk by on my way to the shop," she admitted. It wasn't unreasonable, this laundromat was literally two doors down from her shop, and Vee was so grateful for Durran's sudden appearance that she simply pushed any questioning to the back of her mind.

"Ah, yes. I realized I'm down to this," Vee admitted, gesturing at her current outfit, "or the one dress I own."

"That would certainly be a sight," Durran laughed, having never seen Vee wear a dress or skirt in all the years they knew each other.

Vee could still feel the fae's frustration beside her, and she glanced at the timer for the dryer once again. The fae's wash was done and sitting in the machine. It felt like everyone was waiting for the dryer to give its shrill buzz to indicate it was done.

Five minutes left.

Vee decided she would rather have slightly damp clothes than risk being near this fae any longer, even if she had Durran by her side.

"This is good enough for me," she announced, standing rather suddenly and opening the dryer to take out her things. She haphazardly shoved them back into the laundry bag, not caring that she would, most definitely, have wrinkled clothes until her next laundry day. It was worth it to escape this woman.

"Have a wonderful day," Vee said to the fae, remembering to not be rude, as she turned around gathering her things to head back to her car. Being rude could be worse than if she had given her name.

Durran and Vee made it back to the sidewalk and were nearly to Vee's car before either of them said anything.

"How is it that you can find yourself in precarious situations doing the most ordinary tasks?" Durran mused, watching her shove the laundry bag into the back of her old, decrepit vehicle.

"It's like I'm a magnet to all of you," Vee said, gesturing vaguely to Durran as if she was the representative of all the preternaturally inclined.

"Well, you're just as much one of us…" Durran pointed out, crossing her arms across her chest and raising an eyebrow.

"We don't know what I am. So, I tend to go with the grey zone. Neither one nor the other," Vee huffed, slamming the door since the stupid laundry bag didn't seem to want to cooperate.

Durran rolled her eyes while Vee smiled smugly.

"What's next on the agenda? A big day of early morning lock work to attend to?"

"I wish. No, I have to go to the grocery store now. My house is painfully low on food. Things would get ugly if I ran out of coffee," she grumbled, pulling out the grocery list as if it were the most offensive thing on the planet.

Vee hated shopping. She hated the crowds. She hated too many choices. She hated people approaching her to ask if she needed help. She hated the worthless chit chat some people thought was wanted or necessary with strangers for simply being in the same isle.

"You could always order it to be delivered," Durran suggested, watching her walk around the car to the driver side. The streets were still pretty dead on that balmy Saturday morning, so Vee propped the car door open and gave Durran a playful glare.

"I don't have the patience to go through one of those apps, nor do I have enough money to waste on such a thing. I'll just have to suffer through it," she sighed, giving a weak wave to Durran before she made her hasty exit to the store just a few minutes away.

It was always a little eerie to be out in the early morning after everyone's drunken debauchery. Filth littered the small green places between roads and in front of businesses. Often, she would see someone drunkenly passed out on a bench somewhere, their friends having ditched them partway through their night out. She never really got to have the experience of going out like that with regularity, but honestly, she wasn't interested. Drinking did not help her control her abilities, and this neighborhood had a reputation for crowds and chaos. She would lose it if she was put in such a position, surrounded by various emotions and no control.

In fact, she had lost it the few times she tried drinking when she was younger. Drunk Vee in crowded spaces was not a good mixture.

Her heart sank a little as she saw how many cars were already parked in the massive parking lot. Flanking the large grocery store, there was a strip of smaller stores that also utilized the lot, but mostly, it was a place for people to park their cars before their night on the town began. She hoped most of them were abandoned when their owners found they were not sober enough to drive themselves home and opted for a taxi or a ride service.

Once she parked her car, she took a deep breath, gripping the steering wheel and preparing herself, as if she were going into battle. She walked quickly through the parking lot, avoiding eye contact with the few people she passed on her way toward the entrance, clutching her list in her fingers for dear life. It wasn't just the people in the store or the random conversations that caused her anxiety to spike at even the thought of stepping into the grocery store. People tended to be especially tense when shopping for food. Their internalized anxiety, whether it was over the amount things cost or a diet they were trying to follow, emotions would flood Vee and cause her own heart to race and breath to hitch. This was only further exasperated by it being the second night of the full moon.

The first of three nights were a bit milder. Sure, there was an energy in the air; everyone, preternatural or otherwise, picked up on it, but it was not nearly as bad as night two when the moon was at its full power. There was no escaping the way things shifted and how that made people feel. It was all the moon.

She was halfway through her list, staring down the various granola options, since they didn't have the brand she normally bought, when she felt it, the intense vibration of a new Were. New Weres were extremely volatile, having no control over their animal during the full moon… sometimes for months or years after their first change. For one to be in the city on the second night, with seemingly no other Were around them… It could be a catastrophe.

Vee took a moment to look around, trying to pinpoint where they were, who they were.

Something inside of her told her she needed to know.

She glanced around the larger open area between the isles and the meat counter, but only saw an elderly couple and two sets of teens. It wasn't uncommon for teenagers to waste time in bizarre areas, but one of those girls was the new Were. It was unusual, but not unheard of, for a woman to be born a Were. Women most often became Were by an attack, but even then, the survival rate was low.

She tried to narrow it down between the two groups, but it was to no avail. Teenagers vibrated higher than other humans, and their strong emotions and hum made it impossible to know for sure which one it was. She paused for a moment, collecting herself. She had to make sure her emotions were not showing on her face too much. No need to rouse more suspicion. She already had the fae incident less than an hour earlier.

Once she was satisfied with her own personal level of calm, she decided to try to push the worry from her mind. She had to hope that whichever girl it was, she had a pack leader somewhere that was smart enough to take her to safety before the sun set. She was decidedly a helpless person that could do nothing more about the situation, and she carried on with her shopping, trying to ignore any strange people as they crept into her head.

The store had begun to fill up since she arrived, and having found the last item on her list, the off-brand soda she wanted, she considered the mission to be accomplished and made her way to the checkout line. The cashier's blank face didn't give away whatever internal struggle she was having. Resentment, depression, and jealousy all seeped into Vee as she watched the woman haphazardly scan each item and toss them. Vee could only imagine this woman was either not thinking about this transaction at all, which was honestly, completely welcomed, or she was in such a dire situation in some facet of her life that internally, she was screaming.

Having been recently reminded of the rules of the fae, Vee simply said "I hope your day gets better," to the cashier, who briefly seemed to snap out of her haze to look at her bewildered before Vee made a quick exit out of the store and felt like she could finally breathe again.

CHAPTER 6

S hane woke to the sun in his eyes. His curtains were askew just enough to let the bright morning rays peep through onto his face. It wasn't unpleasant, though, it was the first time in years he hadn't been awoken either by his alarm or someone else. He sat up, taking stock of the quietness of the house. No teenage son breathing in the room across the hall or pack members snoring somewhere else in the house.

Just quiet.

Being the pack leader meant he was never alone. Leadership in your work life, meant your personal life was constantly interrupted. For him, his position as leader was not just his job. It was everything; it was all encompassing.

Hence why he had to change his career situation. After years of switching from one corporate investment firm to another, he had exhausted his options. He had been making plans to start his own independent firm for a few years. Now that people were more used to contacting their advisors via telephone or other digital means, it meant he could more adeptly hide his lack of aging, or at least a bit longer than he usually could.

It also granted him the ability to hire more pack members, keeping things in the family and making situations easier for them to do the things required of the pack.

Having that Friday while the rest of the pack did the run meant he finished everything up and had the rest of the weekend to himself. Time to himself was rare, indeed.

He leisurely went down to the kitchen, fixing himself a tall mug of black coffee. His house seemed enormous with only him inside. The colonial, center-hall style home had all its original hardwood. He had updated it but didn't destroy the history of the house by overly modernizing it like so many people in the neighborhood had. Part of the charm of the house and the neighborhood was the way things had been carefully crafted in days long gone.

He took in a breath, relishing the fact that he had nothing going on that day. No one to help. No clients to meet. No pack to attend to.

Of course, there were still plenty of worries. Thomas said he would keep him posted if they had any sightings of the rogue, but everything had been quiet. He knew he would need to look at the news a little later, to see if there were any new attacks in Missouri, but he decided this rare morning was just for him.

As he sighed again, just enjoying the peace, he caught a hint of that scent again. That locksmith. It was faint, having been a while since she had actually been in his house, but it was everywhere down on the first floor. Coffee in hand, he wandered smelling it, smelling her at the front door, the back door, and the cabinet where they kept spare keys. She was different. Not quite different enough to make her scent stand out amongst other humans, but enough that it caused him to pause.

Her fragrance was like sweet spices lingering in humid air just after a spring rain. Humans smelled sweet, sometimes mildly tangy, but she hung there, clearly long after she had been in the building. It piqued his curiosity. This woman had been all around his house and other pack members' houses several times. The longer he purposefully hunted after her scent, the more intrigued and intoxicated he became. Who was she?

He pulled his phone from his pocket, hesitating for a moment before texting Cora. He didn't want to alarm her with a call, especially since she was with her sister, hopefully enjoying her humanity without the chaos the pack could bring.

[Shane: What was the name of that locksmith again?]

He paced a little, his thoughts racing faster than he would have liked. He should have been resting or relaxing; instead, he was obsessing over this woman.

He began justifying his growing obsession and the intensity with which he was starting to think about this unknown woman. It was for the safety of the pack.

He had to know what was going on with her. He had to know that she wasn't growing wise to anything odd with them. Just thinking of the kinds of destruction she must have seen at their various houses was enough to consider her a threat. Her scent was even on the basement door, a place where he had a room to keep Weres who had lost control.

Had she been in the basement?

What had she seen?

They had always been so careful not to bring attention to themselves. It wasn't easy with so many Weres in one place. For so many years, as the leader, he had kept them safe, kept the preternatural world veiled, and now one silly locksmith could be their undoing?

Or worse… would he have to be her undoing?

[Cora: *The Missing Key* is the name of the shop. I can text you the number?]

[Shane: No. I just want to look into it. Thank you.]

He responded, quickly switching to the browser on his phone and searching for the shop. It didn't have a website, but there was an address and phone number with a picture of the front of the shop from an online reviewer.

Just a tiny store front in Westport.

He was already walking up the stairs to change his clothes before he had fully formed his thoughts around the whole thing. What was he going to do when he got there? No idea. That scent of her still tingled in his mind, and he knew he had to go. He had to see.

He dressed casually, a rare occurrence, but he felt like he'd stand out in Midtown on a Saturday if he dressed in his usual button up and slacks. He decided to take Patrick's car instead of his. Less conspicuous than Shane's Rolls-Royce. Patrick had just turned sixteen, but he had been practicing on the car, a Subaru Outback, he would be driving on city streets. He already had plenty of experience behind the wheel in the country during the day on run outings, but that was more for fun, and less for practicality.

He was headed out at the right time, it seemed. There was barely any traffic on the road, given it wasn't even 9 a.m. on a Saturday. He was about halfway there when he realized, perhaps finally away from her scent, how ridiculous he was being. He had this whole day to himself, and decided he was wasting his time… on what? A girl?

Now that he could think about it with a clearer mind, he was trying to decide what his actual motivations were. Did he really think this person was a threat to them? Well, it wasn't completely out of the realm of possibility, but also, from what Cora told him, and what he read briefly from those internet reviews, she operated that business completely on her own. Why would she lose such good customers?

Clearly, she had helped them many times. Could her shop last without such regular business?

And what of her smell? It was enough to put him into a frenzy. Not that he hadn't smelled it before. Clearly, it had been there in the background, muddied by the smells of his pack, but he had never before had such a reaction to a smell like this. He was wracking his brain, trying to understand it.

The only times he had ever heard of a werewolf having such a strong reaction to another's smell when they weren't an obvious threat was when a Were met their True Mate. But this woman wasn't even a Were of any kind; he knew that from her smell alone. It was an absurd notion that had him almost laughing at himself for even thinking it.

He was nearly there now, and he was conflicted about what he was going to do once he arrived. Would she even be there? It was early still, for a Saturday, but he didn't deviate from his trajectory. He had already come this far. He pulled up in front of the shop. It was a simple store front. No frills or dazzlingly alluring signs. Practical. He could admire that, even though it surely wasn't helping draw business.

He walked up to the shop and noticed the "Closed" sign. No strict hours were posted. He looked through the windows, seeing the minimalist displays of various locks and safes. The wall behind the main counter was covered in an assortment of different key types. There was a silver door that broke up the crowded wall of keys that he assumed led to inventory rooms. Again, not messy at all, but not pristine.

That backroom door was still locked with several padlocks, and she wasn't in the showroom, so where was she? At this point, he just wanted to have a look at her, to be able to know her when he saw her.

"What are you doing here, wolf?" came a voice from behind him. The voice was low, but feminine, laced with malice. He took a deep breath, taking in the creature's scent before he turned around.

Sweet and mildly ozone.

Watcher.

"I was just planning on purchasing a safe," Shane said, turning around to look at the Watcher. She was a little shorter than he was, her hair blunt and cut short, black, and messy. Despite the heat of June, she was still wearing a duster, a glamor most Watchers used to hide their wings. Her eyes were a piercing red brown that glared into his eyes.

"There's no reason for you to be here," the Watcher said, crossing her arms and tilting her head. "Leave her alone."

So, this locksmith had a Watcher. That definitely changed things. What was so important about this woman that the Elders would keep her safe?

"I merely came to have a look. She's been doing work for us, and I wanted to know she is safe for the pack," Shane said, honestly, despite his urge to be argumentative. This Watcher was challenging his authority, and his urge to fight about it was growing.

"She won't say anything. Go before she gets back" was all the Watcher said, before climbing into an old, black Buick Shane had parked behind and speeding down Westport Road.

Shane growled as the Watcher left, his hands had curled into tight fists. Maybe it was the scent of her all over the door that he was standing in front of, or maybe it was simply the Watcher trying to tell him what to do, but he was filling with rage over being told to leave her alone.

He was the Westport Pack Leader. If he determined someone needed to be looked into, that was his prerogative. He took a deep breath to calm himself, the full moon's energy was clearly at play, bringing his wolf to the surface, and with that, heightened emotions.

This wasn't the time or place for him to do anything, and she wasn't there anyway. What was he going to do? Confront her? No.

He went back to his car, careful not to slam the door too much. Once inside, away from her scent, he was still angry, he didn't like the Watcher's tone, but he thought more clearly. There was something about this woman. Something he wanted to know so badly, but he couldn't risk bringing the wrath of the Watchers on him. With a sigh, he pulled away, giving the quaint locksmith shop a final glance before he sped back to his home.

CHAPTER 7

After racing home, throwing her now clean bag of laundry in her room, and hastily putting away her groceries, Vee was finally on her way back to her shop to open for the day. Her cell phone hadn't rung at all, but it was barely 10 a.m. She wasn't really surprised. The streets were picking up with Saturday traffic from people finally getting out to do their errands or enjoy their day off. If she had more people in her life, she might consider a day off to be more meaningful, as it was, there really wasn't much of a need for it.

Being alone meant she didn't have anyone to rush back to. It meant she had plenty of time to work on side projects during her down time. It meant she could go in early and stay late without being concerned someone would miss her presence, but even though those things were benefits, she still longed, sometimes, for companionship.

She managed to find a spot to park a little up the hill from her shop, almost excitedly getting out and walking towards her door. She was eager to pull her mind away from more depressing thoughts and get to her projects. It was still rather humid, but she didn't mind the heat, and the sky was clear. Perfect.

As she switched on lights and set things up, she thought about what a strange day she had already had. She was happy to finally be in her shop. There were very few people and their emotions around to bother her. She could finally think and feel on her own and focus, the objects of which still lay incomplete on the counter, waiting for her.

She was even more eager than usual to get to something she knew, something soothing and ordinary, after her strange feeling the night before and the bizarre morning she had just had.

"Nothing is changing," she said out loud to herself, willing it to be so. In fact, right there in front of her were two perfectly normal lock projects, that she just needed to focus on to get her mind straight.

She turned on some music, donned her magnifiers, and went about finishing up the safe first so that Monday morning the owners could come collect it. The hours passed; her mind fully concentrated on the task at hand. It was so simple to her, putting the pieces together like a puzzle. She didn't have to worry about the parts changing or becoming hostile like the emotions of people. The pieces fit, or they didn't.

There wasn't much left to the repair, but what was left required precision. Blocking out the rest of the world, she had just placed the last piece and began to carefully screw it in, when her phone rang.

She sucked in a shaky breath. Had she jumped at the phone she would have had to redo everything she had just spent hours on. Carefully putting her tools down, she picked up the phone.

Eliza.

The feeling crept back almost immediately.

She had just been thinking about Eliza the day before, and now she called? Hesitantly, she answered the phone, "Hello?" She tried to keep the questioning tone from her voice. She didn't want to scare her sister away.

"Victoria, I need you to come over here," Eliza said, into the phone in a shrill tone. She was clearly worked up. The only person who ever called her by her full name was her sister. Victoria was the old her. The person of the past that didn't know who she was or understand what she could do. Vee had changed, but in Eliza's eyes, she would always be her little sister, Victoria.

"Well, it's just now four o'clock on a Saturday. I'll be closing my shop in a bit, can I come over then?" Vee asked, after having glanced at the clock on the wall. A young couple walked in. She waved at them, smiling as a welcome.

"No, I need you here now. Our spare key is not in its hidden spot. Someone stole it! You have to come change all the locks!" Eliza nearly screeched into the phone. Vee winced at the sound, certain even the humans that entered her shop could hear her sister through the phone.

"Okay, I have some customers in the store. Let me help them, and I'll head over to your house with new locks."

"Fine," Eliza snapped, abruptly hanging up the phone.

Vee sighed, setting her phone down. The customers were, as she suspected, looking at the heart locks that she had on display.

"It's a beautiful Saturday," Vee said, trying and failing to not sound awkward. She had good customer service as far as taking care of her customer's needs, but she struggled in the small talk department.

"Yes," the girl said, her eyes bright as she looked over the assortment, not seeming fazed by the awkwardness.

"We're getting married in a few months and decided we wanted to make a time capsule to open on our anniversary," the boy said, glancing at his fiancée. They had that twinkle in their eyes, an unspoken devotion. Vee felt it rolling off of them. It was overwhelming. She just watched them for a moment, letting herself get taken over. That was a feeling she was certain she would never have with someone else.

"Do you do engravings?" The girl asked, snapping her back to reality.

"Um, yes! Do you see one color or size you particularly like?" Vee asked, moving around the counter with an order sheet in her hands.

She took their order, did a quick price quote, and got their deposit.

"It should be ready by Tuesday, but I'll call you if it's sooner," Vee told them as they happily waved and walked out of her shop.

For a moment Vee went about getting back to her repairs, but as she donned her magnifiers once again, she remembered.

Eliza.

"Shit," she hissed under her breath as she hurried to switch her voicemail and signs. She might as well consider herself closed for the day, even though she felt like she was barely open. By the time she finished changing all the locks for her sister, it would be long past her normal Saturday closing time, and she'd have to come back to balance her register and finish closing it down. That couple took a little longer than she had originally thought when she had gotten off the phone with Eliza. Part of that was probably her fault for letting herself get lost in their feelings for one another.

She went to her back room, pulling out replacement locks. She had only seen Eliza's house a few times when coming to grab old things of hers, but if she recalled, she had black fixtures. Vee found a matching set of six, not remembering how many exterior doors she had, and threw them into a larger bag. Her road tools where already in her car, so all she needed was to get there.

She headed toward Ward Parkway; it was the fastest way to get south from her shop, and Eliza also lived right off of it. The houses that typically flanked that thoroughfare were massive mansions to say the least. Vee turned off the parkway, heading toward her sister's all white and black, perfectly manicured house. Her beat-up car looked horribly out of place being parked on her pristine driveway, but it couldn't be helped.

Vee cringed as her car door screeched as she got out. She tried to take a deep breath to steady her own anxiety before she went up to the house, gathering her supplies as a cover to collect herself. She had to keep herself in check when she was around Eliza. Though she loved her sister, seeing her always brought out the frail, cringing girl of her past. That wasn't who Vee was anymore.

As she headed toward the door, she felt Eliza's panic. Vee had felt it many times before. Every time they were late on a bill or Eliza had to miss work because Vee was sent home sick from migraines. The panic was very visceral, it reached deep into her core. Vee held back tears as she knocked with her stomach in knots and a lump in her throat. Eliza opened it, her face clearly pained. Her complexion was much fairer than Vee's, eyes brown, but sharp. Her brown hair was in a tight bun, she wore a white blouse, and designer jeans. They were very much opposite of one another in the way they dressed, and only mildly similar in appearance.

"I thought you weren't coming! Doing another disappearing act on me!" Eliza said, her voice shrill. Vee winced at the immediate mention of Vee running away. Eliza was an expert at guilt trips.

"I told you I had customers at the shop I had to take care of first," Vee said, trying not to let her voice tremble. She loved her sister, but it didn't mean the wounds of the past didn't still hurt after all this time.

"So how many locks need replacing?" she asked, following her sister into the foyer. Mansions had those.

"Front, back, and two side doors. I can't believe it's gone! I can only imagine who would have taken it," Eliza said, this time a little quieter. The lie of those words stung a little in Vee's mind. Another interesting aspect of her abilities. She could feel when people were lying to her. It made things much more illuminating. That little burn behind her eyes told her that Eliza had some idea of who took the key.

Vee let the little lie go. There was no point in bringing up her gifts; it would only prove to exasperate her sister more. Instead, she smiled to herself, knowing she had accurately remembered at least something in her sister's house. She had chosen the replacement locks to match the fixtures, matte black.

"I suppose I'll leave you to it. Mary should be waking from her nap soon." Even at the mention of Mary's name, Vee was a little blown away at the waves of devotion she felt from Eliza. Taking care of Vee had been an obligation. Taking care of Mary was purely out of love.

Vee set her bags down and took a moment to look around. From where she was at the front door, she could easily look in the rooms flanking it. The rooms were massive and spotless; they were decorated as if they were going to spotlight on one of those home and garden shows. All the upholstered furniture was white with black accents and coffee tables. Every now and then there would be a throw pillow or a vase of flowers that had a pop of color that matched. This time the color was light blue.

Vee, for the second time in two days, felt like she was out of place. A dirty shoe print on white carpet, but she started changing the locks out. It wasn't particularly difficult, she had changed a hundred locks before, and these were not old, so there wasn't corrosion or rust to contend with.

She finished the front door and was nearly done with the first side door before she heard another peep. That was when footfalls started on the stairs, and she turned to see Eliza holding Mary in the archway into… the living room? Vee wasn't sure what room this was supposed to be. The room on the other side could have been a living room too, they both had couches and coffee tables. Either Vee wasn't cultured enough to know the difference, or there honestly wasn't one.

"Almost done with this one, and I'll move to the back door," Vee said, finding it hard to resist grinning and waving at the sleepy toddler in her sister's arms. Eliza smiled at Vee and looked down at her shy daughter. She knew Vee would be a great aunt, but the life she had made didn't involve her little sister. Frank, her husband, didn't much care for really anything about Eliza's former life before him. She made herself into the woman she needed to be, and that woman had no one but him and now their daughter.

"Okay, Frank will be home soon. You know it's probably better if… well, never mind," Eliza said quietly, looking at her sister nervously, knowing she could feel the sadness she felt, but having no way to keep it at bay.

Vee was a little startled at the feeling. She had felt the sadness at other times, nearly every time Eliza let her guard down a little and when Frank was mentioned. She had suspected, but never knew for sure, that he was part of the reason they didn't have a relationship.

She moved to the kitchen shortly after Eliza had left the room and there they were again. Sweet little Mary was in her highchair as Eliza cut up little pieces of fruit for her to munch on.

"So where do you normally keep your spare?" Vee asked as she took the old lock out of the door. She was trying to make conversation. She needed something, anything, to distract from the awkwardness.

"We have a rock by the back door. It matches the rest of the edging rocks, but it's gone. Without it there… well, it was obvious to me it was missing right away."

Vee wondered who would have taken the whole rock, but not broken in immediately. Sure, there was theft all over the city, but that was quite a bold move to fully take the rock and not steal anything while you were there.

"Frank will think this was an excuse to bring you here, but I honestly am so scared these days with how many break ins there are," Eliza told her, her breathing becoming a little uneven as her anxiety crept back.

"I'm fixing it now, Eliza. There's nothing to worry about," Vee said, looking over to give her sister a comforting glance, but instead saw Frank standing in the entrance of the room.

"What's going on?" His voice was already raised. Vee turned back to the lock and tried to go more quickly. Eliza moved over to him and touched his chest, putting herself between him and Vee.

"The hide-a-key went missing this afternoon. Just gone! She was the fastest locksmith we could get to come change them all. I didn't want us to worry about someone breaking in," Eliza explained, her voice calm, but her words coming out quick and deliberate. It was obvious to Vee that this was a regular occurrence. Eliza had clearly had to calm him before.

"I'll just get the last one done and head out on my own. These will be the new set to use," Vee said, standing and placing the keys on the counter. She moved quickly to the last side room, passing the dining room, which looked like no one ever ate a single meal there, before doing the fastest lock change she had ever done. Albeit, at this point, she had just replaced three of them in a row and had it down to a science.

She could feel Frank's anger and hear their hushed voices talking about her rooms away. If she was unsure about Frank's feelings toward her before that day, she was certain he didn't want Eliza to contact her ever again.

As she said, she finished the final lock and moved as fast and quietly to the front door as she could. She felt like she was sneaking out of the house with how quietly she tried to close the front door. It was a relief to be outside of there. It was strange being around Eliza and her mixed feelings, but it felt downright dangerous to be anywhere near Frank.

She ripped open her car door, haphazardly throwing her things into the passenger seat, and climbed in, hoping that she could make a quick exit back to her shop before it started getting dark. Somehow it was already 6:30 p.m., and she had at least an hour of clean-up and closing duties to do before she could go home.

As she began to back out of the driveway, she was suddenly reeling from another wave of intense anger. Before she could look toward the house there was pounding on her car window, so loud she thought it might break. She turned to see Frank there, now gesturing wildly for her to roll her window down. She did, but only enough to hear him clearly. She feared he would try to rip her out of the window with the amount of absolute hatred he was feeling toward her.

"I will find a way to make sure you're permanently out of our lives someday. I don't need the black stain of your filth ruining our family. Eliza is mine now, and you'd better stop trying to weasel your way back to her. She's not going to take care of you anymore," he said, his voice shaking in his effort to remain collected in front of his neighbors. Without missing a beat, he tossed a wad of cash through the narrow opening in the window and stormed back to his house.

Vee glanced at Eliza for a moment while his back was turned. She was standing in the doorway, clearly trying to quickly swipe away tears from her eyes. Vee finished backing out and made her way to the closest street to take her home.

Her breath shook as she tried to calm her own nerves and turned onto State Line Road. It wasn't as fast as Ward Parkway, but that might have been for the best. She questioned how much she should be driving at that moment, but she knew she had to get away. Saying anything to him would have only made things worse.

She was trying her best to dissociate from it. It wasn't like she had really had a relationship with Eliza since she came back. Her moments with her sister were fleeting and usually laced with bad feelings anyway. She struggled with the fact that despite how much she prided herself on being alone and how that solitude granted her peace, she still craved having people that were hers. Eliza had been that for her, even if it was at a distance.

CHAPTER 8

It seemed like she hit every red light on the way home and she was trapped behind the slowest driver in all of Kansas City for a stretch, but she finally made it back to her shop. She parked and realized the sky was already turning. The Saturday night crowds were swarming toward the heart of Westport, and she still had work to do. So much for closing the shop early.

She hauled all the remaining supplies from Eliza's back to the shop and closed the door. She tried to be quick about putting things away, but she knew her Monday self would not appreciate the hastily discarded bits, so she slowed down and actually put things where they belonged.

Time seemed to fly by. She had just finished balancing the register and went into the back room to put away the two locks she hadn't used at Eliza's. She went to update the inventory sheet when she felt it again. That feeling she had felt in the grocery store came back. It was faint, they were at a bit of a distance from the shop, but not by much. It was the thumping in her head that seemed to vibrate in her own chest, creeping in, getting increasingly more intense. She dropped the inventory paper and quickly moved to the show room, looking out the windows at the street. It was getting dark now. The full moon was visible.

The Were was struggling now, feeling the uncontrollable effects of the moon, and she wasn't prepared for it.

Shock. Panic.

Where were they?

It had to have been one of those teenage girls.

Fear. Pain. The Wolf.

It was taking over Vee's mind as the girl was fighting it.

It was a noble effort, but no Were can resist the first change.

Vee raced out of her shop now, frantically trying to look up and down the street. She didn't have time to pause and think about what she was doing. There was no other option but to help.

There they were on the corner of the block, a group of girls all huddled together. Vee ran. She moved faster than she ever before toward them, her mind racing trying to figure out what she was going to do as the Were's feelings became increasingly overwhelming.

She slowed as she approached, not wanting to scare the girls. How was she going to get the other girls away from her?

"Lori, what's wrong? What can we do?" one of the girls said, panic clear in her voice. All the girls were panicking, and the one on the ground, curls shaking with pain and the effort of trying to hold back the beast, was fighting for her life… and the lives of her friends.

If Vee didn't get her out of there, these girls would be ripped apart. She couldn't think about it; she just had to act.

"I know her, she must have had an allergic reaction to something. What did you eat?" Vee lied, pushing through the circle that had been created around Lori. None of the girls questioned her as she knelt down beside the shaking girl, whose eyes were already changing, glowing and wide.

"Um… w-we ate at Westport flea market earlier," said one girl, her eyes glued to Lori as she referenced the landmark and misnomer of a restaurant, just blocks away.

"She's lactose intolerant!" Vee hissed, saying the only thing she could come up with at that moment to explain why this girl would be writhing on the ground in pain. Vee fished through her messenger bag, pulling out her business card and quickly scribbling, 'Her inherited allergy was triggered' on the back. "Call her parents and tell them this. *Exactly this*. And where she is," she hissed, pulling the small girl from the pavement. She didn't know where she found the strength to do that. Had to be the adrenaline.

"But…" the girl with the phone started as Vee placed Lori's arm over her shoulders.

"I'm getting her in my shop. It's on the card," Vee said as she turned, dragging her around the corner. She knew her inventory room would suffice to hold the new wolf until one of her own could come to get her. Other than her inventory, the room was well reinforced, with doors made of thick steal.

Lori was breathing fast and heavily, her hands were clenching and unclenching on Vee, nails that were already turning to claws unconsciously digging into her skin. The smell of blood was not helping Lori's control, Vee could tell, but she couldn't stop. That would be a disaster. They made it to the door of the shop, and Vee was thankful she had left the inventory door open, her inventory spreadsheets strewn on the floor where she had dropped them.

"I can't… I can't hold it," Lori sobbed as Vee let her collapse to the floor between metal shelves.

"It's okay. I'm closing the door. They're safe. You're safe," she assured Lori, locking eyes with the girl one last time before she slammed it closed.

With each lock she latched it was a struggle. Lori had relinquished control to her wolf, and the pain of her first transformation made Vee gasp. As she barricaded the door, she could hear ligaments snapping and bone popping. Lori's cries morphed into inhuman growls and roars. It was so loud Vee barely heard the sound of her shelves knocking over, hundreds of pieces of hardware and locks scattering across the floor of the room.

Vee was struggling to withstand Lori's emotions. Her whole body shook with the pain. This was the slowest transformation Vee had ever felt, but she hadn't felt a first-time change before. She tried to think of calm, a trickling stream, the quiet of the woods, a beautiful sunrise. She built up that calm peace within her as much as she could, and she pushed it out. Training her eyes on the barricaded door, she forced the calm past the door and toward Lori.

As the feeling engulfed the wolf within the room, it helped, only enough that she was no longer thrashing around, so Vee was able stand still for a moment without shaking. She pulled out her phone to see how much time had passed. The pain had been so excruciating it seemed like time stood still, but as the phone lit up, she realized an hour had already passed.

Where the hell were those werewolves?

She stood at the front of her shop watching out the glass door for someone from the wolf pack to come, careful to continue sending the calm to Lori. It was getting a little harder as she was struggling to not feel anxious herself. Vee was still shocked that it seemed like Lori had been totally unaware. She knew female-born Weres were not terribly common, but she assumed all children were watched, monitored, just to be safe. Who in their right mind would let a teenager get into this situation?

Vee's anger was only exemplified by Lori's as she thought about it. She began anxiously and angrily pacing at the front of her shop, wondering when the parent of this child or someone responsible would arrive to assist. This situation was dire, and that room would only hold her so long. She couldn't understand why they weren't there yet.

Shane had been diligently researching the Cross Country Killer, as the news had so aptly named earlier that evening. They always had to come up with some catchy name for serial killers, despite not knowing if this was actually a person or not. He was trying to determine if this lone wolf had just recently been turned, and that was why he suddenly seemed to pop up with murderous intent. The most likely scenario was that this person had already been a murderer in their human life and once turned, had new tools at their disposal.

He knew he had to change at some point, his wolf was growing restless now that the sky was dark, but he wanted to know. He had to know.

His phone rang, snapping him out of the trance he had fallen into. It was Thomas. His heart skipped a beat. Thomas was already on his way back from the Ozarks. Did something happen? Did they come across the creature?

"Thomas," Shane said in greeting.

"Lori, Lori's changed," Thomas said, his voice shaking more than Shane had ever heard. Absolute fear and dread laced his words.

There was silence between them for a moment as Shane tried to process what Thomas had just said.

"What?" Shane finally asked, standing from his desk and rushing down the stairs. "How do you know?"

"You have to get to the locksmith shop," Thomas said, ignoring Shane's question. Shane could hear Thomas's engine straining as he raced back to the city.

"The locksmith shop? What?" Shane was utterly confused and now enraged. What did that locksmith have to do with Lori's change? He grabbed his keys off the counter where he had discarded them this morning and headed out the back door.

"The locksmith saved her! She somehow knew! She took her before Lori could, could… one of Lori's friends called Cora," Thomas half yelled, half stumbled to say. He was horrified for his daughter and at himself. How could he not have known? How could they not have seen it? "I'm 30 minutes out, but—"

"I'm on my way" was all Shane said as he slammed the car door and sped out of his driveway furiously.

He took the twenty-minute drive in ten, frantically trying to understand the little bit Thomas had said. How did that woman know? How could a human save Lori from… he shivered at the thought. Lori could have massacred that neighborhood. He pulled up behind a beat-up Chevy Lumina and looked the little way down the street to the shop.

He could see the locksmith through the windows. She was nervously pacing behind the front door as she waited for someone to arrive and help the newly changed wolf calm. Her straight dark hair fell over her shoulders like a sheet, and it glistened as she moved. Her body was lean and graceful, hidden beneath the frumpy clothing she chose to wear.

He could see through it though, the way the fabric pressed against her sides as she turned and how soft her long neck and fingers were. His anger and fear, still there, but now stifled slightly by curiosity. He knocked on the door quietly, tentatively, not wanting to frighten her more than she already was. When she turned and noticed him through the glass door, she seemed relieved as she unlocked it and pulled it open.

"Oh, thank god! Are you her father?" she asked, ushering him inside her little shop and closing the door as if someone would notice them.

"No, the Westport Pack Leader. Shane Keenan," he said, offering a hand for the introduction. He didn't want to admit to himself how he felt a small hit of excitement bubble up inside him that he was finally meeting her. Her scent was still intoxicating but having her actually in front of him changed the urgent need to see her, to a desperate desire to know her. She looked at his hand briefly, waving it off as if it insulted her, which confused him.

"Why the hell weren't you watching that girl? She could have killed four others tonight and wouldn't have been able to do a damn thing about it. She's confused and scared. I don't want an introduction! I want you to help her! That's why you're here, right?" she hissed. Her brows pulled together to form a wrinkle between them, and her amber eyes were blazing with a protective fury he had only seen within other wolves.

He was taken aback and unsure of how to respond. That certainly never happened. She knew what he was and yet still had the courage to snap at him.

"Where is she?" he asked, finally, after trying to carefully hide the surprise on his face.

With Shane's arrival, Vee's hold on the calm had slipped away. Lori's wolf's emotions had taken back over, the absolute rage was disconcerting.

"In the back room. I got her in there before the change completed, but—"

There was a crash and an inhuman roar that made the reluctantly hospitable locksmith flinch, and the pack leader turn toward the door just beyond the counter.

He walked to the steal door and touched it, taking in a breath of air so he could get a better feel of the state of his new wolf. She smelled of fear and anger. The pain of the change had subsided, but the beast of the newly changed wolf was certainly fighting to escape its confinement. He looked over at Vee whose eyes were trained on the door, not him, as if she could see beyond the steal at the wolf within.

"Lori, calm down," he said, his voice demanding and powerful, his wolf coming through a bit, so his voice sounded gravelly. It was as if Lori's wolf already knew that he was in charge, that she should listen to him, which was somewhat unusual for a newly-turned wolf. He didn't want to but knew he had to plan to change in front of this woman, in case Lori could not be controlled when leaving. The last thing he wanted was for her to attack the person who just saved her.

But surprisingly, the crashing and monstrous sounds instantly ceased, and he turned to look at the owner of the shop.

"Care to open the door?" he asked, gesturing to the elaborate locks that were in place. She ripped the keys from her pocket, glaring at him as she stomped to where he was. She unlocked each lock with a strange sort of care and precision that he had never seen anyone do. Such care left no scratches on the surface of it.

He felt Thomas's arrival, and he looked out the shop window to see him getting out of the car. His face drained of color, and his eyes pained as he started approaching. Shane held up a hand and nodded for him to stay at the car. No need for more bodies in the store to complicate matters.

The locksmith finished unlocking and removed the furniture she had used as a barricade.

"Unlocked," she said, mimicking his gesture at the door.

When he opened it, he looked down upon the new wolf. Lori's wolf form was small, but she was also young and a female. Females tended to be smaller in size. Her coloring was exactly like her father's, a strange black that had flecks of red sprinkled about. Her eyes were as shockingly blue as her brother's.

She wasn't completely calm, by any means, but she was controllable, maintaining composure while she was beside Shane.

"Come, Lori. Your father will take you now," Shane said, patting his thigh as if she were a dog and leading her to the front of the shop where her youthful father waited outside, worry lines evident on his face. Lori's wolf climbed into the back of her father's SUV. "I'll meet you at my house. Just take her straight to the basement," Shane told Thomas from the front passenger window.

As Thomas and Lori drove away toward his house, he went back into the shop, where the woman stood strangely still in the middle of the showroom. Her arms were wrapped around her torso as if she were holding herself together. He had to know how she managed to do this. How had she known Lori was going to change? Not only that, why had she helped

Lori? For whatever reason, she had saved not only Lori but also her friends.

"Can I trust you to keep this secret..?" he asked, pausing to get her name.

"Vee," she said quickly, still staring at the spot where Lori's wolf had climbed into the back of her father's car. "And I won't tell a soul," she whispered, her voice as haunting as her gaze when she turned back to him.

"Good" was all he said before he turned to leave. He wanted to say so much more, ask so

many more questions, but now was not the time. He had to attend to Lori at home, and his wolf was begging to come out.

CHAPTER 9

Vee stood in silence. It was all so still now that they had left. She was grappling and gasping slightly with the fact that the emotions she was feeling now were, in fact, her own. Relief, sure, now that the girl was in the proper hands. The shaky anxiety after that surge of adrenaline, yes. But also absolute, utter fear.

She revealed herself.

She had made herself known to a werewolf of all creatures.

She slowly walked to the front door, locking it with trembling hands.

Change.

The goosebumps on her skin, the warnings that she had sensed all around her had come to fruition. This was the beginning of... of what? Certainly not returning to normalcy. The werewolves didn't know what she was, but they were now aware she knew what they were.

She closed her eyes and took a deep breath, willing herself to turn around and see the destruction in her inventory room. From the open door she could see the claw marks gouging the concrete floor, blood and scraps of Lori's clothes, screws and the remaining shreds of her spreadsheets all scattered across the floor. Her eyes welled with tears.

Every moment of this day had been warning her and now, there she stood in the entrance of her back room, looking at the complete and utter demolition of everything she had built for herself.

She was vaguely aware that her phone was ringing in her pocket. She pulled it out without looking to see who it was.

"Hello?" She answered, her voice flat and emotionless.

"Vee, let me in," came Durran's voice. She turned around and saw her peering through the glass door, phone at her ear.

Vee walked over to the door slowly and unlocked it again, her feet incapable of going any faster. She had transitioned into feeling numb now. It was all too overwhelming. She just wanted to be alone and process everything.

"Vee, are you okay? What happened?" Durran asked, her voice panicked as she locked the door behind her.

"I… I…" Vee's words fell short at her tongue. How to explain what had just happened?

"I saw the Westport Pack leader leaving…" Durran said cautiously, watching Vee's face change from stunned to confused.

"I saved one of them," she whispered, turning to look at the leveled room behind her once more. Durran's brow furrowed, not sure of how to take that information in. How could this little creature save a werewolf?

"What?"

"She didn't know she was turning, and the girls were all just standing there. She would have killed them" was all Vee could manage to say, looking up into Durran's eyes, which had turned bright red. Vee had never seen her eyes so bright.

Durran stood silent for a few moments. The realization she had failed as Vee's Watcher was dawning on her now. They knew about Vee, or at least to some degree. This complicated everything. That wolf had already been snooping around her and now… Had they planned that? Did they purposefully put those people in danger to expose Vee?

Durran was furious. Vee looked at her and her confusion deepened.

"Why are you so angry?" Vee asked, stepping away from Durran a moment to try to understand the emotions she could feel coming off of her.

"I'm just… how could they let that happen?" Durran ground out through clenched teeth, her hands in tight fists at her side.

"I don't know!" Vee exclaimed, throwing her hands in the air. She was having a hard time not letting Durran's emotions affect her. Her control was spent.

"Do you know how dangerous this is?" Durran continued, starting to pace across the shop.

"I'm *very* aware of how dangerous this is. I can't handle your emotions right now," Vee warned, placing her hands in either side of her head, as if it would somehow help her block Durran's anger and fear.

"What are they going to do now?" Durran asked, mostly herself, as she continued to pace.

"For now, they are focused on their new Were, not me," Vee said, glaring now as her friend was clearly not listening to her.

"This could be a disaster… you'll have to—"

"I am not doing anything more right now. I cannot take any more tonight. Go." Vee's words weren't loud, but icy as they came from her mouth. Durran looked at Vee, assessing her more fully than she had when she had come in.

Her normally emerald eyes were vivid amber, without even feeling her emotions, Durran could see the rage radiating, making the air seem to throb and ripple around her. She was pale and shaking. The shirt on her right shoulder was stained with blood. Vee was a complete mess at that moment and Durran's presence was simply making it worse for her right now.

"I-I'll call you tomorrow," she said quietly, nodding shortly before unlocking and heading back out of the shop.

She would have to be more conscious of how she let off her emotions surrounding this. Her very real feelings for Vee clouded her actual objective, which was Vee's protection, and she had definitely failed in that on this occasion.

Vee let out a little sob as soon as Durran was far enough away, and she could no longer feel her. There was nothing she could mentally handle doing at that moment, and it was far later to be leaving with all the activity going on in Westport now than she would have liked. She closed the steel door, breathing deeply with the knowledge that she had days of work to get it even remotely resembling what it had been before. Days of work that would mean no money was coming in.

She turned on the alarm and left the shop, exhausted, but not knowing if she'd be able to sleep. There were too many unknowns now, and she didn't have an ounce of feeling left in her to fully process what she had been through.

She somehow made it home, despite the traffic, and she notice Midi perched in Una's window, watching and waiting for Vee's return. She appreciated that sweet cat. At least she had someone watching out for her. The drive home had given her a little bit of time where she could block out the feelings around her, but now that she was there the presence of her neighbors' minds as they dreamed didn't provide the comfort it usually did.

It was like she was an exposed nerve. Everything affected her more than it usually would at that moment. She sluggishly moved through the building. Climbing the stairs took far more strength than it should have, and she arrived in her apartment, out of breath and in tears.

Somehow, going through the change of Lori's wolf with her had ripped off her emotional skin and left her raw to everything around her. She knew it wouldn't help anything, but she decided to break out the liquor. If she was drunk enough, maybe she would just black out. She dropped her things on the floor, not really caring where they ended up, and went immediately

to the kitchen. Snatching the liquor bottles from the cabinet and taking them with her to the futon. No glass required. She turned on the television, mostly as a distraction from the quiet. The silence only proved to allow her to think more, and right now, she didn't want to think about anything. She didn't want to feel anymore.

Shane woke on one of the less-than-comfortable couches that he had in the basement. He looked across the room to see Thomas, sitting on the floor, one hand on Lori's arm and the other bracing his head as he slept. Lori was stretched across the couch, covered in a soft warm blanket. She had fallen asleep as her wolf just a few hours before. Once she had returned to her human form, Thomas had carefully placed her on the nearest couch, and they had wrapped her naked body so she would feel less exposed when she woke up.

Over time she would feel more comfortable about the nudity. They all had to grow accustomed to it at the beginning. Shane and Thomas, having been able to change at their own will, still had their clothes to change back into once she had fallen asleep.

Shane sat up and placed his head in his hands. He wasn't sure what to do. Not that he could do anything about Lori. She was a werewolf, and she would, of course, be welcomed into the pack. It would be a difficult time for her, but she would adjust. She *had to* adjust to survive. He stood up, looking at the father and daughter sleeping peacefully. He would give them time alone when she woke up. Thomas would want to talk to her privately. There were other matters, however, that Shane had to decide on.

Vee.

He went to his kitchen, checking his phone which he had left on the counter the night before. No additional phone calls, just a text message from Margaret saying the rest of the pack was fine. No other Weres had been detected so far, but they were still going to patrol widely, making sure to get close to the interstate. It was the most direct way from St. Louis to Kansas City.

It was about noon at that point. He wanted to wait for Thomas to wake up before he left again, but he knew he needed to talk to Vee at some point. He didn't see her as any sort of threat. No, her eyes told him she could be trusted when she promised not to tell anyone, but he needed to understand what happened. How did she know Lori was going to change?

He searched for *The Missing Key* again and pulled up the phone number. The shop was listed as closed on Sundays, which he was mildly disappointed about. Part of him wanted to just drive back over there and talk to her again, but she certainly would be lying low after last night. He called the number anyway, deciding he would leave his number there for her to call back at some point. Hoping she would.

The answering machine picked up after a few rings.

"Thank you for calling The Missing Key. *We aren't open right now, but if you have an emergency lock situation, you can call our emergency number at—"*

Shane turned around searching for anything he could write the number down on. He managed to find a piece of mail and a pencil, furiously scribbling down the number before he forgot. With an oddly satisfied sigh, he looked at it. He speculated it was her cell phone. Now he wasn't limited in the times he could call.

He heard a little movement in the basement and decided to start the coffee instead of calling her. It sounded like it was just Thomas moving, but they would both need a cup of liquid energy before they could actually get into the difficult conversation ahead of them. And that's when he remembered Lori didn't have any clothes. Quickly, but not too noisily, he made his way upstairs. His clothes would be far too large on her, but a pair of Patrick's sweats would probably do the trick.

When he came back down to the kitchen, Thomas was pouring some coffee. His youthful face was showing his age behind his eyes.

"Some of Patrick's things for her. I'll need to start keeping smaller sizes here just in case," Shane said, offering a small smile to his friend as he set the clothes on the counter. They had been pack members and friends long before Shane had become the leader. Thomas was probably Shane's oldest friend, and he was gratefully. So many other people they had cared about in the past were gone, and they still had each other.

Thomas smiled weakly back.

"Thank you… she's still not awake, but I think she will be soon. That was not an ideal first change," Thomas said, gripping the counter tightly as he leaned on it, Shane could see the muscles in his shoulders tensing.

"I know. Tonight will be better. We should take her to Maple Woods. She needs to hunt, but we can't go too far," Shane told him. Maple Woods wasn't very large, but it was both close enough for them to get to and from quickly, as well as filled with smaller animals for her to go after. The first changes were all instinct and no control. The basement had been somewhat of a battleground the night before with brief moments of calm when Shane's wolf exuded his power.

Thomas looked relieved that Shane had some sort of plan.

"Wha- where... *Daddy*?" Came Lori's voice from the basement, confused and shaky. Thomas and Shane quickly went back down to her. She was sitting up on the couch, the blanket wrapped around her tightly. She looked at both of them as they entered the room with an expression that made her seem like she had just seen a ghost.

"I'm here, Lori," Thomas said, crouching before the couch in front of her.

"Where are we?"

"Shane's house. This is the basement," Thomas said, looking around the room. It was rather intimidating looking. While it had the couches, there was little else in the way of comforts. The walls had shelves of supplies, mostly for the security company, but there were also silver chains, various bladed weapons, and a massive cage. She had never been allowed down in Shane's basement, and it was terrifying.

Lori shook as she looked around. She was not expecting to wake up to this at all. She narrowed her eyes, furrowing her brow as she tried to think of the last thing she remembered.

Pain.

The horrible pain as her body ripped apart, morphing into… a wolf. She gasped in realization, eyes welling with tears.

"I…"

"You're one of us, honey," Thomas said, nodding and reaching up to wipe the tears from her cheeks. Shane went back upstairs then, leaving the sweats nearby for her to change into, but giving them room. She needed time.

He decided he wouldn't call Vee. Not right now at least. So, he simply texted her.

[Shane: Vee, this is Shane. We will need to talk.]

For now, he would leave it at that.

CHAPTER 10

Vee woke to the sound of her phone notification going off. She was in a very uncomfortable position on her futon, and her head felt like it was going to explode. She realized she had no idea where her phone was, but after a moment of trying to recall, she decided she didn't care anymore. Ibuprofen was the only thing on her mind.

She got up, went to her bathroom to find the cure all, and after grabbing the bottle and closing the medicine cabinet again, she saw her reflection.

Her reflection was quite the sight. Her hair was a mess, face puffy from tears she didn't recall shedding, and her shirtsleeve was stuck to her shoulder with her own blood. Now that she noticed the blood caked against her skin, and the stiffness of her sleeve, she felt the pain there too. As her shoulder started throbbing worse than her head, she started laughing uncontrollably at her own appearance. It was ridiculous. It was horrifying. She was in serious danger, but she just couldn't stop.

She had felt the pain in her shoulder when Lori's claws dug into her skin but had completely pushed it to the side while everything had been happening the night before. Now that she was looking at her blood-soaked shirt, she couldn't ignore it anymore. She couldn't ignore any of it.

Last night happened.

It wasn't just a nightmare she cooked up from her fears the day before. Her laughter died in her throat, and she swallowed the ibuprofen. Nothing would fix this situation, but she had work to do. Distraction would keep her level. She went into her room, to look at her alarm clock. One in the afternoon. Well, it could have been worse. The shop wasn't open anyway, but she would most likely be pulling an all-nighter to get that inventory room back in some semblance of order so she could function on Monday.

She started her shower water and went to the living room to grab her hastily discarded bag of clean clothes from the floor and right beside it her messenger bag. That's when she remembered what woke her up in the first place. Her phone.

She pulled the phone out of its pocket at the side of the bag and saw a message from a number she didn't recognize.

[Shane: Vee, this is Shane. We will need to talk.]

The pack leader. Of course, he would get her cell number. She had it clearly listed right on her voicemail.

She considered the words he chose. He wasn't demanding to talk now, just saying it will need to happen at some point and for that she was grateful. She didn't think she could handle another prolonged Were situation today. She texted back, saving his number in her phone.

[Vee: Yes. We will.]

She knew this wouldn't be the last time she would be dealing with him, so might as well have him in there, just in case. She turned back to her tasks at hand. Showering and dressing herself proved to be more of a challenge with her injured shoulder than she would have liked to admit. It would inhibit how quickly she was going to be able to put back the pieces of her life, and her shop. She pushed that from her mind, continued getting herself ready, ate a small bowl of cereal, and headed to the shop.

By the time she got there, it was nearly 2 p.m., and she was growing increasingly anxious about what she would find in that room. She saw it last night, but she felt certain she didn't remember it all correctly. She hesitated to open the steal door after dropping her bag on the counter next to her still unfinished projects.

It was worse than she remembered. The torn clothes and blood were left exactly where Vee had dropped Lori. Blood was also splattered all over the shelves and on the ceiling. Vee was shocked. She had seen werewolf transformations before, but they never involved blood. Maybe this had something to do with the first change?

She grabbed a box of gloves from under the counter, threw her hair into a messy bun to keep it out of her face, and got to work.

Hours passed and Vee paused to look at how much was left to do. It was still so horribly disorganized; she had just thrown similar things together in boxes. She had managed to put back the shelves where they belonged, and at least most of the blood was gone. Bleach was her friend, and she was glad it was something she kept on hand even if she rarely used it.

It was well past 9 p.m. at that point, and all she had eaten was cereal before she left the house, so she had to get something in her. She grabbed her bag and headed to the gas station just down the road. It wasn't ideal; she would have preferred real food, but she didn't have time. She walked through the aisles, grabbing a couple bags of chips and then wandering over to the soda fountain. She would need a little more caffeine to get her through the night.

She felt the vibration of a Were enter the store then, just as she was hitting the cup to the ice dispenser. She froze. Not only was this a Were, but she knew they were… hunting. The feeling of a predatory urge slithering through her mind. They had to be in their human form, a giant wolf would have stood out, and the few people in the gas station would have been screaming.

She really didn't need anything else to go wrong right now. Too many new variables in her life were piling up. She steadied herself, finished filling her cup, and moved to the register. The Were was going the opposite way down the aisle beside hers. She didn't look directly at him, but she took note of his appearance. A black motorcycle jacket, light brown hair... or maybe dirty blond. He wasn't terribly tall, in fact, a little shorter than average but still taller than her.

When they passed each other, with the shelves between him, he froze. This was no longer a search for his prey. He had found it. Vee kept going, remaining seemingly unaware of him, though internally she was trying to tamp down on her terror. He'd be able to smell her fear.

"Weird night, huh?" the clerk asked when she set her items on the counter, making Vee chuckle a little nervously.

"Yeah, I guess so" was all she said in return, trying to keep her eyes trained forward, even though she felt the Were getting closer.

"Full moon the last few days... brings out all the crazies," the clerk continued as he scanned her handful of items and rang up her soda.

"That's what they say," Vee said, swiping her card in the reader. "I hope it gets less weird for you," she said quickly, but not hurriedly, heading straight to her shop.

As she had left, he seemed to stay behind. She made it back inside, abruptly locking the door behind her. His mind and emotions were distancing from her, as if he remained at the station for her whole trek back.

For a moment she was relieved, breathing in a sigh of relief and turning back to her task at hand, but then she felt him getting closer again. Her stomach churned, and the food in her hands might as well have been ashes. The door was locked, but the whole storefront was glass. That wouldn't hold a Were long. She continued to pretend she didn't know he was there, keeping her back firmly to the door as she returned to the back room. There was a back exit, and she had installed locks on that side of the steal door as well, but she wasn't sure if Lori's activities the night before would have damaged it too much to keep the internal locks from lining up.

As she turned around to close it, she could see yellow eyes peering at her through the front window. She managed to lock the top and bottom deadbolts, but there was a very large gash at the middle of the door preventing her from securing the others.

She raced to the back exit, peering out the peephole to see if he was coming around. Though, it had only been moments ago he had been looking through the glass. No, he wasn't. Good. The building stretched the whole block with several shops only separated by a wall. He didn't seem to be in any sort of hurry and was taking his time to come around to the back as though he was enjoying the hunt.

Was this one of Shane's men? She thought they were going to talk! She didn't think that meant she would be hunted down and apparently slaughtered.

The Were's mind dissipated again. She wasn't going to fool herself into thinking she was safe, not after the predatory way he was feeling. The hunger and lust rolled together with a complete and utter need to kill.

She pulled out her phone and to text Durran, who for some reason hadn't called her today, despite saying she would.

[Vee: There's a situation at the shop.]

She hit send as she looked around for a weapon. What good it would do, she didn't know. With her right arm being at half capacity since her injury she didn't really see herself capable of overpowering a werewolf. Durran texted back immediately.

[Durran: I was about to come by.]

[Vee: There's a Were. I think it's hunting me.]

There was no response. Vee could feel the Were's approach again. Still at a distance but not by much. She could feel him coming down the alley.

Durran hadn't been lying; she was about to come by. She had hesitated all day about calling Vee. Not sure if her presence would make things worse, but both her duty as a Watcher and her feelings for Vee couldn't keep her away all day. She originally went by Vee's apartment, which was still dark, and she could tell she wasn't home. The only other logical place was the shop, and as Durran had pulled up on the opposite side of the street, she saw the Were at the door.

At first Durran thought it could have been one of Shane's pack members, keeping tabs on her until Shane could conclusively decide if she was a threat to them or not. That would have been standard in a situation like this, but no. This man was trying to get to Vee. He eagerly looked through the darkened glass window and sniffed hungrily at the air. As he started to walk up the sidewalk, Durran realized that he was heading for the back entrance, and that was when Vee's text came through.

She had sensed it too.

Durran quickly got out of the car, looking up and down the busy street. She didn't want to use her wings if she could be seen, but Vee's life could depend on it. Hoping no one around was paying attention, she let her wings expand, took off into the air, and landed on the roof of the shop.

She could see him coming down the alley behind the building. He wasn't rushing, but his stride showed his eager anticipation. What was he planning on doing?

Did Shane know this wolf was in his territory?

Durran's eyes narrowed, and she jumped down several feet in front of him, halting him in his tracks.

"Not this one," Durran said, her voice lower and reverberating.

He smiled, sticking his hands in his pockets. His hair was blond but darkened by grease. His leather jacket was worn, but in good condition, perhaps the only object he cared about. The smell coming off of him was dirty musk tainted with predatory phero-mones. His stance was filled with arrogance, eyes twin-kling with a humor that barely masked the murderous intentions hidden there.

"I don't know what you mean, but I've never seen anything like you before," the Were said, taking in the sight of Durran whose wings were still outstretched, blocking the rear entrance from view.

"If you don't know what I am, wolf, then you are too young to be tangling in the likes of this level. This one is not for you," Durran said, chiding this creature and reiterating her demand. He was arrogant and naive. A creature made, but not taught. Perhaps he survived an attack by mistake.

"I was just looking!" he said, laughing, his words insincere. Like a child promising they wouldn't take the last cookie, his face glimmered with false assurances.

"Go" was all Durran said, growing her height a few more feet and towering over the man.

"For now…" He smiled again, raising his eyebrows and glancing at the door one last time before turning on his heel and walking back down the alley.

The way he strutted away with confidence made Durran feel more certain about his intent. She knew this man was going to go find someone else to prey on, but her duty was to Vee. She returned to her human appearance and turned to the door. She could tell Vee was just on the other side, having listened to the full exchange.

"One more thing I have to do, Vee," Durran said, pulling out her phone from her pocket and dialing. She had only ever had the one conversation with Shane, and didn't know his number, but she knew others who would be able to get in contact with members of the pack. It seemed like it was time to acquaint herself with the Westport pack, something she had been trying to avoid.

"This needs to reach Shane Keenan. I just came across a lone wolf hunting in his territory… within the city." That was all she needed say before she hung up the phone and went to the door.

"All good now?" Vee asked through the door. Her voice was a little shaken, but she was trying to use a more lighthearted tone.

"Yes," Durran said, lightly placing a hand on the door as Vee began unlocking it.

Vee's expression was hard to pinpoint. It seemed like it was flitting between relief, happiness, and utter exhaustion. She stepped aside to let Durran in, taking a moment to anxiously glance out at the alley before slamming the door closed and securing it once again.

"You seem to keep finding yourself in precarious situations, Vee," Durran said, looking over the chaotic back room. She had only ever seen this room when the door was open from the showroom. This was a far cry from what little bit she would normally see.

The shelves were where they belonged, but everything else was haphazardly thrown into boxes. The metallic scent of blood still hung in the air as well as the sting of cleaning products. There were trash bags with discarded, broken supplies piled near the back door, and deep gouges from claw marks were on the floor and the steel door that led to the show room.

"Yes, yes, well it's become my life's work," Vee said sarcastically in response, going to her discarded food stuffs on the floor, and snatching them up. She still didn't have an appetite, but she knew her body was hungry, and she needed the distraction of chips crunching.

They were both quiet for a moment. Durran looked over the room and Vee watched her, trying not to let her anxiety consume her.

"Was it one of Shane's?" Vee asked, surprised at how easily the man's name left her mouth, as if she had known his name longer than a day.

"No, that was a lone wolf. I don't think Shane even knows he's in the territory," Durran told her honestly, turning away from the claw marks at the door and letting her eyes fall on Vee's shoulder, which she knew was bandaged under the clean sleeve. It was rather remarkable that she got as much accomplished in this room as she did with that injury. Most humans would not have been able to move their arm for days, let alone put shelves back in place.

"I seem to be some sort of Were magnet these days. I should just hide out at home on full moons from now on," she grumbled, not fully hiding in her voice how much better she felt knowing that Shane wasn't trying to kill her. She wasn't quite sure why it mattered to her so much, what Shane thought of her.

"I think we should get you home, now, Vee," Durran said seriously, picking up her bag. Panic crossed Vee's face, and Durran assumed it was about leaving when that Were might still be out there. "He's gone for now. You're safe."

"There's so much work left to do!" Vee said, gesturing around exasperated. Durran chuckled.

"Tomorrow," she told her, unlocking the steel door and ushering her out to the showroom.

"But—"

"No. I will even come by to help," Durran said as she waited at the front door for Vee to set the alarm. She did, even though she was a little shaken by Durran's words. Not that Vee ever really wanted anyone's help, but Durran had never done more than suggest Vee should hire someone. The fact that she had offered to help get the shop back in working order shocked her.

They went out the front door and after Vee locked it she turned very briefly wrapped her arms around Durran. She hated feeling powerless. She hated depending on others at all, but she was grateful she had a friend. She had someone in her life who cared, and she wanted to reciprocate in the only way she knew she could in that moment. Durran froze initially at the contact, shocked by the affection. After a moment of letting the euphoria of Vee holding her so close sink in, she too wrapped her arms around the little woman before her. For a brief quiet moment, they stood their holding each other.

CHAPTER 11

It was the early morning hours. The moon was still prominent in the sky. Shane's wolf stood a little ways away from where Thomas and Lori's wolves were playing. The moon would soon fade as the sun made its appearance, but for now, they still had to stay in Maple Woods on their own mini-run with Lori. They had both been quite shocked at the amount of control she already seemed to have. She didn't go rampaging through the woods when she changed into her wolf with the last full moon of this cycle.

In fact, when she stepped into the woods, her transformation had been so smooth. Normally the first few changes were wrought with flesh tearing and agony until the human part of them learned to accept the wolf. Lori had apparently very easily come to terms with hers. Maybe it was because she had grown up around them. Maybe because she was female. There would probably be no good explanation for it.

The conversation earlier in the day about her actual change was extremely illuminating. Lori couldn't explain how Vee had known what she was, or that she was changing, but the gratitude in her voice as she talked about it was astounding. How that small woman had basically carried Lori into her shop, Shane didn't know. She was definitely something preternatural, the likes of which he had never seen.

Lori mentioned how there were points while she was in the room when she could somehow feel Vee comforting her. The pain had been unbearable, and the loss of control to the wolf within her had been frightening, but Vee assured her it would be okay. Somehow Lori knew that she was safe the moment Vee had told her she was.

At the thought of Vee, Shane had a strange, uneasy feeling. She looked over and locked eyes with Thomas briefly, making sure the two of them were okay for the time being. Thomas signaled they were, and with that knowledge, he felt a little better about changing back to check his phone.

Just as he picked it up, it rang.

Margaret.

"Yes," he answered, confused.

"The rogue is in the city," she said, the noises behind her were chaotic sounds of frantic packing, a few wolves howling. "I've already sent six of them back, but…"

"How do you know this?" Shane asked, pulling his clothes on as quickly as he could.

"Emily's hawk friend called. A Watcher saw it," Margaret said, as a car door slammed and the engine roared to life. Emily was a newer pack member, if by new you considered a year. She had been a lone wolf for some time and made friends with some other groups of shapeshifters in her travels. Some of which she still spoke to, like the small kettle of werehawks that lived in southeastern Nebraska, and it was nice to have connections like that if the need arose.

Shane was coming to terms with what Margaret had just said. A Watcher saw it. Shane froze for a moment, turning back to Thomas and Lori.

Vee.

"Just get home," Shane ordered, hanging up the phone and heading over to them. "I need to go. Some of the others are already heading back. It's in the city," Shane told Thomas's wolf, who clearly was torn between wanting to go with his leader and his newly turned daughter. "Just come back as soon as you can," Shane told him, before taking off through the woods toward his car.

He drove, first to Vee's shop, his car screeching to a halt just out front of it. It was so early in the morning still that no cars were on the street. It was that strange window when everyone seemed to be asleep. The storefront didn't seem to be disturbed; the darkened shop cast only in the eerie streetlight. He got out, taking in a deep breath.

Yes, a Were, but not one of his own, had been there.

He continued to follow the scent, envisioning how the creature pressed against the glass, his greasy handprints still there, following his movements around the long building to the back alley. As Shane followed he became angry. Not only was this man in his territory, but he was after Vee. Her scent wasn't even back here behind the building. He had been hunting her, trying to find a way into the shop to get to her.

As he approached the back entrance, he finally smelled the Watcher. The same one he had come across the day before when he had come here to investigate Vee.

"It's long gone," came a voice from above. There, the Watcher crouched on the flat roof of the building, watching him. It dropped down in front of him and leaned on the back door.

"You know who I am, but I only know you're a Watcher," Shane said, folding his arms across his chest. If this were a battle of dominance, Shane could tell they would be on equal footing, but this was more about respect. Shane was in charge of this territory; it was his, as far as most other preternaturals in the area were concerned. They would, undoubtedly, be crossing paths more often, seeing that they now had Vee as a connection.

"Durran," she said, her eyes flashing red for a brief moment as she said her name. "It was stalking her. I don't know if it will come back to her or not, but for tonight she's safe," Durran told him, watching as his body only slightly relaxed at the word of Vee's safety.

"How can you be sure?" Shane asked, seeing as how Durran was before him and not watching over Vee, wherever she was.

"It found someone else to suit its needs for the time being," Durran said quietly, guilt coming over her face at the admission. She felt partially responsible for the death of someone else, a death she could have prevented had certain rules not been in place.

Watchers were forbidden to kill a Were in wolf territory.

Shane was still. This wolf killed someone on his ground. He growled uncontrollably. Whether the rogue knew it or not, he had just drawn first blood.

"I expect you'll keep me informed if you see or hear any more about him," Shane said, pulling his wallet from his pocket and producing a card. Durran moved closer, taking the card from his outstretched hand and looking it over. Just a simple white card with his name and phone number. This was not the business card he used with humans.

"Expect nothing from me, wolf," Durran said, her voice cold as she looked him in the eyes.

Shane narrowed his but said nothing more as he left the alley.

Vee slept restlessly the night before, like her brain was searching for the feeling of a Were around her apartment subconsciously, rousing her from slumber every time even the mildest change in her neighbors' moods happened. She was awake, staring at her ceiling when her alarm finally went off.

She had been thinking about what she should do with this situation she found herself in. It seemed like preternaturals were coming out of the woodwork now.

The last time she had been threatened with exposure to that world, she fled. This time, she had put down roots. She had a business, and although she was alone, it would be exceedingly difficult to just pick up everything and walk away like she had before.

She sat up, looking at the brightening sky out her window. If there was any time she would be safe, it would've been now. She checked her phone, even though she had checked it frequently throughout the night. Somehow, she thought maybe she had finally missed something. No. Still nothing.

Coffee and fear would be the only things keeping her going today, and she was seriously lacking in the former. Her coffee pot was still gurgling as she wandered in to get some, her television was on from the night before but down low enough to not disturb her neighbors. She, however, caught the distinct words "brutal murder" and immediately rushed to the futon her coffee lacking its milk but still in her hand.

"The Cross Country Killer seems to have made it to Kansas City, now. A body was found in the wooded area just around Gillham Park. This attack is outside of the similar conditions seen in the more recent prior cases, being that it was directly within the city, instead of the outskirts, leading some officials to suspect there may be a copycat in our midst," the field reporter said while they stood in front of a series of apartments, the backs of which faced Gillham Road. There were small, heavy patches of trees that lay just around there with basically no light. It would be easy for someone to murder someone there.

It was minutes from her home.

She just knew it wasn't a copycat. The way his energy pulsed with the hunt as he came for her. *He* was the killer.

Vee's heart sank. She lived, but someone else wasn't so lucky. It was supposed to be her. She had a hard time shaking that knowledge from her mind as she slowly got herself ready to go and headed for the door. The sadness that ate at her didn't stop her from being vigilant as she left her apartment and walked to her car. Thankfully, there were still no Weres tingling at her brain as she drove.

The humidity wasn't letting up, and she was already sweating by the time she arrived. It was early enough in the day that the only traffic was the Monday morning commuters. She hurried inside and locked the door behind her before turning off the alarm. She felt the approach of a Were causing her to freeze in place, trying to feel out their emotions. However, they were feeling curious, remorseful, grateful, not anything like the cold-blooded intentions of the Were from last night.

She turned and looked at the large man standing outside her door. It wasn't Shane, obvious from his deep brown skin and shaved head, but she recognized him from Saturday night as Lori's father. She went to the door, unlocked it, and stepped away to give him room to enter.

"Vee, right?" he asked, once he had closed the door behind him.

"Yes," she said, trying to give him a little smile, but she wasn't good at faking emotions. This was uncomfortable, and she was scared. She we certain he would be able to tell those things, even if she had been a good actress.

"I'm Thomas. We didn't have chance to meet the other night," he said, extending his hand. She shook her head at the hand slightly.

"Sorry, I don't really shake, but thank you," she said, trying not to be dismissive of the gesture. She didn't like touching anyone normally, since it only amplified their emotions, but even more so at the moment. She was still much more sensitive after having shared in Lori's change.

He nodded and put his hands in his pockets.

"I wanted to thank you. You don't understand how much you've done to help my daughter," he said. The sincerity washing over her was unexpected. She wasn't sure what to say. She would be lying if she said anyone would have done it. These days people were more likely to ignore or record rather than help someone in need.

"I would like to say anyone would have done it, but…" she murmured, mirroring her own thoughts.

"We both know that's not true," Thomas said, smiling kindly at her, the little crow's feet at his eyes the only part of him that revealed a little of his age. They stood there for a moment awkwardly.

"Well, I have a lot of work to do…" she started, glancing at the door to suggest he could head back out. He looked around nervously.

"That wasn't my only reason for being here; I'm sorry to admit," he said, now rocking on his feet a little.

"Oh?" Vee asked, raising her eyebrow skeptically.

"Until the lone wolf is caught, Shane wants someone here with you," Thomas told her, unsure of what her reaction would be.

Vee's eyes narrowed. She was mildly relieved, despite knowing that Durran was going to be here with her all day, but her stubbornness had won out. She couldn't handle a werewolf on her own. She would never win that fight, but the audacity to send someone to guard her without at least speaking to her about it first made her incredibly angry. How *dare* Shane?

"I am clearly capable of taking care of myself, Thomas," she said, turning away from him now and throwing her bag onto the counter.

"You are brave, Vee, and smart, but that's nothing in comparison to a wolf that wants you for their prey," he said quietly, following her to the back of the shop, but still giving her space so as not to upset her further.

"I didn't sign up for being babysat when I decided to save your daughter," Vee snapped, turning to look at him just as she went to open the steel door.

"I know that. He knows that. But... well, think of it as his way of thanking you. He doesn't want you to die."

"He doesn't want me to die before he's had a chance to interrogate me," Vee corrected, opening the door now and turning on the light.

The smell of Lori's blood hit Thomas, and had he been in his wolf form, his hackles would have raised. He watched her for a moment as she pattered into the room, looking around and deciding where she would begin that day. He stepped forward to stand in the doorway; his eyes traveling around the room. It was as if he were trying see what Lori's first change had been like, alone in this room. He could see the blood spatter on the ceiling where Vee couldn't reach, the claw marks on the concrete floor where Lori had dug as her body ripped apart on its own accord only to be put back together again in wolf form.

Vee turned around, feeling his sadness. She watched him as he crouched down, touching the marks on the floor gently.

"I don't know if I'll ever be able to forgive myself," Thomas whispered, closing his eyes.

"She's okay, though," Vee said, still not sure of how true that was but hoping it was.

"She is, but I should have known," Thomas said, looking up at Vee, his regret was palpable. It echoed what she had thought that night. Someone should have known, but she would never say anything like that to them. It was painful enough, an oversight that could have been quite costly.

It was that moment, without either of them having sensed a thing, that there was the sound of the door opening, and then suddenly Durran was at Thomas's back, hand positioned at his throat.

Vee gasped at the sudden protective wave of aggression that came over her from Durran.

"No, Durran!" Vee yelled, and Thomas growled, his eyes glowing and fists clenching. Durran paused in her assault, breathing heavily as she looked up at Vee. "This is Thomas, from Shane's pack!" Vee said, her hands up as if it would stop Durran.

Durran violently released him from her grasp, stepping back into the doorway. She was breathing heavily, her eyes glowing red.

"What is it doing here?" Durran hissed through clenched teeth, speaking to Vee, but glaring at the back of Thomas's head.

"Shane sent him here," Vee said, standing still and looking between her and Thomas. She wasn't sure the threat was over. Thomas had just been attacked, and Durran looked like she was ready to murder anything that moved. They all just remained still in silence for a moment, taking in that there was no threat.

"Shane mentioned a Watcher," Thomas said quietly, remaining crouched but now looking at Vee, his normal eyes had returned. He was feeling calm, unthreatened now, and that was enough for Vee at that moment.

"Um… yes, this is Durran. Durran, Thomas," Vee said gesturing between them. Thomas stood now, his form towering over even Durran. Vee knew, and so did he, that Durran's form didn't attest to her true strength though.

"Looks like you don't need me to help today, Vee," Durran said, her voice clipped as she looked at the Were between them.

"But—"

"I have wards that need watching" was all she said before she turned sharply and walked right back out the front of the shop.

Vee was speechless. Was it like Durran to just leave? Yes, but Vee had never seen her so angry.

"That one is a real charmer," Thomas said after a few quiet moments, his attempt at lightening the mood.

"Yes…" Vee said, finally allowing herself to deflate a little, after holding herself so tensely. Durran was her friend, but all these intense emotions were taking a toll.

This was why she chose to be alone in general and certainly why she tried to stay out of preternatural affairs. With them came drama. "I need to get to work," she said, finally turning back to her piles of boxes. If she engrossed herself in her task, maybe she could pretend her life wasn't falling apart.

"What can I do to help?" Thomas asked, noticing the worry on her face.

She sighed, bending over to grab a box.

"Do you want to start sorting parts?" she asked, shifting her eyes from him to the jumbled contents. He raised his eyebrows and chuckled a little, taking the box from her.

"I did offer."

CHAPTER 12

The day passed rather uneventfully. Thomas at some point changed places with Tommy, his son, so he could get a few hours of sleep. Vee was surprised at how willing they both were to help her. They sorted the jumbled boxes, while she reorganized the shelves and started to get the inventory sheets redone. Off and on Vee would stop to text Durran.

[Vee: I thought you said you were going to help me today?]

[Durran: You seem to have all the help you need.]

[Vee: Apparently I can't send him away so I might as well use the extra hands.]

Vee retorted, irritated that Durran was pouting like a child.

[Durran: Thomas, still?]

[Vee: His son, now.]

She set the phone down, rolling her eyes at the lack of response. She decided to continue on, getting engrossed in her spreadsheets. It was becoming increasingly obvious how much inventory she had lost. Her heart was sinking. There went the new vehicle fund. Weres had nearly funded it… and Weres almost instantly took it away.

Vee had made easy enough conversation with Thomas, talking about Cora and Lori, but once Tommy had gotten there, she was a little conversationally spent. She didn't normally talk this much. He seemed to be grappling with his own feelings. His emotions were laced with concerns for his sister.

"So, you're here, your dad is sleeping, what's the rest of the pack up to?" she decided to ask, noticing him become slightly intrigued when she started the conversation. She got the feeling he was normally talkative but was holding back. She wasn't sure if it was of his own volition. For all she knew, Shane had told him to keep quiet until he could do the questioning.

"Shane and some of the others went to the site to catch the scent. I went earlier with them, so I would know it for this." Mild pity. She found that bothersome, but she decided not to bring it up. Pity was one of her least favorite things to feel from a person. She loathed it when it was aimed at her. "Now they're off trying to track him," he concluded. It wasn't as much detail as she would have liked. For some reason, it intrigued her, the inner workings of the pack. She knew some things but only had a broad understanding from years ago.

"So, they will just try to hunt him down?"

"That would be ideal, but he's managed to get away from so many others," Tommy trailed off, thinking about how the St. Louis pack just let him slip through their fingers.

"Don't you think he'll stay away with you here? He's bound to smell you, right?" She asked, wondering if the smell of other Weres would be enough to deter him.

"Shane thinks he has selected you as his prey. Just because he killed someone else, doesn't mean anything will make him change his mind. He's… well… he's not normal." Tommy couldn't think of a better word for it. Clearly, he wasn't normal. If he was, he wouldn't be running across the country ripping innocent women apart.

They both sat silently for a moment, dread filling the room.

Vee's phone rang, making both Tommy and Vee jump a little.

"*The Missing Key*, this is Vee," she answered, setting her clipboard down to pick up a scrap of paper she eyed on the floor.

"I'd like to see if you can do a full lock change for my house?" came a woman's voice over the phone.

"Yes, that's a service I provide. How many locks will we be replacing?" Vee asked, starting to jot information down.

Tommy watched her subtly from his seat at another shelf. She was, by far, one of the oddest but most interesting people he had ever met. She didn't seem to shy away from ordering him to work as soon as he came to replace his father. It was strange that a little human woman, knowing what they were, seemed unfazed by it.

She talked back and forth a few minutes, getting the details of the customer's needs and quoting a price.

"Okay, well the only thing that's holding us up is that I need to get some in that color. What day were you thinking?" She finally asked, pulling a little book from her bag and flipping through the pages. "That is perfect, I'll see you on Thursday," she said as an end to the conversation, hanging up the phone.

It was then that Vee realized, as she looked through her planner, that the safe repair was getting picked up the next day, and so was the custom lock order for the engaged couple. Her eyes whipped over to the doorway, landing on the counter where they still sat. She needed to somehow finish updating her inventory as well as finish those orders, and it was nearly 5 p.m. already. She didn't want to risk being there after dark again, even if the shop was being protected.

She turned to Tommy, her eyes remorseful.

"I am so sorry, but I have to finish these orders," she said quietly, unable to hide the panic she was feeling. Too much to be done, and not enough time. He was a little confused at why she was apologizing to him. He was there to protect her but had also become rather invested in getting the room out of the shambles his sister's wolf had left it in.

She first headed to the counter of her darkened showroom, inspecting the safe. Thankfully, she had forgotten she had already finished it but just didn't place the face plate back on it. She had been interrupted by Eliza's call two days ago. It seemed like weeks ago. She placed it back quickly but, carefully, gave it a good wipe down and taped the completed invoice to the front. Then she moved on to the custom lock.

Tommy watched her a little as she started looking through boxes. He wasn't sure what she was looking for exactly, but her face was quite serious. It was almost laughable that she exuded such a sense of authority and dominance when she herself took up such little space.

"Is something humorous to you?" Vee questioned, still not looking at him as she dug through a larger box he had sorted just an hour earlier. He froze, not saying anything. Had he chuckled and not realized it? She looked up at him, having found the pink-hued heart-shaped lock she had been searching for. "You were amused," she said as if it were obvious to anyone.

"I was… but…"

"You might as well know now. Doesn't seem like I'm getting out of this with any sort of privacy. I can feel emotions," she said, turning her focus back to the task and passing him again to grab her Dremel from her little front workstation.

Tommy was a little shocked to say the least. He turned his head awkwardly to follow her. What did she mean she could feel emotions? He turned back to his task, trying to change how it made him feel, now knowing she could feel it too. It made sense though. Somehow she had known his sister was changing. It both made him feel better that Vee had been there and also horror at how differently things could have turned out had Lori and her friends chosen to go somewhere else.

The shop door opened, and Tommy got hastily to his feet, pushing those thoughts aside for his duty to his pack, to Vee.

"It's just Durran," Vee said, not looking up from the lock through her magnifiers.

"Ah… the Watcher," Tommy said, continuing to fill the doorway of the inventory room intimidatingly. His father had given him a short briefing about the incident and what Shane had told him about her.

"I'm going to take her home, so you can leave now, wolf," Durran said, glaring at him from the entrance. Vee stopped the Dremel and looked up at Durran.

"Excuse me?" Vee asked, eyes now locking with her friend. She didn't like decisions being made for her or about her. This day had already been full of unwanted Weres, and now Durran was deciding when and how she'd be going home?

"It's going to get dark soon" was all Durran said for an explanation.

"And I still have work to do," Vee said, gesturing to the lock she had been engraving.

"Tell him to go," Durran grumbled, moving closer to her.

"Fine, but that doesn't mean I'm leaving right now," Vee spat back, before turning to Tommy. "Thank you for your help today, but apparently Durran is here now, and you can go," she said, her voice letting on her irritation.

"Shane said—"

"I don't care what Shane said," she snapped, cutting him off before she gestured for him to scurry away. "Shane will eventually come talk to me. Durran is capable of keeping me safe, or whatever it is that you all think you're doing while hanging out in my space."

Tommy nodded, walking slowly past the Watcher and out the door. Once he was in his vehicle, Vee started the Dremel again, putting the finishing touches on the lock.

"He's not leaving, you know," Durran said, watching her and leaning against the counter as she wiped the lock down of metal fragments and packaged it away in a box.

"He has orders, and *you* can't kill a Were in their territory, right? So, he has to stay," Vee said, giving a sarcastic smile as she put the actual facts of the matter back in Durran's face. She didn't like being in the middle of things, and Durran would have to learn to play nice with them since this didn't seem to be ending any time soon. She also loved to remind Durran that she wasn't as naive about the preternatural world as she let on.

Durran didn't want to accept it, but Vee was right, at least about killing a Were in wolf territory. What she would have preferred was to just whisk Vee away to somewhere safer until this whole thing was resolved, but knowing Vee… well, she wouldn't be going anywhere if there was work to be done.

Vee finished up a few more boxes of inventory and checked the time again when she noticed the sky was turning a faint pink. The cleanup wasn't nearly as close as she wanted it to be, but it was markedly better than the day before.

"Ready yet?" Durran asked, as Vee finally started turning off lights and picking up odds and ends.

"Yes," Vee murmured, turning to the alarm panel. She could still feel Tommy's presence outside as he sat in his vehicle, and she glanced at the pick-up truck outside before locking the door. She had assuredly replaced the lock on that very truck when the handle had somehow gotten ripped off. Oddly, based on how laid back he seemed to be, she didn't suspect it had happened out of anger. More likely he accidentally used his full strength. She couldn't help the small smile that crossed her face imagining it.

Durran had clearly picked up on the smile, and based on her fluctuating mood, let a little confusion in as they walked to Vee's car.

"Are you riding with me?" Vee asked slightly astonished as Durran didn't head to her car, but rather opened the passenger door.

"Yes," she said simply in return.

"But…"

"I'm coming."

"How will you get home?" Vee asked, raising her eyebrows as if she had already won with that argument.

"I'll walk. Or fly, who knows!" Durran said wiggling her eyebrows as she climbed in. Vee hadn't ever seen Durran's wings, but she knew about them. Given the opportunity to tease, Durran loved to remind her of that.

Vee hadn't had anyone in her car… well, ever. She didn't particularly like it. It was like an extension of her apartment. The car was part of her solitary place. She was alone here, but now Durran was there, fiddling with her radio and looking at the few things she kept in there, all of which were tools for work. And behind her was Tommy following along in his pick-up truck.

They pulled up to her apartment, and Vee got out. She stopped Durran in her tracks after she closed the door.

"I'm going in alone," Vee said, holding up a hand as if she expected Durran to try to barge through her.

"I didn't think you'd let me in your little fortress of solitude," Durran reassured her with a smirk, turning her head to glance at Tommy who was parking just down the road a little. "I told Shane already, but I want you to know… this Were that is following you… he was someone to fear even when he was a human. Do not take this lightly, Vee," she whispered, her eyes softening as she looked over Vee's face.

Vee looked at Durran, heavy-handed, yes, but a true friend to Vee. She had her own wards to watch, yet she had chosen to come here and make sure Vee made it safely home. Vee certainly didn't make it easy to be her friend. In a very uncharacteristic move, Vee bridged the gap between them and hugged her tightly for the second time in two days. It was brief but it oddly felt like exactly what she needed at that moment. Durran relished it.

CHAPTER 13

It was a little after 9 p.m. The sky was fully darkened, and Shane had decided to do one more sweep of the neighborhood around Gillham Park. His phone rang.

"Did you find anything?" he asked as a greeting to Margaret.

"We're following a lead up into downtown, but it seems unlikely," she said, the sound of the wind through the windows of her car more prominent than her own voice.

"Circle around and head back. There aren't enough trees there for his usual tastes," Shane said, hand rubbing against his forehead in frustration.

"Should we regroup at the house?"

"Go back to the house, switch out who is patrolling. I'm going to Vee's," he told her starting his car as he said it. It hadn't been his intention to go there originally, but he had to talk to her and something told him he needed to be there.

"But Tommy—"

"I'll call you if plans change."

He hung up the phone, quickly referencing Tommy's text from earlier with Vee's address and taking the quick trip over to her house. He didn't want to admit it to himself, but he ached to be there all day, jealous of the time that Thomas and Tommy had with her. She was strong and stubborn; he had seen that much from their brief interaction. What little insights into her personality had they picked up? What did they glean from her that he hadn't had time to see for himself?

He parked behind Tommy's truck, who got out to join him on the sidewalk across from the apartment building.

"No movement for the last few hours. I haven't sensed anything preternatural since the Watcher left. She's just been up in her apartment this whole time," Tommy debriefed, shoving his hands into his pockets and looking up at the third-floor window that still had the lights on.

"How is she, you think?" Shane asked, following Tommy's eyes to the window and staring. It was an odd question coming from Shane. He wasn't really one to question or wonder about anyone else's feelings normally unless it was Patrick. Tommy paused for a moment, taking in Shane's expression. No. He had never seen Shane look like that before about anyone.

"She's scared, but is trying not to show it. She ordered me around all day," Tommy chuckled. Shane smiled at that. That sounded about right.

"I don't want you to leave. Just stay here for now. Touch base with Margaret for me," Shane said, before heading to the apartment door.

He was looking at the buttons at the entrance trying to determine which one to buzz for Vee's apartment when someone came out. Just a little old lady with a small bag of trash. She paid him no mind as she grumbled to herself and walked out the door, leaving it slowly closing behind her. He took the opportunity to slip in the door before it closed, walking up the stairs to the third floor.

He wasn't sure why his heart was beating with anxiety so loudly. This wasn't some huge threat. It was just a woman. Why did he react this way when he thought about her? He knocked at her door, which was quite plain in comparison to her neighbors. The other apartments had doormats and various decorations hanging over their doors. Hers had nothing. Nothing to let anyone on to who she was.

Her smell was thick in the air here, and his breath hitched a little taking it in. He heard her move through the apartment, bare feet on the creaky wood floor. A number of locks had to be unlocked before the door finally opened just a crack for her to peer out.

"Vee," he said as her emerald eyes took him in.

"Shane," Vee said back, eyes slightly narrowed. She assumed Tommy would tell Shane where her she lived, further complicating things for her, but it couldn't be helped. Now, he stood outside her apartment, dressed as if he had just gotten home from a business meeting, and took off his jacket and tie. The only thing that gave away the chaos of the last few days was the stubble that was forming over his face. Not that she minded, the grey hairs peppered in it somehow added contrast, making his deep brown eyes seem warmer. His cool, collected demeanor didn't give away the anxiety and excitement she was getting from him.

"I figured we would talk," he said, raising an eyebrow and glancing at the still mostly closed door.

"Not in here," she said quickly, shutting it and stunning him a little with the abruptness. He could hear her quickly moving around, picking up keys, and slipping on shoes. She opened the door again, this time just enough for her to slip out. She shut it behind her, turning to lock it with that same odd precision that he had seen days before. He barely got a glimpse of the apartment within, but the few things he saw spoke to her quaint existence. Mismatched shelves with books and movies and a small table for two in a dining nook that had a few things strewn on it were all he had seen.

"Where, then?" Shane asked, as she turned to him, her expression mild exasperation and a little surprise at how close they were. He hadn't thought to step back as she came out, being too engrossed in learning what little he could about her.

"Um… let's just go to that little clearing across the street," she said, moving her own body away from his. She could feel the heat coming off him. It was far closer than she ever really was to anyone, and Weres ran notoriously warm.

He followed her down the stairs, watching her movements with intrigue. She was not as clumsy as most humans; she moved with the intuition of an athlete who knew their body and how it adapted to the environment. Most everyday humans moved through the world as if things would jump out of their way. She was graceful and strong behind the loose-fitting clothes she hid behind.

Once outside, they both paused to look around. Shane was smelling the air to be sure the only Weres he scented were himself and Tommy, and Vee was trying to sense the same thing, only picking up the vibration of him beside her and, mildly, Tommy in the truck down the street a ways.

They made it to the clearing. Vee took a seat at the lone picnic table, looking out at the darkened grass ahead of her. Shane sat across from her, even though his instincts begged him to be right beside her. He didn't like picnic tables generally. They were clumsy to get in and out of and not ideal in an emergency if one had to move quickly, but there was nowhere else to sit.

"Where to begin?" he finally asked after the long silence.

"I suppose you want to know how I knew Lori was changing?" Vee asked, looking in his eyes. She was not angry or irritated, which surprised her a little. She had resigned herself to the fact she would have to share what she could do with him over the course of the day.

"Yes."

"I can feel things; I guess you would call me an empath," Vee started, waiting for the scoff that she assumed would come. There really wasn't a better way to describe her abilities. When most people heard the word empath, they immediately thought of humans who would say that. Not that some of them weren't, but in most cases with humans, it just meant that they were very good at picking up queues. It was a bit more than that for her.

"You're a true empath?" he asked, eyebrows rising.

"You're curious, anxious… excited, although you seem to be just as confused about that excitement as I am," Vee said, smirking a little.

He chuckled a little at that. The confusion was lessening as she spoke. He was excited to get to know her. She had sparked his curiosity and invaded his mind since he realized her smell… realized she was already part of his life without him knowing. He didn't have an explanation for the draw to her, but he had concluded he wanted to see where it led.

"But you knew what she was, that she's a werewolf?" he confirmed, watching her nod slightly.

"You all feel different to me, preternaturals. I figured out why when I was younger."

"Interesting, so you just figured it out?" he asked. It wasn't completely out of the realm of possibility. There were some humans who could see through the inherent magics that were designed to make preternatural activities harder for them to spot.

"Not exactly. I had always felt the differences, but I didn't know what it meant until I became friends with some Weres," she admitted, finally averting her eyes from his and fiddling with the strap of her messenger bag. He sat up at little more at that. Who had known about her and never said anything to him? How could a Were give away that secret to someone who at least appeared to be human?

"Here?"

"No. I was living in St. Louis at the time. I ran away from my sister when I was fifteen. They found me living on the street," she murmured, the memory more painful now, recalling her last interaction with Eliza.

"So, the St. Louis pack knows about you? Told you about us?" he asked, anger rising in him at the thought that a pack leader would allow someone outside of the preternatural community to know such things.

"No, they were also runaways. It was just the four of us kids. All a little weird in our own ways. Two were Weres," she said, looking up at him as she felt his anger.

"Who are they?" he demanded, staring into her eyes as if it would force her to tell the truth. His anger only made her more determined not to tell him. If he thought she would give up their names because he demanded it of her, he was sorely mistaken.

"I won't tell you. You'll just hunt them down, and I wouldn't do that to them," Vee insisted, lifting her chin in defiance.

"And the other?" he asked through gritted teeth. He was willing himself to calm down about this. It was far in the past, but the urge, the need, to protect his kind was powerful. He could tell his reaction irked her, and the last thing he wanted to do was push her away over something that happened more than a decade ago.

"A witch. She was a white witch, who was cast out by her mother because she wouldn't do the sorts of things they had wanted her to. Black witches. Somehow the Weres had stumbled across her, and they decided to take shelter together. She hid their resting place from others, and they managed to live there in the city, unfound by either the coven or the pack leader in the area," Vee told him, letting her eyes fall away from his again.

"So, what, they just told you about preternaturals?" Shane asked, narrowing his eyes.

"They weren't going to, but they could tell I was different. I wasn't trying as hard to hide myself from them in my weakened state. I hadn't eaten in days, and it's a lot harder to block out most things when I'm weak," she murmured, remembering how weak she had felt the day before after being so wrought with emotions from Lori's change. She hated losing control.

"They told you what? About Weres?"

"And the others. They didn't know much about the Watchers. I learned the basic ins and outs of a Were pack. I also figured out how I could feel the differences between preternaturals."

They fell into silence then, as Shane digested what she had just told him. He took a deep breath to calm himself, but his thoughts were racing. If they were friends, why did she leave them? They were safe there, and they accepted her. She could have had a life with people, albeit preternatural people, but at least she wouldn't have been alone.

"Why did you leave?" he asked, looking over her solemn expression. The sadness in her face darkened further at that question.

"The witch was taken, and we couldn't find her. So, the Weres decided to leave the area, and I came back home. I never found out what happened to her, but without her, we weren't protected anymore," Vee whispered. The image of their little apartment ransacked sent shivers down her spine.

"And you came back here…"

"My sister had a husband by then. Three years without me, and she had married a man with a boatload of cash." She smiled eerily at the memory. "She didn't want me to be part of her new life, so I got a job, saved my money, and became a locksmith," she finished, looking at him with those emerald eyes.

"Interesting" was all he said to her. She may not have been a Were or a witch, but she was certainly a preternatural. She wouldn't tell their secrets because she had her own secrets to keep.

The silence resumed, but their eyes remained locked. She could tell he wasn't a threat to her; if anything, he seemed to be feeling more and more protective. For most of the day, she had been under the impression, despite Thomas and Tommy's feelings, that Shane was only having her protected because of obligation. Not only was a lone wolf hunting and killing in his territory, but she had also just saved a pack member. Now, she realized it wasn't just that. It confused her but made her feel better about having told him.

"You are fascinating," he said aloud, even though he didn't mean to. It made her blush just slightly, averting her eyes from his. That blush made him happy he made the small slip.

It was in that moment that she felt the presence of another Were. It was distant but coming toward them quickly. It was familiar, the buzz of the approaching presence. Her stomach rolled and her mouth turned to ash as her eyes whipped in the direction he was coming from. She stood from the picnic table, body tensing, as she turned her focus to the north.

"He's here" was all she managed to say before it went black for a second, and she found herself lifted off her feet. She was moving quickly The only things in her view were the picnic table broken and flipped over and two men changing into wolves as they began running after her.

Shane was right on their heels, having immediately ripped his shirt off while sprinting. Tommy was behind him a few hundred feet. She looked up, seeing she was tucked under the arm of the Were from last night. His eyes glowing ominously in the dark as he ran at inhuman speed toward Main Street.

She struggled in his grasp, digging her nails into his arm and thrashing around. She didn't want to scream as that would only draw human attention. It was bad enough that they were all running full force, even in their human forms. She looked again at Shane and Tommy. They had stopped their transformations, having seen that he was headed toward even busier areas in Midtown. It was too early in the night for everyone to be home. People were still out and about, especially in this area.

She cursed her lack of strength, trying to will herself out of his iron grip on her, which he only intensified as she squirmed. Horns honked as they dodged in and out of traffic. Vee's panic only increasing as the man's confidence doubled. She could almost smell it off him, the metallic tang of pheromones. He leapt over a car and headed down a side street, going south, she noticed.

Where was he taking her?

Back to Gillham Park?

That would have been idiotic since it was still a monitored crime scene.

Her eyes closed briefly as she tried to think and tried to channel an emotion that wasn't fear. He seemed to be feeding off it. It was futile. She was too distracted by the chaos of her capture and the danger they were all in to focus on a different emotion.

They popped out of the quiet residential street on to the hilltop of Gillham Road. This twisted sharply at the top, right at the Nelson-Atkinson Museum. He leapt over the short stone wall, dashing across the grass. She jostled a little as he landed causing him to tighten his grip, sinking his nails into the skin of her side. As she cried out from the pain she realized it wasn't just nails, he had partially changed, meaning three-inch claws were tearing into her flesh. She looked up at him, horrified, to see he was open-mouth grinning, drooling with anticipation as her blood hit the air.

CHAPTER 14

Shane was further behind them than he had been, only jumping the wall once they were about to round the northwest corner of the massive building. He had been just as fast as this creature originally. She suspected he had slowed some when they were crossing the busier streets. His golden eyes were shining in the dark, never leaving her, until her capturer took the turn.

She had expected him to keep running down the length of the museum's yard through the sculpture park south, but he deftly popped over parked cars on Oak Street, heading straight into the adjacent Southmoreland Park. It too had a stone retaining wall, but he managed to fly over it in at breakneck speed, heading south from there toward yet another busy street, Emmanuel Clever II Boulevard.

She couldn't struggle against him anymore. With every movement, he dug his claws deeper into her flesh. She was almost more fearful of what would happen when he eventually took them out. She tried to think of something, anything, that would get him to slow now that they were nearly to the boulevard, and she saw no signs of Shane behind them anymore.

Had he abandoned her?

Where was he?

The creature didn't slow as they got to the street. He wove in and out of cars and jumped over others. He was not being subtle; in fact, his face lit up by the street and car lights revealed his gruesome, partially changed face to her. It was still his human skin but stretched tightly over an elongated face. His teeth, too large for the opening of his mouth, were sharp and glistening with the gathering saliva. Her stomach churned at the sight of it, not fully knowing what lay ahead for her.

Would she be torn apart by this monster? Not quite man or wolf.

They were on the other side of the boulevard now, having crossed the intersection diagonally to Frank A. Theis Park. There was some tree coverage there, but she had a sinking feeling he wasn't going to stop just yet. They were still heading south although she could tell now he was slowing a little, tightening his grip and causing her to moan in pain.

"Soon I'll have you. You thought your Watcher and your wolf protectors would keep me away," he laughed, hauntingly, his voice somewhere between human and wolf. "I always get what I want," he said, glancing down at her, his eyes glowing wide and wild.

They got to the end of the park, where there was a ledge that dropped down to the walkway along Brush Creek. He cleared it effortlessly, immediately jumping into the disgusting, polluted creek water and swimming to the walkway on the south side. Vee choked and gasped as her head went in and out of the water. She couldn't tell where they were in the creek anymore and was just trying so hard to remain alert despite the pain and now serious lack of oxygen. She realized he was using the water to clear their scent.

Shane was either gone or too far away to see their trajectory. He would have no way of knowing where they ended up on the other side of this creek if he was even coming for her still.

The creature hauled her up the side of the creek by her side. She could feel muscles and ligaments tearing in her torso with the exertion. They were further down, not across from the spot he had jumped in, having swum a little more east with the current to an overpass bridge. She expected him to keep running, but instead, he grabbed her shoulder with his other hand and slammed her into the concrete wall.

She could see his monstrous face better now that he was right in front of her, despite the lack of light. He was grotesque and feverishly panting as he looked her over.

"Now I can have you all to myself," he said quietly, pressing his body against hers but not removing the claws from her side, if anything he dug them in deeper. "I wish I had more time to play with you like I did my other girls, but I'll have to take what I can get with you. The memories will be just as sweet." With that, he licked her from the top of her chest, up her neck, to the side of her face. She could smell him under the stench of the creek water like the dirty musk dogs get when they are between too many baths combined with the rank stench of human sweat.

She shivered in disgust, her hand clamped firmly on her large set of keys in her messenger bag. She had gotten ahold of them at some point while he had still been running, but the odd angle and her injured shoulder had prevented her from using them thus far. Now that she was upright and he was unsuspecting, she forcefully jammed them into his ribs causing him to retract and back away from her with a wolf like yowl of pain.

She pushed herself off the wall, running as fast as her legs could carry her to the open walkway just ahead. She wasn't sure how far they had traveled down the creek, or how far she would make it. Her canvas slip-on shoes had been lost at some point along the way, and she could feel the rough concrete tearing into the soles of her feet. She saw Shane on the opposite side of the creek at least a few hundred yards from where she was, jogging her direction sniffing the air, trying to catch a scent.

"Shane!" she screamed, catching his attention just long enough for them to lock eyes, just before a clawed hand grabbed her hair and pulled her back into the shadow of the overpass.

Shane watched in horror as she was being dragged into the darkness. She was soaking wet, the right side of her shirt and pant leg red with blood. Without a second thought he leapt as far as he could into the creek, swimming the rest of the way, and pulled himself over the edge. He crouched there, taking a moment to rid himself of his remaining clothes, forcing the change into his wolf as quickly as possible. He no longer cared who saw it. He had to do it.

He ran toward the overpass, eyes blazing with fury as he saw the glowing orbs of his enemy ahead of him. Out of the shadow stepped the creature. He was more than half changed, his lower jaw protruding unnaturally, sharp teeth sprouting out in odd angles. His hands had twisted into monstrous, elongated half claws.

"She's mine!" he roared, holding her out in front of him by her hair. She was still conscious, but barely, her hands hanging limply at her sides as she looked toward Shane with half closed eyes.

Don't give up, he thought within his wolf, wishing he could shout it to her. He was thinking of the best way to attack without more injury coming to Vee, but he knew the moment he moved, the creature would attack her.

"I'll rip her apart in front of you, wolf," the creature said, his voice rough and jagged as it went between human and wolf growls.

Vee had no strength left. The last few days had already exhausted her, and now with the blood loss… she was fully spent. She looked at Shane's golden eyes, feeling his conflict and his hope. She recalled the feeling she got from the creature as they ran through the city. His excitement and boost of adrenaline at the smell of her fear. She looked at Shane one last time, just as she felt the familiar presence of Durran coming closer.

Yes, this monster fed off her pain and panic, but how much could he handle?

She slowly reached up, pressing her hands to his forearm and sent him every ounce of fear, panic, sadness, anxiety… everything that she had been feeling over the last few days. She pushed it into him. Wave after wave of it crashing into him.

He started to shake, howling loudly as his grip on her hair loosened enough for her to fall to the ground. Durran swooped down at that moment, pulling Vee into her arms and quickly moving so that Shane was between them and the creature.

He sank to his knees clutching at both sides of his head as if he were going to explode. Shane was confused by this sudden reaction, but he didn't pause to think about it, taking his opportunity to strike. He charged, opening his massive jaws to clamp around his neck. Not to kill him, but incapacitating him. There would need to be justice served by all the packs he invaded, all the territories he hunted humans in so brazenly.

Tommy came running slowly up the other side of the creek. He was clutching his arm, which drooped from his shoulder, obviously and painfully dislocated. Durran looked down at Vee, who was slumped in her arms. She didn't want to leave her now that she was safely in her arms, but Tommy needed to be capable of helping his pack leader right now.

"I'm going to help Tommy quickly, and then I'll be right back," Durran assured her, as if Vee thought she was abandoning her.

Durran jumped the width of the creek with ease, landing next to Tommy and making him startle slightly.

"Is Vee okay?" Tommy asked, looking past Durran to see her clutching her side weakly.

"Not in the slightest. What happened to you?"

"Didn't quite dodge a car," Tommy admitted, looking down at his limp arm.

"Humans okay?" Durran asked, inspecting the shoulder between glances at Vee. She was still breathing.

"Yes. I made sure. Their car is totaled, but I have the license plate number," Tommy told her. Durran nodded in approval, watching him wince as she placed her hand on the shoulder. He looked away, eyes darting between Vee and Shane, still holding the incapacitated man who had returned to his human form.

"Tommy, right now you need to focus on me. I'm going to count to three," Durran said, catching his eyes and holding it there as she grasped his wrist. "One, two—" With a movement faster than a human could see, she pulled up and pushed his shoulder back into place with an audible snap.

Tommy made a horrible guttural sound, gasping afterward, but managed to not scream out. They made it this long without attracting too many human eyes; he didn't need to be the thing that caused them to finally take notice.

Only giving himself a moment to breathe, Tommy pulled out his phone and immediately called his dad.

"Is everything okay?" Thomas asked, his voice still gruff from sleep.

"The rogue attacked Vee. Shane has him, but we need back up, and Shane will need clothes," Tommy said, noticing the shreds of Shane's pants on the ground not far from Vee's feet.

"I'll call Margaret. Where are you?"

"Brush creek… hard to explain. I'll share my location," Tommy told him, before hanging up the phone and sending his location to his dad's phone.

"I'll bring you over," Durran said once Tommy looked up from his phone and back across the creek.

"What?" he asked, confused at the suggestion. He figured he would just walk up to the overpass and cross over that way. How would Durran, who looked to be less than half Tommy's bulk, bring him to the other side?

"I'm bringing you," Durran said, not wanting to waste the time explaining, she simply stooped over, scooping Tommy up in her arms with ease, before jumping back over the creek gracefully.

She dropped the stunned man, heading back to Vee to finally look over her wounds. Shane growled in that general direction, unable to release the man in his jaws until Tommy came to take over. He wanted to be the one to look over Vee. He needed to see if she was going to be alright.

"Oh, shut up, wolf! You can't right now," Durran hissed, not taking her eyes from the wound on Vee's side.

"It's not life threatening," Vee said quietly, her voice flat and tired.

"Shush," Durran said back, peeling Vee's hands away from her side.

Shane's wolf made a sort of whine sound, making Tommy look over to him, instead of watching as Durran tore the bottom of Vee's shirt off to get a better look. It was still bleeding but not profusely. Nothing that wouldn't mend with time. Tommy realized what

Shane was asking, that he take over holding the unconscious man so Shane could go to her.

"Hey… I liked this shirt," Vee said weakly, giving just the smallest smile.

Once Tommy took over, Shane walked over, still as his wolf, to the two on the ground. His gaze moved over the holes in her side. He looked into her eyes, hoping Vee could feel his request. She searched the golden depths, feeling somehow so safe with the two of them, Durran and Shane, beside her.

She was hurt, but she wasn't dead.

For all her irritation over them guarding her, they did what they set out to do, which was keep her alive, and she was grateful. She saw the pleading in Shane's eyes and felt his worry as he broke their locked gazed to glance at her wounds. She realized, with some embarrassment, that he wanted to clean it for her.

Normal canine saliva was antibacterial and helped stop bleeding, but werewolves had their own magics. To clean and heal another wolf's wound was reserved for pack members. They were giving of their sacred magics to another. For Shane to be offering that to her, it meant something.

"I'm not worth that, Shane. I'll live with or without it," Vee told him, turning now to Durran. She didn't want to see the disappointment in his eyes that she could feel from him. "Take me home? I can clean it there," she whispered.

Durran looked down at Vee. She was battered, bruised, and bleeding. There was nothing Durran wanted more than to spite the wolf beside them by giving in to what Vee asked, but she knew that Vee's recovery would be much more difficult without it.

"You should let him, Vee," Durran told her, making Vee blink with confusion. That was not what she was expecting at all. She felt Shane's massive paw rest lightly on her leg to get her attention again. She looked back into his pleading eyes, then nodded very slightly, closing her eyes, and bracing for pain.

But there was no pain. It was like the best pain reliever was being applied directly to her skin in the form of a soft warm towel. It radiated from her gashes, all throughout her body. Magic tingled with more intensity in her wounds, but it glided through her veins, reaching other parts of her too.

When he stopped, she opened her eyes looking into his once more.

"Thank you," she murmured with tears welling in her eyes. She barely knew him, but he made a huge sacrifice for her in that moment.

"Dad's here!" Tommy said, looking up at the overpass and waving for them to come down.

"I'm taking her home now," Durran told Shane, lifting Vee from the ground. "You'll let me know when he's secure?"

Shane's wolf nodded once, before Durran jumped into the air, disappearing into the low clouds above them.

Shane then turned his attention back to his duty. Thomas and Margaret had made it down to where Tommy was. Thomas was busily both tying and shackling the offender while the other two held him in place. He was still unconscious, but they weren't taking any chances. As Shane approached, Thomas paused to jerk his head toward the pile of clothes he had brought for him so he could return to his human form.

Shane ducked into the shadows of the overpass, taking his time. It was exhausting to switch back and forth in such quick succession, not to mention he had barely slept for the last few days. For a moment, he just sat there, naked on the concrete. He looked at the pool of Vee's blood against the wall and on the ground. He had been so close to losing her.

The panic he had felt when he watched her suddenly disappear in front of him at that picnic table caused a visceral reaction in him. He didn't think before he ripped the table in front of him apart to get to her and the way she looked at him as he ran after her. She was afraid, but she was confident. Confident in him.

He found it so strange that he already felt so strongly about a woman he had barely had two conversations with. It was like she had bewitched him somehow, but she was no witch. He sighed, trying to shake the thoughts of her from the forefront of his mind. He changed into a black jogging suit, one pack members used when on certain security details, and went to his torn clothes to gather the remnants of his things. Thankfully, his wallet and keys were still safely in his pocket, his phone, however, was dead and waterlogged.

"Okay, Shane. We're going to load him up," Thomas said, taking the head for Tommy, while Margaret took the feet.

"I'll be there," Shane said, looking around at the other smaller pools and smears of Vee's blood which were dotted everywhere.

"I'll stay and make sure the others get this cleaned up before morning," Tommy assured him, using his good arm to touch Shane's shoulder.

"I don't want anything catching a single whiff of her. We very nearly were exposed tonight… she doesn't need to deal with the others," Shane said seriously, thinking of what the vampires would do if they came across her blood. If he had such a reaction to her scent, they certainly would.

"We'll get it all, Shane, don't worry," Tommy said, watching his leader's brow furrow more intensely, eyes gliding over each visible speck.

It shook him how close it could have been. One wrong move and she would have been torn apart in front of him. He didn't want to admit that if Durran hadn't been there, things could have gone much differently. He hated that he was powerless in that moment, as she dangled from the creature's hand. Shane looked over at Tommy, letting a bit of pride seep in.

"I trust you," Shane said, giving him a smile. Those words struck Tommy profoundly. Not that he didn't know Shane trusted him, but to hear it was quite another thing. Shane didn't often express those sentiments. Perhaps it was something about this Vee that was bringing it out in him.

Without another word, Shane headed to the cars above. He climbed in the passenger seat of the SUV that they loaded the man, nodding at Margaret to take them home. He was already overly tired and had a long night ahead of him.

CHAPTER 15

Vee woke up on her futon in her living room. She stared at her ceiling, trying to piece together how she got there and what exactly happened. It seemed strange to be real, but the pain was too intense to have been a dream. Her hands traveled to her side, touching the fabric that was wrapped there. She sat up slowly, her muscles aching in places she didn't know could ache.

She didn't recall how she had gotten home. In fact, the last thing she remembered was being scooped up by Durran after… She looked, now, at the crude bandage over her stomach, her blood caking the fabric to her skin. She thought to remove it but decided better of it. She would look at it when she took a shower.

She glanced around, noting she was fully alone, even her neighbors were all out of the building, no hum of their presence in the back of her mind. The sun flooded the room through the front window, and she suddenly realized it had to be late in the day. She was late for work. She shot off the futon, instantly regretting the sudden movement and pausing to wince. This was not going to be easy. She couldn't rush herself.

She headed to the bathroom, her feet stinging as she took each miserable step. Once she got there, she turned on the shower water before turning around to look in the mirror. She looked like absolute garbage. Her hair was everywhere, tangled and weirdly matted from having been whipped around and then dunked in the creek. Her face was pale but otherwise unharmed, save for a small scratch on her chin that wasn't very noticeable. She was thankful for that. Last thing she needed was to scare customers away because she looked like she had been beaten up.

Then she looked down at her body. Taking off her clothes would be a task. She decided to start with the remnants of her shirt. It was torn off just above her belly button, leaving the band logo intact, but she wasn't one for wearing crop tops, so she didn't see herself keeping it. It was quite the struggle to lift her arms over her head, but she managed it. With extreme care, she pushed her pajama pants and underwear past her hips, stepping out of them instead of bending over.

It was then that she took a deep breath, preparing herself for the mangled remains of her side. She was sure it was going to be monstrous to see. Delicately, she peeled the fabric from her skin, letting it fall to the bathroom floor with the rest of her clothes. To her surprise, the wounds were there, five gashes, but they were already closing. She was certain she would have scars, but it wasn't nearly as bad as she expected it to be, given how painful it was the night before.

She touched it, remembering Shane licking the wound. Why had he done that?

Her heart beat a little wildly remembering his face when he raced after her. His eyes only looking at her.

She tore her eyes away from her stomach, shaking her head to rid herself of the thought. He was just protecting her out of obligation to his territory, as payment to her for helping Lori. Nothing more.

She got in the shower, sighing at the glorious hot water cascading over her. Clean water. She slowly scrubbed, partially because she didn't want to move too fast and hurt herself more, and partially because she needed to feel clean. She felt like she had a layer of creek grime coating her skin.

She slowly walked from the bathroom once she was done, cursing herself for not having taken the time to put her clothes away after Saturday. She dumped the clothes out on her bed, which took far more effort than she thought it should, and gingerly picked the first things she saw that were easy to put on.

That's when her phone rang. She couldn't help herself as she raced back to her living room, her phone on her makeshift coffee table where it had been when she left the apartment with Shane.

It was Durran.

"Hello?" she said, wincing at the pain she caused herself from moving too quickly but trying to hold in the guttural sound from it that threatened to escape.

"I opened the shop for you. You needed to rest," Durran said quietly. Vee could hear what sounded like metal clinking in the background.

"What do you mean?" Vee asked confused, pulling the phone from her ear to look at the time. It was nearly 5 p.m. How had she slept so long?

"Both your customers came and paid. You had a few others too. I scheduled you some house calls, but I warned them they may not be fulfilled in their time-frame," Durran continued, her voice so nonchalant, it almost made Vee feel like she was audibly hallucinating.

"I… um… you opened my shop?" she stuttered, still not past that bit of information.

"Yep. I finished some organizing of this back room too. I saw where you were going with these spread-sheets." To say Vee wasn't absolutely flabbergasted would be an understatement. "I'm not sure how you like to reconcile your register, though. So, I was won-dering if you'd talk me through that," Durran admitted, letting a little unease fill her tone. Vee seemed to snap out of her shock with that. She didn't want Durran messing up her register.

"I'll come there…" Vee murmured, looking momen-tarily for her canvas shoes but remembering they were lost somewhere between the museum and the creek. She instead slipped on some sandals. The sandals were not kind on her scraped feet, but the thought of bending over to tie shoes was enough to make her tense. She quickly swept the apartment with her eyes to find her keys. Durran must have taken them. Thankfully, she had a spare set hidden in a little, ceramic plant-less planter on her bookshelf.

"No, no… just tell me," Durran tried to insist, but Vee was already out the door and headed down the stairs.

"On my way," Vee said before hanging up.

She didn't *race* to her car, per se, more like walked as quickly as her body would allow. The drive to the shop was longer than usual, the roads being clogged with rush hour traffic.

She pulled up behind Durran's car, slowly getting out and walking to the door. The closed sign was already on the door and there Durran sat behind the counter, eying the tablet that Vee used for the register with distain.

"Don't mess with it," Vee said as she locked the door behind her.

"I told you just to tell me," Durran grumbled, clearly exasperated by the technology in front of her.

"You managed to ring up my customers, but you can't figure out how to reconcile the day?" Vee asked, smirking as she slowly rounded the counter to Durran's side.

"Your methods are clearly flawed, otherwise I'd be able to do it." Vee chuckled at her frustration, turning the tablet to her and setting about getting it closed.

"You just don't know how to deal with technology," Vee told her, turning it back to show the screen as it read, "Day Closed." Durran scoffed, standing from the stool she had been sitting on and pacing around for a moment with irritation. Vee turned to watch Durran's movements, still finding amusement when she looked at the inventory room and noticed it looked put together.

Vee's face fell into shock, unconsciously moving forward to get a better look. The room was clean, the boxes she had left on the floor were neatly set on the shelves, labeled appropriately. The trash bags had been hauled out and clipboards with spreadsheets were hanging off the corners of the shelves where they belonged. Days of work she thought she had were done for her in the course of one day. She was sure that there were things she would change around to suit her better, but this helped her tremendously.

She felt Durran approach her from behind, but Vee was too stunned to move.

"I can't believe you did all this," Vee whispered, her breath hitching a little as she continued to look it over.

"I told you I would help," Durran said quietly, humor radiating as she recalled the way the previous day's conversation had gone.

Vee came up with so many words to say. So many different ways of saying how appreciative she was, but they fell short at her lips as she simply let her mouth hang agape. Finally, she turned back to Durran, her eyes welling a little.

"Thank you," she whispered.

The whole house on Morningside was a buzz with activity. Everyone was on high alert. Various pack members were sitting at tables, notepads before them, as they called person after person, informing them that the rogue had been captured. Shane couldn't simply kill a Were that had affected so many other packs without letting them know. He also needed to determine when and where the creature had been created.

He had set the younger ones, Patrick and Lori, to researching him. They had taken his wallet from his back pocket before they locked him in the cage in the basement. His name was Todd C. Downing. He had hunting permits for New York State and an NRA membership card with his New York commercial driver's license. He was a cross-country trucker.

So far, they had discovered he was a previously convicted rapist in the early 2000s but had been let out on good behavior. There was no way to determine how long he had been a werewolf, but Shane suspected it wasn't long. They had dosed him with massive amounts of benzodiazepines to keep him asleep while they alerted the other pack leaders. It took a lot of drugs to affect a Were, their bodies naturally had a higher metabolism, but they still worked for a time. They didn't need him causing a ruckus until it was time to interrogate him.

Shane was trying to sleep on the couch in the living room. He kept waking off and on but finally decided to get up when he could smell food wafting through the air. As he walked into the dining room, he saw everyone grabbing from the bags of various fast-food places. Cora was trying her hardest to pass it out, so everyone had an even share, but as usual, they were too hungry to do it in any sort of logical way.

"Set your food down and behave like civilized people for once," Shane said loudly enough for everyone to stop and quiet. They may have been werewolves, but they didn't need to act like a ravenous pack of animals all the time.

"Thank you," Cora said, her voice about as exasperated as she looked. She had had quite a trying time herself in the last few days yet was still taking care of everyone. That call from Lori's friends on Saturday night had shaken her. Her daughter could have very nearly killed her friends, and she could do nothing but call Thomas and wait.

Shane nodded, trying to be reassuring and express his appreciation to her as he moved past them into the kitchen. Thomas was just getting off the phone and scribbling on the notepad before him.

"Ah, you're awake. Good. I finally got ahold of the Albany leader. He was telling me that a small group of lone wolves came through there about four full moons ago and requested to run with them. They left shortly after," Thomas told him, as Shane filled a glass with water.

"And it was the next full moon the attacks began?" Shane asked, coming beside him to look at the notes scribbled.

"Yes. Downing wasn't one of those wolves, so I imagine he was attacked on that run and turned the next month."

Shane narrowed his eyes as he thought about it. What lone wolf in their right mind would attack a human? And if they did accidentally, why would they not seek to help them through the change?

"And what of the other leaders?" Shane questioned, wondering if any of them would seek their own retribution. It would make things more complicated if he would need to facilitate a transport over state lines or worse, mediate between two leaders who had been wronged worse and therefore had the right to kill him.

"Sounds like they all would rather just call for the Sha to handle it. Not that I blame them," Thomas told him, shaking his head.

Yes, getting the Sha involved made things complicated, but there would be no questioning their decision. They were the originators of all shapeshifters. Each type of Were-creature branched from them. There were few of them since new ones could only be born, not turned, but they were extremely powerful, and as such, they were the final say when it came to any Were matters, especially when it involved multiple packs.

"Are these the lone wolves?" Shane asked, glancing over the list in front of Thomas. His eyes widened slightly when he saw the third name written there. Ethan Keenan. "Ethan…" Shane muttered, closing his eyes. Of course, his oldest son would be wrapped up in this. He had a striking ability to get into trouble.

"I know. But there's no actual evidence it was one of them," Thomas said, trying to be comforting.

"No… but depending on what the Sha have to say about all of this, no evidence might mean nothing," Shane said quietly, clutching the counter, instead of the water glass.

Ethan, his older son, was a lone wolf. He had left the pack as soon as he turned eighteen. It was years ago, long before Shane's late wife was even in the picture or Patrick a thought. It was unfortunate that Ethan never stayed around long enough when he came through to know his little brother, Patrick. Shane and Ethan's relationship had always been tumultuous, but he was still his son.

"You think the Sha should be involved?" Thomas asked, his face turning grim.

"Multiple packs have been affected, not just wolves. I would find it surprising if they didn't at least want an explanation. And now with all of them wanting the Sha to make the final say… what choice do we have?"

The whole house had quieted listening to their exchange. Once the Sha were brought into the mix, it became deadly serious. Cora came into the kitchen now, holding two sandwiches she had salvaged from the others.

"It seems like you just said someone had died by the way everyone stopped talking," she said, setting the food in front of them and then setting a box on the counter in front of Shane. It was a new cell phone. "Tommy mentioned yours was done for after last night. I wasn't sure if you had any more spares since Patrick seems to break his phone once a month." They all chuckled momentarily.

"I'm clean out of spares. Thank you, Cora," Shane said taking the box and looking at it. Same phone, newer model, so he wouldn't have a problem adapting. His dead phone had been discarded on the counter by the coffee pot when they had come in. It took quite a few of them to wrestle Downing to the basement and into the cage, and he rid himself of his pocket contents as soon as he could.

Quickly, he pulled the SIM card, which was thankfully dry, from his old phone, popped it in the new phone, and booted it up. He had many calls to make, he realized. The others had made calls to the effected packs, but he needed to call Ethan and the Sha… and Vee.

First Ethan. He needed to figure out what Ethan knew before he reported the capture.

"The drugs will wear off soon," Thomas warned, taking a bite of his sandwich.

"These calls don't usually take long," Shane assured him, walking out the back door to stand in the grass. It was about 8 p.m., the sun starting to set and turning the sky pink. He let the feel of the grass on his bare feet ground him before he dialed Ethan's number.

With each ring of the phone, Shane grew more concerned. He rarely called, but when he did, it was important. Ethan knew this and would normally pick up on the first ring.

No answer.

Shane called again.

This time he answered.

"I'm busy," Ethan said, his voice short.

"So am I. That serial killer is a Were," Shane told him, beginning to pace the yard.

"And? I thought it was pretty obvious." Ethan's tone did not hold back his annoyance.

"You might be implicated in his turning. You and your other lone wolf friends were visitors of the Albany pack a month before the murders started." Shane let that sink in for a moment, listening to Ethan's breathing as it changed with his words. They were distant and they butted heads, but Ethan knew Shane loved him and even with a strained relationship, he wouldn't lie to his father. The silence intensified as time went on. "Ethan?"

"We lost control on the second night. I don't remember exactly what happened," Ethan said quietly, his voice shaking slightly.

"What do you mean? How could you lose control?" Shane asked dumbfounded. Once a Were accepted their wolf, they were one in the same. There were only a few reasons that would happen and none of them were good.

More silence.

"What did you do?" Shane's voice was cold now, angry.

"We found something… it's hard to explain," Ethan said, his voice barely a whisper.

"Come home" was all Shane said before he hung up. It took every ounce of self-control for him not to throw it across the yard. Ethan could have made a deadly mistake, and it wasn't something Shane could get him out of.

CHAPTER 16

"Soundproof the door," Shane said to anyone who was in the kitchen as he stormed back into the house and headed directly down to the basement. He slipped his phone into his back pocket and rolled up his sleeves. Standing in the middle of the room, his eyes burning, he stared at Downing, who sat quietly in the cage. He seemed to have been awake for some time, but unable to move much from his confines, deciding instead to listen to the activities upstairs, or what little he could.

Thomas, Margaret, and Tommy had all followed Shane down, dismissing the lower ranked pack members who had previously been guarding the monster.

"I'm going to ask you questions and how you answer them will determine your ultimate fate," Shane said calmly. Just looking at the man made him boil with rage, but he stayed collected on the surface.

Downing's eyes were cold and unfeeling as he stared back at Shane. Dead, black, soulless. He was ugly, even in fully human form. His nose was too long, his eyes deeply set and small for his face, and his jaw was sharp in an unflattering way. His hair was dirty, and not just from the creek, as if he didn't care to bathe with any regularity. The light brown hair, Shane suspected, was usually dark blond but darkened with grease. He said nothing, opening his hands, palms up as if to say "continue."

"How did you come to be a werewolf?" Shane asked, grounding himself where he stood and crossing his arms. Downing straightened his back slightly and turned his head, looking over the four in front of him through the bars.

"I'm sure it's unpleasant to see someone like me, turned into a wolf instead of born one like all of you," Downing said, smirking slightly. Margaret laughed then; her eyes glowing.

"You would be mistaken if you thought we were all born this way," Shane told him, a twinkle in his own eye at the thought. Downing's smirk faded at those words, looking more directly at Margaret. She wasn't a petite woman, quite muscular in her physique. It was easy to assume she had been born a Were based on her body type alone, but as he looked at her, he saw her curly, unruly hair was clipped up revealing a large, faded scar encompassing her shoulder only slightly obscured by her shirt strap.

"Packs seem to be a family affair," Downing then said, removing his focus from Margaret and looking to Thomas and Tommy.

"Yes, many of us are blood family, but that's what a pack becomes when you're welcomed into it. Usually, a turned wolf will be brought into that family. Who turned you?" Shane said, bringing the conversation back on topic. Downing's eyes lit up a little, leaning forward.

"Well, they didn't exactly tell me their names," he spat out.

"Then tell me the circumstances," Shane retorted, having a harder time maintaining the calmness in his voice. Downing leaned back again, clicking his tongue and looking at all of them as if he were trying to decide if he wanted to tell them. His arrogance got the better of him, though, you could see the pride welling in him at the thoughts running through his head.

"That human girl you were all protecting… what's her name? Mmm, Vee… yeah… she looked so much like her," he started, letting out a little sigh.

"What?" Shane barked out at the mention of Vee's name.

"Vee smells so good too, doesn't she? Like she got a little extra spice in there," he said, grinning and wiggling his fingers.

It took everything in Shane to remain composed. His short nails dug into his palms with his closed fists, eyes now ablaze.

"Who did she look like?" Shane asked, his voice gravelly with anger, but trying to keep composure to get back to his line of questioning. Downing chuckled a little, eyes alight with pleasure.

"She's small, easy to pick up. It was like snatching a child when I grabbed her right in front of you." Shane went rigid now, his whole body tense. If his words before hadn't struck a nerve, those had. It had been one of the more horrific things that had ever happened to him, watching Vee be ripped away right in front of his eyes. "Her skin is so soft. It was so easy to just push my claws in. Almost like butter. I wish I had been able to do more than lick her. She was going to be such a tasty snack." His lips smacked at the idea, eyes hungrily looking at Shane who's own had turned murderous.

"Who did she remind you of?" Shane repeated, his voice trembling ominously with the exertion it took to keep himself in check.

"Have you gotten to touch her? To taste her?" Downing asked, sitting up a little again and turning his head in mock curiosity. "Hmm… I guess not. Well, I'll give you a little teaser… Her skin tasted even better than she smells, if you can believe it. I'm sure her insides would have been even sweeter."

"Answer the question!" Shane yelled, his whole being vibrating. Thomas placed a hand on Shane's shoulder, trying to anchor him. Downing laughed and sat back again. His laugh was high and villainous, eyes sinister.

"Oh… yes… those wolves attacked me when I almost had her. Months ago, in the woods. I thought I had gotten away from everyone. Took her to the woods, so I could hear her screams fully. I don't like it when I can't hear them. In the city, I have to keep them quiet. I want to know how much it hurts," Downing said nostalgically, as his eyes drifted away from Shane, unfocused as if he were seeing it play out again. He was basking in the memory. All four of them stiffened at his words. Margaret's lips curling up in disgust, watching as Downing clearly physically reacted to the memories of his victim.

"They attacked you," Shane prompted, trying to steer him away from his sick fantasies. Downing's eyes returned to Shane.

"They must have heard her."

"And they what…? Tried to kill you?"

"That seems to be what they were trying to do. They should have torn me apart, but they just bit and tore at my flesh… left me bleeding in the woods," he said. At the mention of his own pain, he shivered a little. "She got away that time, but I finished what I set out to do a little later." He concluded with a malicious grin.

Shane's rage had dissipated slightly, knowing the reason Ethan and the others attacked. Of course, they lost control. He would have too, seeing a girl being assaulted by this psychopath. He looked at Downing a little more thoroughly now, noticing the scarring on his neck. It was light, but it was there. If four wolves had attacked him, there were bound to be more scars. A human shouldn't have been able to survive an attack like that.

"How did you survive?" Shane asked, narrowing his eyes and returning to the more collected demeanor he previously had.

"Once they had left me there, I used my own blood with dirt to stop my bleeding. I laid there until that next night when the full moon came out. It seemed to heal me, or at least enough that I could move." He shrugged a little, making the chains that held him rattle against each other.

"You didn't try to seek out other Weres? Didn't think to find some of your own to help you?" Shane asked, internally doubting this man would have ever been taken in. The air around him seemed like poison. No pack leader in their right mind would ever trust him.

"I play by my own rules. I do what I want. I get what I want. I've been a lone wolf, even when I was human," Downing said, his smile unfading.

"That's not how any of this works, and you would know that if you had tried to learn more about what you had become, Downing," Shane said, crouching down to look him straight in the eyes. "The punishment for killing a human in another pack's territory and endangering the preternatural community is death," Shane told him, eyes still molten and shimmering as he stared into Downing's dead ones.

"Try it," Downing said, spitting at Shane as he said it.

"I don't have to. The Sha will be notified. I have everything you just said recorded," Shane admitted, smiling smugly as he pulled his phone from his pocket and waved it in front of him.

"What's 'The Sha?'" Downing asked, clearly becoming mildly concerned and staring at the phone. The four of them chuckled as Shane stood up.

"You'll find out" was all he said before he turned around and headed back upstairs.

Once the door had closed to the basement, he gasped a little. He had been holding in so much rage and contempt for that creature as he spoke. He wanted to rip that man's head from his shoulders for the things he said about Vee. Shane was certain his imaginings of what he would have done to her, had he not been interrupted, were far worse than Shane could even comprehend.

"I have to call the Sha," he said regretfully.

He didn't want to for a couple of reasons, Ethan and Vee. Ethan could face punishment for his actions, as could the other three lone wolves he was with. How severe the punishments were going to be was questionable. Vee on the other hand was mentioned quite a lot by Downing, and Shane's own reaction to him saying her name was not, he hated to admit to himself, friendly acquaintance-level reactions. It wasn't unheard of for a Were to take a human as a partner. Thomas had a human wife; Shane did once as well, but he was worried about what Downing had said about her smell. It was different. Not different enough for them to think anything of it in passing, but if they were tipped to knowing she was in any way unique, it may lead to inquiries. If they wanted to, they could see fit to bring her in and question her.

Shane went to his car. It would provide him with some sort of mild privacy with the whole pack in the house. As he closed the car door, he gave himself a moment to lose control. He yelled loudly but didn't let his wolf come out to howl. That would have been enough to bring the pack running. No, he made it brief, releasing as much of his anger as he could afford to. Taking in a shaky breath, he lifted the phone. He was dialing the number for Min, their Sha contact, when he really wanted to be checking in on Vee.

"I suspected we'd hear from you soon, Shane," Min said, without greeting.

"We've captured the rogue Were. The one the humans named the Cross Country Killer," Shane told him, gripping the steering wheel in front of him.

"I suppose the others have decided we need to deal with him if you're calling for us?"

"They have," Shane affirmed.

"Tell me what you know."

Shane told him everything he needed to know about Todd Downing and the murders. He only mentioned Vee as the last human he was trying to attack, but of course Min picked up on his slight change in tone.

"And who is she to you, Shane Keenan?" Shane cringed.

"I have interest in her," Shane stated truthfully.

"Interest?"

"We haven't gotten very far. We've only known each other a few days," Shane admitted.

"Her full name?" Min asked, clearly planning on doing a background check on her. Shane's mouth fell open as he realized he had no idea what her full name was.

"I... I don't actually know," he admitted, putting his hand over his face. How could he not even know her name?

Min was silent for a bit. The quiet made Shane worried. The last thing he needed was to push Vee away by the Sha demanding to meet with her.

"She has been through enough. No need to bring a human into these affairs any more than she already has been. We will be there in three days. I expect to see your son there as well," Min told him. Relief for Vee. Horrible panic for Ethan.

"He should already be on his way," Shane told him honestly. He knew that when he told Ethan to come home, it was not a request that Ethan would ignore. He may have been a lone wolf, but he wasn't stupid enough to avoid the Sha.

CHAPTER 17

Vee's phone rang. It was late, but she had already slept most of the day, and although she was achy, her brain had trouble shutting off. Too much stimuli from the last few days. She was watching a comfort movie; one she knew all the words to and had watched nearly a hundred times. She didn't even have to pay much attention to it, just the familiar sounds in the background helped her feel a little less anxious about how drastically her life had changed.

She looked at who was calling, and her heart skipped a beat. It was Shane. She had expected a call much earlier in the evening. She had been too embarrassed to call him herself.

"Hello?" she said as she placed it to her ear.

"Are you okay?" he asked, his tone letting some of his worry come through.

"Sore, but otherwise okay," she told him, feeling it was better to play down her soreness. He didn't need to know she had been walking around like a tin man all day. She hesitated slightly, looking down at her loose shirt that covered her claw marks. "Is it... over yet?" she decided to ask, trying to keep the fear from her voice and hoping that the monster was dead.

"He can't hurt you, but it's far from over," Shane said. Vee held back a chuckle only because she hadn't even considered the creature was a threat to her anymore, somehow. For whatever reason, she trusted Shane to have that taken care of, but she wouldn't feel settled until she knew he couldn't breathe the same air as everyone else.

"So, do we know what happened? How he... came to be...?" she disjointedly asked, trying not to fidget too much, he'd be able to hear it over the phone if she did. The question was vague, but she knew he'd understand. He sighed.

"Yes... I feel like we should talk about this in person. I have a lot to tell you," he said seriously. She nodded to herself. She was expecting that he would rather discuss it away from the prying ears of the pack.

"You can come to the shop tomorrow. I have house calls in the morning, but otherwise..."

"I'll come at six. That's about when you close?"

"Yes," she said, trying not to read into the slight eagerness she heard in his voice or the flutter she felt at the thought of seeing him again.

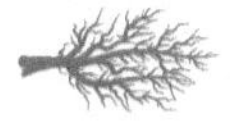

Vee's Wednesday was relatively uneventful. Other than her continued soreness, which was markedly better than the previous day, she got her work done. Running by the hardware store to re-up on some of her supplies, dropping her deposits at the bank night drop, and filling her gas tank all before she opened the shop felt good. She was relieved to finally be having a normal day. She made her house calls getting to the last one about 3 p.m.

It was odd, but welcomed, that so many homes needed lock changes. As the woman at her first stop had said, the city seemed to become rife with thieves. Perhaps people would rethink who they gave their house keys out to.

She pulled up to the address, of the final house call of the day, only then realizing it was on Eliza's block. She momentarily felt a trickle of anxiety about Frank seeing her so near, but she shooed the feeling away. She wasn't there to see Eliza, so there should be no problem with her doing her job. She gathered her tools, trying not to wince as she walked to the house. Part of her wished Shane had licked her feet too, when he was cleaning her side injury. They seemed to be the slowest thing to heal so far.

She knocked at the door, listening to people moving through the house. A heavier-set woman answered. She was adorned with so many pieces of jewelry, Vee wasn't sure where to look.

"I'm Vee, from *The Missing Key*," Vee offered, noting the confused look on the woman's face as she looked her over. Vee assumed that the look of a woman in baggy overalls and a bag full of tools probably wasn't something this woman normally encountered.

"Oh! I wasn't really expecting a woman," the home-owner said, causing Vee to raise her eyebrow a little. "I mean, I thought the person who had taken down my information was a man," she backtracked. It was a little odd, considering Durran had scheduled this appointment. Vee supposed Durran's voice was quite low and could be mistaken for a man.

"Ah, well, I had someone helping me with calls the other day. Sorry," Vee said, pulling out a card from her pocket to hand to her.

"Not at all! I'm Vivian. I just need the front and back doors replaced like I said. I wasn't sure what colors you had…" The woman barely looked at the card, instead gesturing for Vee to follow her in the house.

"I brought a few different types for you to decide on," Vee told her, walking through the lavish home. This house was quite different from Eliza's. Its size was the same and general layout, but it was more traditionally extravagant. Gold-plated, ornate picture frames, cla- footed furniture, and intricate upholstery and rugs adorned the home. Vee should have guessed it would be this way inside, based simply on Vivian's attire.

She set the options out on the marble counter of the kitchen island. She already knew the woman would be going with the gold option, but she still went through the game of pros and cons of each color with her.

"I suppose the gold *does* compliment my aesthetic," the woman concluded after twenty minutes of this. Placing her hand on her chest to fiddle with the necklaces there.

"I think so," Vee told her, smiling, mostly out of amusement. It was then that Vee felt the void of a mind. She furrowed her brow as the woman kept talking about various aesthetics. What would Durran be doing here?

She looked at the back door, where the presence was growing stronger and met with the view of not Durran, but a tall, thin, red-headed man. His hair was to his shoulders and naturally curly and his eyes were that familiar reddish brown, like Durran's. He came through the back door and looked at her as if he already knew her.

"Oh, Mac!" Vivian said, grinning. She was clearly smitten with this man, a stereotypical housewife. "Vee, this is our handyman, Mac. He's going to need a key. He comes by to fix this or that, but he suggested you when we were talking about getting new locks," she told Vee as she saddled up right next to him, placing her hand on his chest.

"I heard about you through the grapevine. Good to meet you," he said, reaching his hand out to shake hers. The hint of a lie twinged in her mind. She hesitated, finally meeting his hand. His emotions hit her like a ton of bricks. This Watcher did *not* like her. At first, she had been unsure whether the subtle hatred he was giving off was for the woman of the house, but as she touched his skin, getting the full brunt of his emotions, she knew it was aimed at her.

Her spine tingled. How did this Watcher know her, other than through Durran?

"Thank you," she said, pulling her hand away quickly. "Well, I better get to these locks." She decided to start at the front door, so she'd get a moment away to think. This was probably one of the more bizarre encounters she ever had. Watchers were rare. Coming across Durran and becoming her friend was unusual enough. Coming across another Watcher was entirely unprecedented.

She swapped the lock, trying not to be too suspicious. Maybe this Mac was watching over this woman, or someone in her family. That seemed unlikely, but she was trying hard to not panic. Too many strange occurrences had happened in such a small amount of time. Surely, she was just being paranoid. As she finished that lock, wincing as she stood back up to move to the back door, she felt him coming around the corner to her.

"You okay?" he asked, watching her strange, stiff movements. His words came out sounding sincere, but the feeling behind them wasn't.

"Oh… yeah. Just had a rough couple of days," she said truthfully, moving past him back to the kitchen. He followed her of course, curiosity and disdain surrounding her from him. Vivian had left the kitchen by this time, and Vee desperately hoped she'd come back before the second lock was finished.

"So, you do this all by yourself?" he asked, as she unscrewed the old lock from the back door. It was odd that she felt a tingle of a lie when he asked that question. He already knew the answer. A second small lie in only a few sentences. Her unease around him was growing by the second.

"Yep," she said, keeping the conversation as minimal as she possibly could without coming off too rude.

"That must be hard. No one to watch your back." She paused. That seemed vaguely threatening.

"I have a few people that help me from time to time," she told him. It wasn't entirely untruthful. She had had several people helping her as of late, both of the Watcher and Were variety.

"It's important to not be alone," he said, stepping a bit closer. Vee quickened her pace, but of course this particular door needed a bit of widening to make the new lock fit properly.

"It's more important to be content," Vee told him without looking at him, choosing to remain focused on her task as she pulled out her narrow sander, smoothing the hole, and trying the lock again.

"You're a bit strange for a woman," Mac said, then, the first genuine thing he seemed to say. She stopped and turned to look at him. He was leaning against the kitchen island, eyes a bit more red, but not glowing. His brows were furrowed and head tilted in speculation, as if he was trying to figure her out, simply by looking at her.

"I've been told," she responded, her voice flat. This was a tiresome conversation she had had time and time again with a variety of males. The only difference this time was he was a Watcher.

"Well, if you ever need any help…" he trailed off as he pulled a card from his pocket, holding it out to her between two fingers. Vivian made an appearance again, and Vee turned back to the door to put the final touches on, ignoring the card. She did not need to have any connection to this Watcher. She knew it was dangerous.

"Are you trying to fish for work with this girl? Trying to leave us?" Vivian asked as she paraded back into the room.

"Oh no, Vivian. I'm very happy being this neighborhood's handyman," he said, smirking and making her blush. The lies came so easily from his mouth, Vee's nose was almost burning as her head became engulfed in the feeling.

"Well, Miss Vivian, I'm all finished here," Vee said as she stood, having placed the last screw.

"Do you take cards?" Vivian asked, brandishing a thick black credit card.

"Of course," Vee said, pulling her swiping tool from her messenger bag and snapping it on her phone. She was actively avoiding Mac's eyes as Vivian paid.

"You've been a delight. Can I have some more of your cards to give out?" Vivian asked as she walked Vee back to the front door, Mac in toe. Vee handed her some, thanked her, and headed back to her car.

Thankfully, Mac didn't seem to be watching or following her at that moment, but she was absolutely shaken by him. She felt like she suddenly had a target on her back. As if, no matter what she did to maintain her little solitary life she had made, she was being stalked, followed. Preternaturals were being attracted to her at an alarmingly fast rate, and she didn't know how to stop it.

She purposefully turned around to avoid driving by Eliza's house, the pain she felt just being in proximity was telling enough. She didn't need Frank potentially seeing her car drive by and escalating things since she had managed to avoid him noticing as she worked on

Vivian's locks. His threat to her days ago seemed inconsequential in comparison to the preternatural threats she had been facing as of late. The pain of remembering that she essentially lost her sister was still a bit more than she could take at the present moment.

Once back at her shop, she sat in her car for a moment. She had a sinking feeling. She couldn't quite put her finger on it, but she felt like there were things about her that she didn't know. She was being left out of the loop on something. She wasn't even sure who to address. She blamed herself, partially. She had kept herself away from the preternatural world. One foot in to know it's there, but not draw attention to herself.

But now she had.

Attention was drawn and she couldn't escape it.

She thought about Mac. Such hatred from a person she had just met. How could he have had such strong resentment, having never met her? Perhaps before she had met Durran she would have suspected he loathed her for being skilled at something he wasn't, but that wasn't it. She could feel the tendrils of distrust creeping in.

Could she go to Durran with this?

Did Durran know this Watcher?

Of course, she knew him. Two Watchers in the same city were bound to know of each other's presence.

She hated this. She hated the mystery. The life she had built for herself didn't have room for that. The biggest mystery she had signed up for was not knowing if she was going to save enough to buy herself a new car. She didn't want excitement. If she did, she wouldn't have spent her twenties scrimping, saving, and learning so she could start her own business. She gripped her steering wheel, trying to pour all her frustrations into it so she wouldn't explode.

With a deep breath, she tried to let it go. She had gotten through hard times before. It took work, but she could do it again. She could get back to her life. She got out, collected her things, and headed inside to immerse herself in her work.

CHAPTER 18

The pack had been busy, cleaning and preparing for the visit from the Sha. In the few rare times that they came to the territory, Shane or his predecessors would have taken them to the property in Pleasant Hill. It was expansive and much more private. If it was practical for the pack to operate there normally, Shane would have them all move closer to it, but as it had been for many years, the city was the hub of the pack. Despite how much Shane would have preferred the Sha not come to his home, it would prove to be too difficult to move Downing out there.

Shane felt the nervous excitement of the pack, especially Patrick, who hadn't even been born when the Sha last visited. He understood the excitement but feared it. While the Sha were often their allies, they could also be the downfall of his oldest son, depending on which way they took the attack on the creature.

He wasn't sure when Ethan was arriving. It had been a few years since he had last seen him. He was happy that he would be seeing Ethan but not happy about the circumstances. His mixed feelings were only deepened when he glanced in Patrick's room, seeing him nervously looking through his desk.

"What are you up to?" Shane asked, leaning on the doorframe.

"Ethan gave me something the last time he was here…" Patrick said, not looking up from his task.

"And you've lost it?"

"Well, I couldn't wear it at school at the time. No jewelry," Patrick told him, his voice somewhere between irritation and panic. Private schools had strict dress codes and one of the rules for the elementary school Patrick had previously attended was strictly no jewelry what-so-ever.

"Jewelry?" Shane asked, curious about what sort of thing Ethan would have given him as he watched Patrick open a side drawer on his desk and pull out the contents.

"It was a pendant he got in Ireland. He said something about it being made by a werewolf blacksmith in one of the packs there," Patrick's murmured, spreading the objects out on his bed. Shane had no idea Ethan had brought anything like that to Patrick. It gave him a little comfort that, though he was rarely there and they weren't close, Ethan still tried to have some sort of a connection to his younger brother.

A bit of metallic shine caught Shane's eye and he pushed off the doorframe to go to the bed and grab it. The pendant was a round piece of iron, a slew of Celtic knots intricately carved into it that shaped the head of a wolf. It was beautiful. Shane held it in front of Patrick's face, causing him to stop rifling through his things to grab it.

"Oh, thank goodness!" Patrick exclaimed, snatching it from his father's fingers and eagerly putting it on.

"Once you're done cleaning this up, I think Tommy is heading to the store to get some things. Why don't you and Lori go with him?" Shane posed it as a question, but Patrick knew it wasn't. He rolled his eyes.

"Why can't I help around here?" he asked, not being able to hold back the slight whine in his voice.

"Because you're still a kid, and Tommy will need the extra hands," Shane told him, touching his shoulder and giving it a squeeze.

Shane went to his room to get cleaned up before he went to talk to Vee. He found himself growing increasingly nervous about it. Over the course of this short span of time, she had become one of the most important people in his life somehow, and it shocked him. He had never had such an all-encompassing feeling about anyone. He knew she was important. He knew she was something, someone, he couldn't lose.

He was buttoning his shirt and glanced at the picture on his side table. It was his late wife, Patricia. She had been lovely, warm, caring and taught him how to slow himself, to calm down, and not be so beholden to his wolf's whims. She had tamed him, in a way, which he needed at the time. Losing her broke him for many years. Being grounded for Patrick and the pack was the only thing that had kept his head above water. He realized that even though he loved her he had never felt such an intense draw to her, like he did to Vee. He felt slightly guilty about it now, looking at her smiling from the picture and realizing that fact.

Patrick chose that moment to walk into his room.

"Are you okay, Dad?" Patrick asked timidly. He had never seen his father's emotions so all over the place. Sure, Shane would get angry, but for all of Patrick's life, that he could recall, he had never seen his father so conflicted.

"I'm okay. Just a lot going on right now. I'm glad you're on summer vacation so we don't have to add school to the mix," Shane told him, giving him a small smile. Patrick smiled back, looking over at the picture of his mother that Shane had obviously been looking at.

"You know… I bet she'd be happy if you found someone new." Patrick hadn't gotten to know her at all, her dying shortly after he was born, but with all the stories he had heard about her, he felt like he knew enough. At least enough to know she wouldn't want Shane to be alone. Shane stiffened a little, following Patrick's eyes to the photo. He wasn't wrong, she would have been happy he had feelings for someone, encouraged him, even, if she could talk to him from beyond.

"Well, I don't have much time for finding anyone. But—"

"I'd be happy for you too," Patrick interrupted, looking at his dad seriously, his eyes holding that same kind of warmth that Patricia's used to. Shane sighed a little, smiling at him before he abandoned buttoning the last two on his shirt to pull Patrick into a hug. He was getting tall, but not quite as tall as his dad. Short enough still that Shane could quickly kiss the top of his head as he squeezed him tightly.

"You'd better go, I think I hear Tommy and Lori already arguing at his truck," Shane said, releasing his hold.

Patrick wandered back out of the room, leaving Shane happy, but a bit more confused than before. His guilt wanted him to push away these feelings for Vee that were just seeming to grow stronger, while his instincts, and apparently his son, were telling him to go for her.

It didn't matter which way he was going to choose to go now. He had already promised to meet her. They had important things to discuss.

His conflicted thoughts continued during the drive over there. He had to tell her about the important issues, but he also wanted to know her more. What little he did know was that she was stubborn. Stubborn and strong. He pulled up behind that same rusted Lumina he had seen before, realizing now that it must have been her car. It was a strange juxtaposition to see his pristine car next to hers.

He couldn't help himself as he got out, and curiosity got the best of him as he walked past the windows. Was she messy? Is that why her car looked the way it did on the outside? Was that why she didn't let him in her apartment before? The little he did see in her apartment didn't appear to be too out of order.

He peered into the back seat, seeing only a few bags of tools placed neatly on the floor. No other debris seemed to be there. There was nothing in the front seat at all but a pair of sunglasses hanging off the visor. It made him internally a little happier, knowing that she may not have had great quality things, but she took care of them nonetheless.

He approached the door then. The "Closed" sign was on the door and the lights were dimmed, but there she was behind the counter busily scribbling on a piece of paper while she looked at the tablet in front of her. Her brow was furrowed and her hair back in a loose ponytail to keep it from her face. He just looked at her for a moment, marveling. He knew very little about her past, but to have basically started all of this from nothing was quite a feat.

Quietly, he knocked on the glass, causing her eyes to shoot up from the tablet to him with mild surprise. Did she think he wouldn't come? She set her pen down and moved around the counter, perhaps less gracefully than she had when walking down the stairs the other day. She had mentioned soreness. Being tossed around and dragged for blocks would explain that.

"Come on in. I'm almost done reconciling my register," she told him as she unlocked the door. She turned around quickly once he stepped through, heading back to her work.

"Take your time," he said, locking the door behind him and starting to wander the shop. Inside display cases, she had quite a variety of safes as well as various combination and pad locks. These were not your run of the mill locks. No, she had built these, made these herself, he realized. "You made these?" he asked, leaning over the counter to see the heart shaped ones.

She glanced up at him from the tablet, feeling out his emotions. He was genuinely curious and extremely intrigued.

"Yes, most of them. Some of the antique locks are refurbished. I have a couple home renovation contractors who bring me old locks that are just going to be thrown away," she told him, putting in the last few numbers into the computer.

"I always thought people who could make beautiful things with their hands were amazing. My hands may as well be claws all the time. I can work with numbers, but don't ask me to make you anything," he said quietly, still looking at the locks, but feeling her eyes on him.

"Well, I'll keep to the locks and maybe you can help me figure out how to get enough money to replace my car before it falls apart," she offered, moving a little down the counter to a clearer spot and leaning on it.

"That might be doable. That car is… horrendous," he told her, smirking a little and looking back at her. She smiled and nodded in agreement.

"So," she said, tearing her eyes away from his and clasping her fingers together nervously. "You had some things to tell me," she reminded. His demeanor immediately changed, hand going to his forehead, rubbing it as if that action would make things easier to say.

"Yes… where to begin…" he murmured, talking a few steps closer to her.

"Who is he?" she decided to ask first. She didn't even have a name for the man who almost killed her.

"His name is Todd Downing. He is a crossroad trucker… also a serial rapist and, I suspect, murderer, based on some of the things he said," Shane told her, anger welling in him as he said the words out loud. She mulled that over for a moment. Before this knowledge, he had only been a creature, a monster that was going to tear her apart. Having his name held a little power. He seemed smaller with that name.

"So how did he become a werewolf?"

Shane's emotions became a bit wild at that question. There was fear, anger, and pity all rolling around her from him.

"I have an older son, Ethan. He's in his forties. He's been a lone wolf for the better part of twenty years now. Sometimes lone wolves get together for brief stints. They go to packs and run with them on the full moon. He and a few of his friends came across Downing on a run," Shane said, pausing, trying hard to pull back his anger. It was horrifying to think about what Downing had been doing. It was also horrifying to think his son was capable of doing what he did to a human, no matter how gruesome they were.

"So, Ethan turned him?" Vee asked, not even trying to hide the shock in her voice.

"Not exactly, that was not the intention of the attack." Shane's jaw clenched as he spoke, rage smoldering in his eyes as he thought of what his son had come across on that fateful night.

"What was it, then?" she asked, brows furrowed, trying not to meet the rage she felt from him.

"Downing was... they heard the girl screaming..." Shane couldn't even utter the words. The very idea of what Downing did, what he had been capable of in human form, let alone as a Were, was unimaginable.

Vee straightened up at that. Her eyes glazing over unintentionally imagining what Downing had been doing. No wonder they attacked. She would have wanted to murder him, slowly and painfully, had she come across a scene like that. She refocused on Shane whose eyes were trained on her face, watching her expressions change.

"I would have too," she said solemnly, her hatred of Downing deepening. Shane let out a breath. He wasn't sure what he had been expecting her to say as he saw the realization come over her face.

"They didn't finish the job… or… they failed to kill him, so he healed. He went through the change."

"And his new rampage began," Vee finished for him, pushing herself from the counter where she had been leaning and starting to pace a little. "What now?"

"The Sha is coming," Shane said, unsure if she knew what that was. She stopped pacing and looked confused.

"The Sha?" She asked. She knew some things, but not everything when it came to Weres. His anxiety had spiked, she noted, as he said those words.

"They are the shapeshifters where all Weres origi-nated. Old… powerful… They are the ultimate say in Were politics," he told her, watching her face deepen in its confusion.

"So, they are coming here to…?"

"There will essentially be a sentencing for Downing. I… I had to mention you," he said quietly, regret lacing his words and feelings. Vee's anger rose at that instantly.

"You *told* them about me?" she hissed, her whole demeanor going from concern to absolute rage.

"You were just mentioned. I didn't say anything about your abilities," Shane tried to assure her, stepping closer, hands slightly outstretched. She simply stood there breathing a little heavily, glaring into his eyes. He wasn't lying to her, but the fact that her name was even brought up to them was absolutely horrifying.

"Why couldn't I have just been some random human he grabbed, like the others? Why would you put me in danger this way?" she demanded, eyes slowly turning an amber hue from their normal emerald. He hadn't seen this transition in person, only the before and after. It shocked him a little. Only preternaturals eyes changed that way. His shock muddied her anger only slightly. "What are you so shocked about? That I'm upset you gave them my name? Connected me with the preternatural world?"

"Your eyes," he said, stepping even closer to her and looking into them. The amber that they were now, glistened as she looked back.

"Stop distracting!" she snapped, quickly moving around him to pace where he had been standing previously.

"Downing mentioned your name. If he did with me, he will when they're here. I had to beat him to the punch, so they wouldn't ask for you," Shane said, turning his head slightly since she was now behind him. He didn't want to mention his own reaction to Downing's mention of her. His reaction had been far stronger than he felt it should have been for someone he barely knew. Maybe it was better if he stayed looking away. She was distracting him. Not purposefully, of course, but something about looking into her eyes made him unable to think clearly. She calmed a little at his words but continued her pacing.

"But they will still be here, in the city?" she confirmed.

"Yes."

"When?"

"In two days."

She stopped, taking a deep breath and moving to stand in front of him again. He hadn't turned around while she had been pacing.

"I'll just stay away from your house, and I'll be fine. I do that anyway, unless I get a call over that way," she said, looking up at him. She was so much closer to him, her amber eyes a little less fiery.

"I don't want to risk it… risk you," he murmured softly, a pang of guilt sweeping through him.

"What do you mean?" she asked, drawing her eyebrows.

"I want to have some of my wolves with you while they're here just in case they seek you out. That way we'll know. We can move you," he told her, his hand unconsciously raising as if to touch her, and then dropping back at his side.

"I can sense if something is nearby. I don't need your protection," she said stubbornly. She didn't like his heavy-handedness. She didn't like feeling weak and powerless. His hands balled into fists. Her hard-headedness was frustrating. He knew his emotions were unreasonable. That she was just saying this because it was an invasion of her life, but he couldn't help his anger.

"Oh? You didn't need my protection from Downing? I should have just let him run away with you?" he barked back, eyes shifting to gold quickly.

"That was different," she hissed, amber eyes burning again to match his.

"How is one threat different from the other? You want me to leave you here, alone for them to seek out? We don't know their intentions, Vee. We don't know if they said they wouldn't call on you to placate me."

"Placate you?" She laughed. "Great! So, I just get to live my life now based on what placates and pleases you, Shane Kennan?"

His eyebrows shot up just slightly at the use of his full name. His feeling of anger was only matched by his urge for her. He couldn't help his hand this time, it had a mind of its own. He reached to her, touching her chin. They paused there for a moment, the touch somehow feeling so intimate.

"What's your real name?" he whispered, leaning his head down slightly. She drew in a ragged breath at his touch. She could feel his emotions much more boldly with the contact. His anger, his worry, his lust, all swirling. She felt her own rise to meet his.

"Victoria Malone," she whispered back.

"Victoria, I *need* you to do this for me. To let them protect you," he said, his face getting closer to hers. His wolf was urging him closer.

Vee closed her eyes, pulling away from him and breaking their touch. The way her name came from his lips made her shiver. Its negative connotation seemed to have the very opposite effect when he said it, and because of that, she knew couldn't do this. She couldn't get more involved with him, them, the werewolves. This would upend her life more than it already was. She was wildly confused by his feelings. This man had only met her a few days ago. Why would he feel so strongly about her already? Why did she feel so deeply for him?

"I… I don't like it when you say my name," she lied, trying to put distance between them but finding her back to the counter. He let his hand drop again, trying hard to hold back his disappointment at the break in contact and her words. "I'll do this just the once. Once they're gone you can't just demand that I let your pack *protect* me all the time. I made it this far without you," she said, hesitating to lift her eyes and look at his again. She had felt his disappointment, though, it and his other emotions were slightly dulled now, somehow.

CHAPTER 19

Shane nodded, bringing his hand again to his forehead, rubbing it. He needed to reel it in. Even if he was consumed by her smell and she was somehow always in the back of his mind these days, she wasn't willing for anything more. He took a deep breath and clapped his hands together, rubbing them slightly as if he were cold. In reality, he was trying to shake himself of the urge to cradle her face in his hands and kiss her.

"Have you eaten?" he decided to say, taking her aback. Her eyes shifted around in confusion.

"Um, no?" she said as a question, now moving herself back around the counter to start putting away her things.

"We could grab something to eat?" he offered, watching her as she placed a few things in her messenger bag and went to close the inventory room for the night.

"I don't really have the money to eat out right now," she admitted. "Someone trashed half my inventory," she joked, smirking a bit and giving him a little playful side-eye. Her eyes had gone back to their normal emerald now. He smiled a little at her playfulness, despite the awkward moment they just had.

"Well, she's going to be one of the wolves I assign to you, so you can get some labor out of her to make up for it," he assured her. Vee stopped short again, just as she was getting ready to put the alarm on.

"Lori is?" Vee asked, turning to look at him. She was a bit shocked, but also a little relieved. She wanted to talk to her, see how she was doing since the change, but hadn't known how to go about getting in touch with her.

"I'll tell you more at dinner," Shane said with a wry smile, eyebrows up playfully. Despite her denials, he still found her utterly intriguing. She was someone worth getting to know. She rolled her eyes, turned back to the panel, and set the alarm. He walked out first, giving her space to close and lock it behind them.

"You'll have to pick what you want, I'm terrible at deciding where to eat," she told him quickly, putting her hands in her back pockets and rocking a bit on her heels.

"Hmm…" he murmured, looking up and down the street. They could travel to the hub of the neighborhood, where there were tons of restaurants to choose from, but with those restaurants and bars, came quite a lot of noise. "Isn't there an Italian place over here?"

he asked, starting to walk a little up the hill away from the hub before she could respond.

"Yes…" she said warily, walking behind him. She knew she couldn't walk behind him like that for long; Weres found it threatening, but she took the moment to look him over. He was taller than she was, but that wasn't much of a feat since she was quite short. He was, perhaps average for a man. She could see his defined muscles through his light-colored dress shirt, sleeves rolled up on his forearms. He, again, was dressed quite nicely in comparison to her worn jean overalls and loose t-shirt. It seemed like he always dressed as if he had just gotten off work at his nice corporate job.

She didn't understand what his attraction was to her. It was obvious he was attracted, based on the lust she felt from him, but in her mind she was very plain, if not downright grubby and forgettable. She also noted that his presence wasn't an irritant to her, like some Weres were. Instead, his buzz in her head was soothing. The only thing she seemed to dislike about his presence was his overbearingness.

She caught up to him, so she was beside him, having noticed his head turn slightly to glance back at her. She kept her eyes focused in front of them, seeing the sign of the restaurant just ahead.

"I haven't been here before. Always wanted to try it," he told her as they entered.

It wasn't a traditional restaurant set up. They ordered at the counter and got a number for their table, like a deli, but the food was amazing. She decided on their cheapest pasta dish, thinking of how much inventory she still had to build back up as she pulled out her debit card. Shane quickly saddled up right beside her, already having his card out.

"I'll get both," he told the cashier, who smiled flirtatiously at him.

She glared at him for a moment, snatching her number and water cup from the counter and heading over to where the tables were before he was done. The restaurant had the main space where they ordered, which had a few tables and the drink dispenser, but also included the building next door. Between the two was a small alley that had a trellis hung above. In the warmer months, they would put out tables there to provide more seating. No one seemed to be out there on a slow Wednesday night, so Vee thought it best to park them out there, as to not be overheard by human ears. Who knows where their conversation would lead them.

Shane was right behind her, going a little slower to look at where everything was. It reminded him a lot of a restaurant with a similar setup in his neighborhood. He noted the few people seated in the restaurant stared at the two of them while they passed. They did look rather strange together. Not that he looked much older than her; in fact, he still looked like he was in his thirties, but he assumed their very different states of dress made them seem like an odd pair to be eating together.

When she went out the door, he was a bit confused but followed, nonetheless. She was already setting her sign and empty cup on at the furthest back table. They were alone out there, which he appreciated. However, the humidity left him wishing they could have found something in the air-conditioned interior. He was going to start sticking to his shirt.

"We have to go back in for water and utensils," she said, her tone still having an edge.

"Upset again so soon?" he asked, failing to keep the smirk from his face. She narrowed her eyes at him.

"I didn't like you paying for my food," she said. At least she was straightforward.

"You said you were low on money," he said with feigned innocence. She scoffed, snatching his cup from his hands.

"I'll go back in. You stay here," she instructed him, as she marched back through the door, even though there was no way their food would be ready so quickly, and honestly no reason for him not to go get his own things.

He sat once she was gone, looking up at the ivy and fairy light laced trellis above. He wasn't completely sure what he was doing here with her. He wasn't sure he was ready for diving into this… whatever it was, after having just met her. She clearly wasn't ready for that sort of change, either. His wolf begged to differ, making his heart pound at her smell as she walked past him, feeling excitement at how straightforward she was with him. He decided he was just trying to get to know her better. That was all.

She came back, seeming to be less irate and set his water and utensils down in front of him before taking her seat.

"So, what's the plan, then? For when the Sha arrive?" she asked, getting right back to the topic.

"The Sha tend to send scouts out ahead of the leaders, so tomorrow I'll have Lori, Tommy, and my younger son Patrick join you at your shop," Shane told her, watching a strange expression flutter across her face.

"Younger son?" she asked, going back through their previous discussion. Yes, he had mentioned that Ethan was his *older* son, but she hadn't understood the implication at the time.

"Yes. He just turned sixteen a few months ago," Shane told her.

"Sixteen… wow," she murmured, nodding her head. Even more of a reason not to fall onto her irrational desires. He was clearly already taken, had a family, and obviously his pack. She shouldn't be getting involved with these werewolves for so many reasons, but this was just the cherry on top.

"What?" he asked, confused by her reaction.

"Not with his mother, then?" she asked, trying to make her voice as nonjudgmental as possible, but she was failing miserably. His emotions went from confused amusement to mild sadness and guilt.

"No. She died," Shane told her, quietly. Vee's eyes widened at that, putting her hand to her mouth as if to make herself shut up. If she could have crawled under something to hide from him, she would have.

"I'm sorry…that was rude," she muttered, horribly embarrassed now.

"No, you didn't know," Shane assured her, watching her shift uncomfortably in her chair. "What about you? Anyone in your life other than the Watcher?" he asked, trying to hold back his irritation even mentioning Durran. Her discomfort seemed to grow at the mention of potential partners.

"No," she said, picking up her glass and taking a drink of water.

"Why not?"

"I don't really have time, and I don't like the disruptions," she told him honestly.

"But you have tried in the past?" he inquired, dubious that a woman like her wouldn't gain attention.

"Tried? Yes. Humans are not great for my abilities," she admitted, sighing.

"Not preternaturals, though?"

"Never tried. I try to stay out of that world as much as possible," she reminded him.

"What's so bad about humans?"

"They have no control over their emotions. I have yet to find a single person, preternatural or not, that doesn't irritate me with their presence after a short while," she told him seriously. He laughed a bit at that, surprising her.

"Humans have no control over their emotions? I think werewolves certainly struggle with that," he said, eyes flashing gold momentarily. She smiled at him.

"It's different… the wolf is…" she paused searching for the words. "The wolf's emotions are more primal. I, for some reason, can attune to that better." He took that in. She wasn't as bothered by the fluctuating emotions of a wolf's whims.

"And has my presence become an irritation yet?" he asked, leaning forward on the table a bit. She measured him. He was genuinely curious with every question he asked her. She could count the number of people who had ever felt that way about her on one hand.

The servers came out with their food at that moment, setting their respective dishes in front of them and taking their signs from the table. Once they were alone, Vee looked at the spread. Her simple pasta, his plate of lasagna, and, apparently, he had splurged on garlic bread for them to share as well.

"Not your presence, but your heavy-handed decisions are becoming one," she finally answered, gesturing to the food before them. He chuckled, picking up his fork to start eating.

They ate in silence for a few minutes, Vee, having not realized exactly how hungry she was, tried not to scarf her food down like a heathen. She had originally planned on ignoring the bread that he had gotten for them, out of principle, but she couldn't help the draw to scoop up some pasta sauce with a piece.

"Why those three?" she suddenly asked after having eaten enough to feel like she could slow down a bit.

"What do you mean?"

"Why Lori, Patrick, and Tommy?" she clarified.

"Lori and Patrick are our youngest members. I would rather them be a little more controlled before they're exposed to the Sha. Tommy is essentially their babysitter," Shane told her, setting his fork down having completely cleaned his plate. Vee hadn't even noticed he was also eating quickly; she had been so absorbed in her own food.

"So, I'm really just a convenient way of getting the teenagers out of your hair?" she questioned, her eyebrow raised.

"It serves multiple purposes. You have Tommy, who knows what to look out for, the kids feel like their helping, and you stay out of the Sha's view," he said, leaning back in his chair to stretch a little. She tore her eyes away from him, trying to resist the urge to ogle. She was internally admonishing herself for being unable to curb these thoughts. She usually was much better about controlling her own feelings.

"I see," she said, deciding she was done eating out of disgust for herself and pushing her plate away a little.

"Are you done?" he asked, looking at her plate which still had about half the food on it.

"I'll just grab a to go box, so you don't have to wait on me," she said, gesturing to his empty dish and getting back up with hers to take it inside. "Bring yours so we can put the dishes away," she told him, as she waited by the door. He did as she instructed, following her inside and watching as she approached the drink station, carefully emptying her contents into a to-go container that was provided there and placing her dishes in a bus tub right beside the trash bin. It was a little odd. He had never been to a place with service like this, unless it was a buffet, but even then, you often didn't have to clear your own plates and fill your own drink cup. He followed suit, and they were back out on the sidewalk, walking back to their cars.

"Don't be mad when they show up tomorrow," Shane said, stepping off the curb into the street between their cars.

"No guarantees," Vee said following him, but turning toward her car. "Thank you for dinner," she said quietly as she opened her door.

"Thank you for the conversation," he replied, realizing this had been the first normal conversation he had had with another adult that didn't have much to do with business, and more to do with getting to know her, in a long time.

She smiled and looked at him one last time before she got in her car.

CHAPTER 20

Vee pulled up to her parking spot at her apartment and saw Durran sitting on the steps to the front door. She hadn't been expecting her, but she often didn't when Durran decided to show up. Seeing her reminded Vee of the Watcher she ran into earlier in the day. Part of her wanted to confront Durran about it, the other part didn't know if she could trust what Durran had to say about the matter. Watchers protected their wards, they were honest when they needed to be, but above all else, they protected their own kind. Vee wasn't sure where Durran would fall with this particular news.

She decided she'd act like nothing was wrong for the time being. Mac hadn't been physically aggressive by any means, but the feelings she got from him had been. What the other Watchers knew about her abilities was still unknown to her, and she wasn't about to ask more questions and bring more attention her way. She got out of the car, grabbing her leftovers from the passenger seat and moving to where Durran sat.

"I really can't get through that way if you're sitting there," Vee said, putting a hand on her hip. Durran smiled faintly and stood. "Are you alright?"

Durran looked at her, eyes turning red a bit. Vee could feel her disappointment and anxiety.

"Inside" was all Durran said, using her head to gesture to the door. Vee went to unlock it, feeling additionally awkward as they silently walked up the stairs to her apartment. Once inside, Vee went to the kitchen to stash her dinner for tomorrow and turned back to watch Durran, who was beginning to pace in the small space.

"Care to share why you're feeling the way you are?" Vee asked, going back to the door to slip off her shoes.

"You shouldn't be... I... Keenan is dangerous," Durran finally said, having a hard time getting the words out. Vee crossed her arms and glared at Durran, who still paced.

"Yes, I know, but I don't really have a choice now, do I?" Vee asked her eyes tracking the Watcher before her.

"You did. You chose wrong," Durran snapped, still pacing.

"Are you serious?" Vee asked, shocked that a Watcher, of all beings, was admonishing her for saving lives.

"Why did you do it? Help her?" Durran asked, finally stopping and turning to face Vee. Her eyes blazing crimson and her anger fully risen to the surface. Vee had never seen or felt Durran this way.

"I couldn't sit by and not save those innocent girls, Durran! How could I know something was happening and not *do* something about it?" Vee yelled, not even caring if her neighbors heard her at this point.

"You are not in a position to be saving anyone," Durran said coldly. Vee laughed angrily at that.

"I am not some damsel in distress. I had the capability and the means to help, so I did." Durran fumed at her for a moment, breathing through her nose.

"Because of this, you were targeted, and who knows who will find out about you." Vee stilled at the thought of others discovering her abilities. She was worried about the Sha but somehow trusted Shane to quell that as best he could, even if it meant having Were bodyguards for a few days. What else did Durran know?

"I would have been targeted regardless of what I did to help Lori. Downing didn't go after me because of what I could do, Durran. He doesn't know. I was just his *type*," Vee hissed back, her nails digging into her palms in frustration.

"You've been exposed! Are you not concerned?" Durran threw up her hands, ignoring Vee's words.

"And what did you do, Durran? You saved me, yes, but you let that monster go and kill another woman," Vee said, her voice chilling and eyes deadly. Durran's face crumpled a bit and her guilt rose. She took a deep breath, realizing her emotions were only proving to make Vee more hostile.

"I couldn't kill him," Durran said quietly. "I cannot kill a Were on their territory."

Vee laughed again. It was her turn to pace.

"Yes, of course not. You can't kill one of their own on their territory. You would bring war to your kind," she said, her tone mildly sarcastic. Durran visibly shuddered at the thought, reaching out to grab Vee by the shoulders and look her in the eyes.

"It's not a joke, Vee. We've kept peace for centuries. All of us. Those wars were unimaginable."

Vee felt the heaviness in Durran's words, saw in her eyes, horrors of the past. She wouldn't have changed her decision to save Lori, but she understood Durran's reason for not killing Downing.

"Okay, I understand, but that doesn't change the fact that I would make the same choice to save those girls, to help Lori, a hundred times, even if it meant my life was never the same," Vee whispered, looking up into Durran's glowing red orbs.

"Why? You fought so hard for this life, Vee! Why would you risk it all?"

"If you don't understand why, then you don't understand me," Vee said, pulling her shoulders from Durran's grasp and taking a step back. Durran's brows furrowed looking at her, she realized now she smelled Were on her, breathing in through her nose a bit more intensely.

"Were you with him?" Durran asked, voice laced with accusation. Vee felt the anger and jealousy rise in Durran.

"We had to talk; the Sha are coming here," Vee told her, looking at Durran with confusion as she felt her emotions.

"He was so close to you," Durran stated without thinking, nostrils flared to take in the wolf's smell.

Vee's own anger rose. How dare she? This whole conversation had been laced with Durran's attempts to control Vee, and now she was *angry* that Vee was too close to Shane?

"Get out," Vee said coldly, her eyes having turned amber for the second time that night. Durran's demeanor immediately changed. She stood up straight, her expression shocked.

"Vee, I didn't mean—"

"Get out," Vee repeated pointing to the door. She didn't have the emotional capacity to deal with Durran's confusing feelings for another moment. Too many of her own confusing emotions were swirling in her head. She saw this as a strange and subtle betrayal from her only friend, and coupled with the distrust she felt, having run into Mac, she didn't want to be anywhere near her. Things were only going to get weirder now that the Weres seemed to be becoming regular fixtures in her life.

Durran nodded, not saying another word as she turned and walked out of the apartment, leaving Vee reeling.

Shane's phone rang almost immediately after Vee pulled away. He had thought to follow her home, just to make sure she was safe, but the phone call set his good mood on fire.

"Dad, Ethan is here," Patrick said. Shane could hear Ethan and some of the others chatting in the background.

"I'm on my way," he told him, starting his car and racing home.

He spotted Ethan's motorcycle on the front walk by the door as he pulled up to the house. The house was still full of pack members and, of course, Downing in the basement. This would be their most interesting reunion yet, he imagined. He walked through the back door, glad to see the arrival of Ethan hadn't distracted them from guarding the basement. Markus, a wolf who had joined them about five years prior, was there.

"Emily and Michael are down there too," Markus said as greeting, noting Shane's expression.

"Good. Are they—" Shane started, planning on asking where his sons were but heard a crash from the living room. "Never mind," he said, following the sound of the ruckus.

He entered the room and crossed his arms, watching as Tommy and Ethan wrestled on the floor. It was clearly for fun, but the lamp on the floor was completely done for. Patrick was sitting on the couch watching. His eyes snapped up to his dad, going from amused to horrified in an instant.

"I'm glad you've made yourself at home so quickly, Ethan," Shane said, causing them to freeze. Tommy and Ethan parted and helped each other up, Ethan grinning. Ethan was built like Shane. His light brown hair was the most striking difference between them. They could have been brothers by their looks and passing age.

"It is my home, right, Dad?" Ethan asked rhetorically, as he stepped forward, hand out to shake Shane's. It hadn't been the home Ethan grew up in, werewolves tended to move about their territory with some regularity, both to keep the humans from noticing their lack of aging, but also so other preternaturals didn't become wise to their central location. That didn't matter though, any home of Shane's was Ethan's home too. Shane pushed the hand out of the way, going in to embrace his son.

"We have a lot to discuss," Shane said to him as they parted. Ethan's face had turned from amused to confused as he breathed in deeply.

"Why do you smell like that?" Ethan asked, leaning a little toward Shane again and sniffing. Shane took in a breath, realizing that he smelled like Vee. She was all over him, clinging to him, as if he had been holding her all night, when, in reality, he had touched her for barely a moment.

"She's not to be concerned with at this moment," Shane told him.

"*She?* You're involving yourself with another human?" Ethan questioned, his voice not hiding his utter disgust. Part of the reason Ethan stayed away for such long stretches was due to his marriage to Patricia years ago. Shane's eyes shifted to Patrick briefly, who's head hung a bit, understanding the implication of Ethan's words.

"It's not a topic for discussion, Ethan," Shane said again, more firmly, turning to head up the stairs. "Clean it up, Tommy," Shane hollered behind him as he ascended the stairs. Ethan rolled his eyes and followed his father up to the office, closing the door behind them. The room was lightly soundproofed to keep the whole pack from hearing more delicate conversations, but it didn't keep everything out.

Shane sat on the edge of the desk, watching until Ethan closed the door.

"The other three are coming too. They should be here by the time the Sha arrive," Ethan told him, flopping into one of the large leather chairs in front of the desk.

"That's good. Don't want to delay them and have them stay any longer than necessary," Shane said, feeling relieved that he wasn't going to have to track down three lone wolves in the midst of all this.

"So, what's the deal? What do you know?"

"Todd Downing. He's a serial rapist, murderer," Shane said flatly.

"Didn't know his name, but that much I figured. How did you catch him?" Ethan asked, genuinely curious. Downing had evaded so many other packs' capture. Shane tried to hold back the shudder at the memory of Vee being carried at break-neck speeds away from him.

"He went after a friend of the pack. He, stupidly, chose to try to take her while I was talking to her," Shane told him. It was true. There wasn't a lie there, but perhaps a bit of an omission.

"*Friend* of the pack? Is that the smell all over you?" Ethan asked, his lips curling a little with his words. Shane sighed.

"Yes," Shane told him, eyes daring him to keep with this path of conversation.

"A little more than a friend, then, to you."

"That's not what it is, Ethan," Shane said quietly, growing irritated now.

"Why can't you just stick with our kind? Even another type of Were would be preferable." Shane gripped the desk. Ethan's distain for human-werewolf relationships stemmed from the pack leader who had been in charge before Shane took over. It was an old and arbitrary way of thinking, and Shane hated it. Ethan smirked at his father's physical reaction to the questioning. "I suppose she does smell intriguing, though. Maybe not completely human, but certainly not a Were."

"This is not a topic for discussion, Ethan. Why are you here? Is it because we have a non-Were as a friend of the pack, or is it because of your actions?" Shane asked, stopping this before it got too out of hand, his golden eyes staring into his son's. Ethan's expression faltered slightly. "To have so much disdain for a human, you certainly may have brought a great deal of suffering onto yourself trying to save one."

Ethan sat quietly for a moment.

"What do you think they'll do to us?" he asked quietly, his expression cold with fear, thinking of the Sha. Shane sighed, doing his signature forehead rub and going to sit beside Ethan in the other leather chair.

"I don't know. I'm hoping, despite trying to kill a human, his actions were enough for them to consider yours called for. Who could sit by and not help someone who was..."

Ethan nodded, slumping a little in his chair at the thought. He had done many stupid things both as a teenager and as an adult, but never had he done something so bad that it brought the potential wrath of the Sha down on him. He understood the gravity of this situation.

"How has the pack been doing? Patrick?" Ethan asked, looking back over at his father who was still rubbing his forehead.

"It's been pretty easy going here since the last time you visited up until last weekend, that is," Shane told him, giving him a weak smile.

"With Downing coming in town?" Ethan asked, more as confirmation.

"Actually, with Lori changing," Shane said, his face letting on his exasperations as he recalled the chaos of the last week. Ethan's eyebrows shot up of their own volition.

"Lori changed?"

"Yeah… we certainly weren't expecting it," Shane said, letting out a breath.

"But isn't her mother…"

"Human, yes." Born werewolves were almost always male. The likelihood that Lori would have been born a werewolf had been slim-to-none, and yet she had turned.

"Wow. I've never heard of such a thing," Ethan said, surprise laced in his voice.

"We're going to have to keep an eye on quite a few of our members' kids now," Shane realized aloud, thinking of the slew of young children that would be coming of age in the next ten years. He briefly wondered if Vee would be able to tell before they hit puberty or not. That would have to be a question for another time. They both sat in silence for a moment.

Everything was a mess right now, and they simply had to play the waiting game before they could move on.

"Let's get you some food and set you up in the room next to Patrick," Shane said, bringing them into the present as he stood.

"What do you have?" Ethan asked, joining his father as he opened the door.

CHAPTER 21

Vee was in the middle of her quick breakfast, having gotten everything else ready for her day, when an unfamiliar number called. It was a bit early for a house call, and her closed message on the voicemail for the shop didn't give out that number anymore, not since Shane had snagged it that way. She took another bite of her cereal, scrutinizing the number one last time before she picked it up.

"Hello?" she said as greeting, her tone questioning.

"Uh… yeah this is Tommy. Sorry it's so early, but—"

"I'm heading to the shop in a few minutes," Vee said, rolling her eyes.

"Okay, we will be there soon," Tommy told her, hanging up the phone.

She knew to expect them, but this was a bit much. All day? What was she supposed to do with three additional people *all day?*

She gathered her things and headed to her car. Most of her soreness had dissipated, which she appreciated, but she still would get the occasional twinge in her side as she bent over or got back up from crouching. She swung by the bank night drop on her way to the shop, just a few minutes out of her way, and pulled up behind Tommy's truck. He shouldn't have been able to get there so quickly. It had been ten minutes at most.

"You were already here when you called, weren't you?" she asked, one eyebrow arching as the odd trio got out of the car. Tommy smiled and nodded sheepishly as he came around to the sidewalk, rubbing the back of his head nervously. Lori and Patrick both looked exhausted. 7 a.m. was far too early to expect teenagers to be functional.

"Come on, then," Vee said, rolling her eyes before she unlocked the door. She moved quickly over to the alarm panel, turning it off, before circling to watch the three Weres move into her shop. It was interesting to see Lori, who, despite her clear grogginess, was looking around at the place with interest. Her curiosity was radiating off her, which Vee suspected had something to do with having already been here before. It was probably disorienting to be back at the place where one of the most traumatic events of her life had happened.

Patrick looked shockingly similar to his father. Like a shorter, leaner, younger version of Shane. She smiled lightly, imagining what type of father Shane was. He had a lot on his plate with the pack. She hoped he made time for his son, too.

"So," Tommy started, looking around the showroom. "What can we do?"

Vee raised her eyebrow at him, a little shocked at the offer. She figured she would be forcing them to work, if she got their help at all.

"Um… well, those two don't look like they're going to be of use to anyone until they have food and maybe caffeine. Are they old enough for caffeine?" she wondered aloud, questioning herself. She was certainly drinking coffee at fifteen and sixteen, but she was also on her own, completely unmonitored.

"That's a good point…" Tommy murmured, looking over at the two zombified teens that were slumped over the counter. "Go to the gas station, and get some food for everyone," Tommy said, pulling out a wad of cash from his wallet and handing it over to Lori. Her eyes brightened up at the sight of that.

"None for me," Vee said, going to unlock the inventory room. She heard their exit as she flipped on the lights back there. With a sigh she glanced around at her sparse inventory, trying to decide what she would use her time doing today. Thankfully, Lori hadn't destroyed the newest box of antique locks that had been brought to her the week before. They still sat, ready for restoration, in the furthest corner of the room.

The idea of picking up that heavy box, the way her side was feeling, was dreadful. She decided instead to wander the showroom, turning on display lights while she contemplated how she would move it where she needed it to be. Or at least to a more accessible spot in the back room. Vee glanced up at Tommy who looked like he was the embodiment of twiddling thumbs.

"You want to grab a box for me?" she asked, making his head snap up to look at her.

"Uh, yeah. Sure," he said, standing a little straighter as if to indicate he was ready for anything. She gestured for him to follow her, heading back in the room and pointing at the large box in the corner, next to the bathroom door.

"I hate to admit it, but I'm still sore. If you wouldn't mind bringing that out to my front workstation…?" It took everything in her not to hate herself for asking a "big strong man" for help, but he was there, and she just couldn't handle it.

"Oh! Yeah!" he said happily, walking back and easily snagging the box from the floor. Not an ounce of pity was coming off him for doing it. Tommy seemed to be very matter-of-fact. He was there to help Vee, and Vee needed a box moved. Nothing more to it.

She smiled a bit at that, following him out and gleefully digging into the old locks once he had set them down. She could get herself completely transfixed in these locks, and hopefully ignore the three additional bodies in her shop for the day.

Lori and Patrick came back, seeming more awake and in better spirits. They had arms full of food and drinks in each hand. Vee watched them walk back through the door playfully chattering about the upcoming school year. The three went on about eating the snacks that had been purchased, Lori put on some music on her phone at some point, while Vee quietly honed in on the locks before her.

Later in the morning, Lori came over and watched Vee as she removed a corroded internal piece of the lock and carefully looked it over, trying to determine if she had a piece to replace or, if she would have to do some welding.

"That must take a lot of patience," Lori said quietly, entranced by Vee's slow, delicate movements. Vee looked up at her from over her magnifiers.

"It does, but it's interesting to see how things were made long ago," Vee said, her voice equally as quiet as she set the small piece down. "I think I might have a piece for that."

Lori and Patrick followed Vee into the back room, watching her as she went to an old library card catalog cabinet beside her computer desk. She didn't often use her computer other than to pay bills online. For the most part, it just sat there, gathering dust. She just didn't feel like she had enough time to fully integrate everything to digital form.

As Vee dug through the little drawers, hoping to find the exact piece she needed, she could feel Lori and Patrick's curiosity as they looked around the room. It was much more sparse than it had been, and Vee could feel the little pangs of guilt come over Lori as she looked at the gouges in the floor and recalled how much more filled the shelves had been, for the fleeting moments she could remember about the room prior to relinquishing herself to her wolf.

"Is this the only inventory sheets you have?" Patrick asked, picking up one of the clipboards hung on the metal shelf. Vee looked up, seeing him flip through the pages.

"Yes?" Vee replied, her voice questioning his inquiry.

"Why don't you have this in your computer?" he asked, eyes shifting from the computer back to her.

"Time," was all she said in response, as she finally found the piece she had been looking for. She smiled at the tiny metal bit in her hand and turned around to look at the two of them.

"I could put this in for you," Patrick offered.

"I'll help!" Lori said enthusiastically, smiling. She had been wracking her brain trying to think of a way to help Vee as a show of appreciation, but not knowing anything about locks, she hadn't been able to come up with anything. Vee looked at them thoughtfully, testing out their emotions and intentions. They both were genuinely happy to help, Patrick seemed like he saw it as a challenge.

"Let me show you what I have set up already," Vee said, causing both teenagers to grin. She went over to the computer, booting it up and going through her files to find her attempt at a digital inventory. It had all her supplies listed and most of the updated prices on there. If nothing else, it was a starting point. "Just don't delete *anything*," she said, standing from her chair to allow Patrick to take a seat.

"Don't worry. I won't make any big changes without showing you," he assured her, as he sat, determination on his face.

The rest of the day went by rather uneventfully. Vee didn't find their presence as distracting or disruptive as she thought she would, getting quite a few locks in good stages to be restored and helping several walk-in customers. Tommy went back and forth between helping the kids and watching out the window.

"When you aren't doing security detail for me, what do you do, Tommy?" Vee asked, putting custom orders into her calendar for next week from the last few people that came in.

"Security for other people," he said, smiling. Vee's eyebrows went up in surprise.

"How do you manage a job when Shane pulls you away for pack stuff all the time?" Vee asked, setting her calendar aside.

"Shane is my boss. He owns a security company too. We only take on short details so that we can be available for pack business."

Vee was surprised, but it made sense. If there was a way to make things easier to move in the world as a Were pack, Shane seemed to have found it. It made sense why this particular city wasn't overrun with bizarre preternatural events that had to be covered up or explained away like other cities had. It was much better to have legitimate businesses for the pack to be part of, rather than essentially having a mob situation, where most of the members couldn't hold down real jobs.

"Shane's pretty smart," Vee muttered, looking over at the part of the showroom where they stood talking the night before.

"He is a good man," Tommy said to her seriously, his tone and feelings verging on reverent.

This pack was far different than the other one she had experienced, or at least known of, in St. Louis. Shane was not leading these people like a *boss*, he was leading them like they were a family. He took care of his members, made sure they had a place in both the pack and in the human world. His son was intelligent and caring, wanting to help her, even though he didn't know her. From what she gathered, the human companions and children were regarded just as highly as if they were members themselves. Shane was a different breed all together, she realized.

Thinking about actual threats, he did things differently than she would have thought a pack leader would have. He clearly wanted to kill Downing the other night, but he held him, captured him, to make sure full justice was served for his actions. From what she remembered about the St. Louis leader, he would have simply torn him apart and brought the repercussions from the other packs down on them.

She both liked and hated how finding out new information about him only made her more drawn to him. They had a strange, natural connection, that much she had gathered, but now knowing more about him as a person and a leader over the past few days, made her like him more. Of course, his heavy-handedness was going to be problematic. She didn't want her life to be centered around the preternatural world. She had chosen to get away from all of that. She had chosen a simple human life.

She had chosen to be alone.

Vee and Tommy's phones chimed at the same time with incoming messages. She pulled out her phone to see a message from Shane.

[Shane: The Sha have arrived.]

Vee glanced at the time on her phone, noticing it was nearly 6pm at that point.

Tommy text back, making her phone chime again.

[Tommy: So, we stay?]

Vee momentarily twinged with irritation at being in a group chat, but let it go. She was more irritated at the idea that now she'd have house guests in her tiny apartment.

[Vee: No.]

Vee texted back in response, looking up at Tommy, her face laced with her seriousness.

As it was most of the time, Durran's form shadowed the doorway with her presence at just the right time. Vee was still very upset with her, but if her appearance kept the Weres from having an impromptu sleepover, she would take it for now.

[Shane: Not for discussion. You agreed to the protection.]

She could almost feel his frustration through the words on the screen.

"It's time to go home, Vee," Durran said quietly, her emotions full of guilt and mild disgust as she avoided going near Tommy. Vee wanted to snap at Durran for trying to dictate when she should be home, but she was distracted by Lori and Patrick coming out of the back room, then.

"What's going on?" Patrick asked, looking warily at the Watcher in their midst. He had never seen a Watcher, but he had overheard some of the conversation about this particular one in the last week.

"Two conversations at once, which is two more than I usually like to have," Vee said, trying to determine how she would text Shane back at this moment. "Durran can escort me home since you all think I need to be watched so closely right now."

[Tommy: The Watcher is here.]

[Vee: She'll take me home.]

Vee silently looked at Durran as if to tell her it was conditional. They would not be having another conversation like they had the night previous.

[Shane: Fine. Bring Lori and Patrick to your parent's house, Tommy. I'll send Markus.]

It wasn't the reply that Vee wanted, but she also didn't want to get into a text battle with Shane either. Yet another wolf would be watching over her apartment. She felt like a prisoner.

"We'll be back tomorrow morning," Tommy said to Vee, glancing at Durran with suspicion. Vee nodded, smiling at Lori and Patrick as they made their way out of the shop.

"See you tomorrow!" Lori said happily, waving as she left.

Once the sound of Tommy's truck had faded into the distance, Durran moved a little closer to Vee as she started her end-of-day tasks at the counter. Vee was trying, very diligently, to ignore the pulsing emotions of her friend, as she went about her duties. It was only when she accidentally kicked the box of antique locks still needing restoration that she sighed and glanced at Durran.

"I'm still too sore to move this, would you mind?" Vee asked hesitantly, gesturing to the large box at her feet. Durran moved around the counter without a word, scooping the box up, and heading into the inventory room to set it down. Without even being asked, she switched off the light and closed the door.

Vee almost felt guilty for the way Durran was behaving. She clearly knew the ins and outs of Vee's routine, having been around for years while she developed it. Up until recently, Durran was Vee's safe space. She had been completely content and happy to have lived the rest of her life exactly as she had been with Durran as the only person she let in every now and then.

Vee wandered over to Durran, who stood latching the various locks on the steel door, and wrapped her arms around her. The silent "thank you" bringing out a deep emotion in Durran that Vee had only ever felt flickers of before. Durran wrapped her arms around Vee and held her tightly in return. She didn't completely trust Durran, and she was still quite irritated with her, but she appreciated their friendship and didn't want to lose her.

CHAPTER 22

Min sat in Shane's living room. The house was eerily quiet save for the sounds of all the heartbeats and breathing. Shane sat opposite him, remaining calm, despite how much he hated that this had to be done at his own home. Min had been accompanied by two other high-ranking Sha and their small entourage of younger, lower-ranked members.

"When do we expect the other lone wolves to arrive?" Min asked, glancing up from his cup of tea that they had provided. Food was offered, but the Sha declined.

"That's a good question," Shane said, turning to look at Ethan, who was trying very hard to be as stoic as his father but failing. The beads of nervous sweat were collecting at his temples, and he reeked of fear.

"I'll go call them," Ethan said, hastily moving to step out to the front yard and away from the prying eyes. They all sat quietly for a minute, listening to the muffled sound of Ethan's phone calls.

"I suppose we can begin questioning the prisoner," Min said, moving to place his cup down.

"You've only just arrived. I thought you'd want to touch base, and then settle in for the night," Shane said, standing with Min. The three Sha smiled knowingly at one another, then turned back to Shane.

"We arrived and settled yesterday." Shane froze at that. How had they not noticed their arrival? How much had they observed without him realizing? "It felt prudent to get here quickly, what with the seriousness of the crimes committed and that the justice would need to be served within the city. Once I spoke with the others, they agreed the three of us should head here as soon as possible," Min told him, dark eyes piercing into him. Shane thought of the moments he shared with Vee the night before. Surely, he would have noticed… or she would have, if there was a Sha in their midst.

"I see," was all Shane could think to say, choosing instead, to gesture for them to follow him through the house to the basement. Emily was at the door, stepping aside to let Shane and the three Sha behind him through. As they descended the stairs the whole house seemed to increase with intensity. The Sha were fully allowing their power to be known, making every Were feel on edge, knowing who was really in charge.

There Downing sat, still chained and tied to the cage to provide minimal movement. He had been given brief stints with heavy guard to walk, use the restroom, and one hand released, on occasion, for food over the last few days. Each time, unsurprisingly, he had tried and failed to attack the pack members watching him. And even though he failed, he had an air of smugness about him, like somehow, he knew he would get the best of this situation.

That smugness evaporated as soon as the three entered the room fully. Min was not tall or overly muscular. His lean, lithe body was dressed in traditional tribal attire, although not any Native American tribe that you could pinpoint. Designs woven into the fabric all felt familiar, but nothing someone could specifically point to. It could have belonged to any native tribe from any land, not just the Americas. His long black locks were braided and hung over his shoulders, tied off with a string of leather. His face, though calm, was not peaceful, by any means, as he looked at the monster of a man before him.

"Todd Downing," Min started. His voice may as well have been a roar at the way Downing shuddered, though it came out soft. "Do you know who we are?"

"The Sha?" Downing asked quietly, eyes downcast and unable to look into Min's. He only knew the name because of Shane, but he understood they held power. He could feel it pulsing from them, almost making the walls of the basement beat like a heart.

"Yes. And do you know what we are?"

Downing looked up now, eyes glancing over all the people in the room, as if one of the Weres who had held him captive here would save him, help him, give him the answer. The silence lasted too long, and

Min clicked his tongue and chuckled mildly, moving a bit closer to the cage and crouching to be closer to eye level.

"We are what all shapeshifting creatures come from. See, while the Watchers and the fae have magic that gives them the illusion of another appearance, our magic fully transforms us into our beasts. You were gifted as a wolf, were you not?"

"I-I was…"

"And you have not used that gift correctly."

Downing's eyes widened. "Correctly?"

"When you were given this gift… what were the circumstances?" Min asked, standing again to slowly and deliberately walk before the cage. It wasn't pacing; it was intimidating, like a predator circling his prey.

"I was attacked by four wolves," Downing said, his eyes downcast again. The way his voice lilted, made him seem like he was some innocent that had been viciously ambushed.

Another Sha stepped forward. Yona. She, too, was small, but the power that flowed from her was enough to make Downing whimper. Her eyes were bright as they bore into Downing's face.

"Why did they attack you?" she asked, her voice callous. The words came out normal, but the shimmer around her suggested she wielded her power. Truth. She had a strong connection to the owls, bringers to truth, and therefore, could pull it from weaker-minded individuals.

He cowered slightly and began to shake, feeling the full brunt of her power brought down upon him. For a moment they were all watching, thinking he was shaking in fear, or even crying, but when he snapped his head back up to look into Yona's eyes, he let out an inhuman cackle. The sound made all their skin crawl as they looked at his maniacal face, eyes bright as if he were to change before them. He slowly stopped laughing, but his malicious grin remained.

"What was the question?" he asked, his voice chilling as he stared at Yona. She narrowed her eyes, leaning forward to stare him directly in the face.

"Why did they attack you?" she repeated. He waited a beat, as if he were trying to recall, licking his lips.

"Because I was raping her. Killing her," he finally said, no remorse in his tone, in fact he seemed giddy. Saying it out loud excited him. The look of disgust on Yona's face echoed the feeling of everyone in the room. She broke her eye contact with Downing, breaking the magic, but it no longer mattered. He didn't care about the façade he had been putting on anymore. Min again stepped forward to crouch in front of the caged monster.

"And when you realized what you were, after they attacked you, what did you do?" Min asked.

"I found her again. She was mine. I deserved to have her. After all that work I put in to get her, I *had to* finish it." Downing was drooling now as he panted, recalling the memory. "She tasted so good, all the fear running through her as I ripped her apart. It was almost sweeter, her thinking she had gotten away."

Min's lip curled into a snarl, his careful stoicism gone listening to the filth coming out of Downing's mouth.

"You are disgusting," he said, not being able to hold it back. Downing laughed again, his face warping a bit, eyes bright, but soulless.

"I give my wolf what he wants. We got what we wanted again and again and again. And we *will* get it again," he said, eyes turning to Shane who stood near the stairs. His eyes were burning golden as he stared at Downing. "I'm going to eat her, Shane. I'll get out of this. I'll find that *Vee* of yours. I'll make her *mine*. I'm going to rip her apart while I take her," Downing said, laughing again as he struggled against his chains. His whole body quivering with the very idea of it.

Shane fought the urge to rush over, tear the cage apart, and rip the head from his body for simply saying those words.

For bringing her name up again.

For imagining those things about her.

For calling her *his*.

Shane growled low in his chest, and Downing chuckled.

"Enough!" Min yelled, stilling the whole house once more, even Downing. "You have been found to be breaking the laws of our kind. Ancient, sacred laws against harming innocent people. Like others before you that were afflicted with this incurable madness, you are not fixable. You are not redeemable. You will be put to death," Min told him, each word vibrating the house with the finality of his statement.

Downing's face changed, twisting uncontrollably into something between shock, rage, and horror. It was as if it finally and truly dawned on him that he wasn't going to escape this. He shook and pulled at the chains and rope, hoping to burst free from the cage, as if this final attempt would be the one that got him his freedom, but it was to no avail.

"No!" Downing screamed as they all turned once again to leave the basement. "No!"

The door closed firmly to the basement and Min breathed in deeply from his nose. Shane had never seen him so angry, even when the last Westport Pack Leader had betrayed them, years ago.

"I have never come face to face with such evil," Yona said, her eyes still glowing and wide.

"How and why the magics chose him..." Min wondered, venom filling his voice.

"There is always a reason," came the third, and so far, silent Sha. Shane had seen him before but never heard him speak. The man, like the others, looked young and vital, but his hair was white as snow, tied in the traditional braids, like Min. He was usually just there, observing everything while other members of the Sha did the conversing.

Min and Yona looked at him, expressions unable to hold back their surprise. Aho only spoke to other Sha, but there, in Shane's kitchen, his voice made everyone stop.

"Aho..." Yona began, hoping to keep him from continuing to speak, but he raised his hand to halt her, turning to look at Shane and gesturing for him to follow to the backyard. Shane did, leaving the others behind them, stepping out onto the green lawn in the moonlight. Aho stood, looking at the waning moon for a moment.

"The moon has given us so much. The magic we hold in us is special. Anyone gifted with the magic holds importance here on this earth, don't you agree, Shane Keenan?" Aho asked, turning his eyes to look at the pack leader. His voice had a cadence to it, giving those who listened to it a relaxed feeling.

"Yes," Shane replied simply, letting his shoulders relax slightly.

"This man served some purpose, and now, with purpose served, he will be destroyed. What that purpose was, I don't know, but I believe you do," Aho told him, eyes twinkling knowingly. Shane took in a breath, thinking only of Vee. Downing didn't bring Vee into his life, but he certainly made him see how important she was to him. "I will not ask you. That secret I will let you keep for now, Young Black Wolf," he said, seeing the momentary worry flash across Shane's face.

"Thank you," Shane said solemnly. They knew, or at least Aho knew about Vee, at least to some degree.

"Now we must determine the punishment for the lone wolves. What would you consider fair?"

Shane's eyebrows shot up at the notion that he would have a say in such an important decision. This whole conversation felt surreal. This man had never uttered a word in all the years Shane had been around them, and now he was asking what he thought an acceptable punishment was. He had given it thought, trying to wrack his brain as to what Ethan was going to face.

"I feel like a hold on being near other lone wolves for a period of time. Perhaps no running with packs unless they have blood relatives." The words flowed from him easily, somehow. As if he were the one doling the true sentence. It wasn't an outlandish punishment.

Harsh maybe, due to the isolation from other lone wolves and other packs, but not unreasonable, considering what they did, what they wrought on the preternatural and human communities.

"Hmm, yes. Maybe a four-year span. One to represent each of them, so they can remember they did this together, even while they are apart," Aho said, nodding, before they lapsed back into silence.

They stood out there for a few more minutes, listening to the summer night insects and feeling the warm breeze. Shane took the moment to be grateful, something he felt he took for granted. Ethan faced punishment, but nothing too harsh, Downing was to be removed, he had been gifted a rare conversation with one of the oldest Sha there was, and Vee was safe. She was safe.

"You are a good leader, Shane Keenan. A good man. It makes sense why the magics chose you for this path," Aho said, still looking at the moon. Shane looked over at him, contemplating his expression. He was staring at the sky, eyes only letting on a hint of wonder. "Sometimes the magics lead you down strange roads. Yours seems to be getting a little rocky, but know that you are headed in the right direction."

Shane thought about all the small pieces that came into place perfectly over the last week. Each moment he followed the pull, his instincts, for the most part, to this moment. He knew he had to be patient, but if Aho was assuring him he was on the right path, he took a bit of solace in that.

CHAPTER 23

Shane and Aho returned to the kitchen, but no one was there to greet them. Even Emily was no longer at the door to the basement, which now stood wide open. A roar emerged from below, causing them both to rush down. It seemed like an army of werewolves were trying to keep Downing restrained. His body had again, begun a half transformation, giving him strangely elongated limbs and a horrifically mutated face. The chains were silver, which didn't hurt a Were, but were supposed to dampen their abilities, and they had been enchanted with Sha magic to prevent this very thing from happening.

Downing was breaking free.

Shane rushed over to help Thomas who was trying, and failing, to hold Downing's arm in place so Emily could tie it to the bars of the cage.

"I will be free!" Downing screamed ending his words with a howl, his voice somewhere between his human and wolf.

No one even acknowledged his words, all simply struggling, somehow, to keep him still long enough to get him restrained once again. Emily got the rope knotted, but Downing managed to draw blood, gouging her arm and causing her to cry out in pain. He laughed as he flailed, managing to break yet another shackle, this time on his foot. It was too far in the cage for anyone to reach and they watched in horror as his foot shimmered and morphed, ripping skin as it changed into a massive back claw.

Shane made eye contact with Min at that moment, silently they both understood how this had to happen, despite the potential consequences. There would be no keeping him restrained any longer. This would not be a simple and easy execution.

"Stop," Min said, his eyes glowing as he stepped away from the cage to stand before it. All the Weres paused, still holding as Downing struggled, but looking to Min. "Let him go," Min said quietly, removing his tunic as Shane joined him a few feet from the opening of the cage.

Hesitantly, they began releasing their hold, the last remaining bonds holding Downing, snapping under his strength. Shane removed his shoes in preparation, as Downing ferociously tore at the cage, bending metal under his partially transformed claws. He ripped at the door enough that it clattered to the floor, bent and mangled.

Even Downing stopped now, for a moment, eyes looking over the room full of Weres, searching for the weaknesses in their defenses. He looked Shane, dead in the eyes, telling him exactly what his plan was without a single word.

He was going to go after Vee.

The quiet moment returned to utter chaos as Downing leapt from the cage, Thomas trying to shoot out and grab him, but instead having his arm twisted and broken in an instant. The snaps of his bones echoing in their ears as his face went from determination to a silent scream. His anguish echoed through their pack bonds, making every Were in the house want blood for hurting one of theirs.

Others tried to grab at him as well, but Downing dodged their lunges, heading straight at Shane. Shane reached as he came close, seeing his human hands barely missing the half-changed creature, as did Min's, and Downing flew past them, up the stairs. There was no moment to spare as they raced after him, following the sounds of destruction in his wake. Downing burst out the front window of the dining room, passing Ethan and the other lone wolves that stood on the front lawn. Their nervousness quickly evaporated as they watched Downing's mutated form, racing down the street on all fours, Shane and Min close behind him.

Ethan immediately started shucking his shoes to follow behind, but Thomas grabbed his shoulder with his noninjured arm, halting him from the pursuit.

"Too much attention if we all follow, Ethan. Let them go," Thomas said, his voice strained with pain.

Thomas immediately pulled out his phone to dial Markus. Everyone knew where Downing was headed.

Vee woke to the sound of her phone's shrill tone. Despite feeling relatively safe, knowing there was a werewolf guarding her apartment, and undoubtedly Durran not far, she had decided keeping her phone in her room was prudent. At the moment though, she was not pleased to be woken from the sleep she had just barely slipped into.

She looked at the screen. It was midnight and the caller was Thomas.

"Hello?" she answered, trying to make her voice sound normal, instead of half asleep.

"Downing escaped," Thomas said, sending an immediate chill down her spine. She shot out of bed, phone still to her ear.

"How?"

"I- he… he basically overpowered us somehow. Shane and one of the Sha are after him," Thomas said, his voice not as reassuring as she presumed it was supposed to be.

"How long?" she asked, moving to her kitchen to see if she had anything she could use as a weapon, although it was laughable that anything that she had on her could keep that monster from tearing her apart.

"It's been a few minutes. I called Markus first," Thomas said, causing her to go to her front windows and peek out. Markus was standing in the middle of the sidewalk leading up to the building. He glanced up at her, eyes glowing in preparation for battle.

"How long do you think it will be?" she whispered.

"Honestly, it could be any minute. He was going top speed," Thomas said, his voice giving away his worry.

"I need to call Durran," she said, her voice wavering. She honestly didn't want to get off the phone with Thomas. Somehow having him on the line made her feel less alone.

Choosing to stay with the small comfort she had, Vee stared out the window. The lights in her living room were off, so her view of the street outside her apartment was clear. Part of her wanted to crack her window to see if she could hear the sounds of him coming, but she didn't want to have a weakened point of entry. She gripped the dull butcher knife she had grabbed from the kitchen, hoping she would be able to defend herself if he somehow got through Markus.

Where was Durran?

The minutes seemed to drag on forever. Her mind racing, thinking of all the possibilities. He would hunt her down until one of them was dead, that much she knew.

She heard a strange sound, then, from the back of the apartment building. It sounded like bricks falling. Her body instinctively turned to the sound, listening as it slowly got closer. She could tell, as the sound slowed, that it was claws gouging between the brick. She could envision it, the look of his ghastly half-turned hands, penetrating the mortar to hoist himself up the building from the outside. She hung up the phone now, not wanting any sounds to alert him to where she was.

Glass shattered, the back window to the hallway that led to the fire escape exploded. She glanced down at Markus who was no longer watching the front of the building but attempting to rip his way into it at the locked front door. She hit the buzzer in a panic to let him in but had to back up as she heard the strange footfalls of the creature in her hallway.

Where could she hide? This place was so small there was nowhere else to go.

But she heard other footfalls now, racing down the hallway and the crash of more shattered glass. Her whole body jumped at the sound, not expecting it. She moved back to the living room window to see Shane on top of the malformed beast, both recovering from the fall that Downing's body had broken. Shane had, quite literally, tackled Downing out the opposite window.

Stunned, it took Markus a moment or two before he began to hold the creature down. Its partially turned form, stronger than his human one, was immediately fighting back against the new restraint. Downing ripped back out of Markus's grasp, pushing past Shane as he leapt back onto the front of the apartment building, heading to the roof.

She saw Shane follow suit, using the holes that Downing made as hand holds to pursue him. He paused briefly at her window, eyes burning golden onto hers. The look on his face was all she needed to know. He was ending this now.

Shane made it to the top of the building, seeing Downing pacing, his form shifting, skin tearing in some places.

"I have to have her," Downing said, his voice gruff and eyes wild.

"You can't have her," Shane told him, slowly stepping closer.

"She's mine!" Downing barked, hunching as if he were going to attack.

"She will never be yours," Shane snarled back.

Downing took a step forward, her back arched unnaturally. Shane anticipated the attack before he even had a chance to move. He lunged now, swinging around so he was at Downing's back. He kicked the back of his knees, making him buckle, and managed to get his hands around Downing's neck. Min joined the rooftop just as Shane let some of his wolf take over. His fingers elongated, like Downing's, but in a much cleaner way, since Shane had been transforming into a wolf for over seventy years.

"Do it," Min said, eyes ablaze as Shane began sinking his claws into Downing's skin. Downing made a wet guttural sound as his throat filled with blood, struggling against the strength of Shane's hold, which only caused his flesh to tear more. The blood hit Shane and Min's noses, causing them both to growl low in their chests, the blood of the prey they had chased triggering hunger within their beasts. With a deep breath, Shane stared Min in the eyes as he ripped the head from Downing's body in one motion.

The intensity of the energy remained for a moment, as Shane stared down at the lifeless body of Downing. His corpse was shifting back to his human form, blood still pooling from his open neck. Min stepped closer, looking over it with disgust.

"I'm sorry you had to sully your hands," Min said, glancing at Shane's blood-soaked fingers which had returned to their human appearance.

"I wanted to," Shane growled, flicking the blood off before bending over to wipe them on Downing's shirt.

"My people will dispose of this. You've done enough for tonight," Min told him, touching his shoulder.

"I'll stay," Shane told him, as he walked to the fire escape opposite to where he climbed the roof. He couldn't say more at the moment. His mind was only on one thing. He just had to see her. To know she was okay.

As he climbed through the broken window, stepping on the glass that littered the floor, she was there, standing in front of her open apartment door. She had been listening to everything. She had felt everything. The power, the hatred, the visceral need to protect her laced in Shane's emotions when he tore down the monster, had consumed her.

Her eyes met his, each of them stood at either end of the hall. The apartment building was still quiet. Somehow the noise hadn't woken her lower-level neighbors. The people on her floor were all, somehow, thankfully, gone for the night.

Shane slowly walked toward her, glass crunching under his bare feet, eyes still golden. His wolf was in control right now. Vee felt its continued protectiveness, perhaps a bit of possessiveness laced there as he looked at her. She walked toward him too, noticing the blood still on his hands. Somehow, knowing he had just ripped a person apart on the roof of her apartment didn't bother her.

They stopped when they were only a foot apart, eyes locked. He didn't need to say anything. She felt it in that moment. He was telling her she was finally safe. That he had made sure of it. She felt that flutter of another feeling. Something deep and powerful. She had felt something similar from Durran earlier that day, but this feeling wasn't fleeting. It was growing.

Shane's hands came up to her face. They hovered there for a moment before he finally touched her. She let out a tiny gasp at the contact. The emotions so much stronger with his touch. Her reaction, and the way her burning amber eyes bore into his, he couldn't hold back. He leaned forward gently pressing his lips to hers.

She melted a little at the contact. It was overwhelming, his emotions and hers, and the fact that she was even being touched this way. She unconsciously put her hands on his chest, feeling his heart beating rapidly there.

It was as if Shane had never kissed anyone else before, the way it made him feel. Such a bold and electric connection, instantly. The kiss grew more intense as Vee slid her hands up his chest to his neck, letting her body settle against his. He turned them, pressing her against the wall and lacing his fingers through her hair.

They were lost in all of the feelings, the beautifully strange connection, the safety, the lust. She found herself only craving more, clutching to the back of his head, as if their lips could be any closer. His hands traveled to her waist, lifting her, so he didn't have to bend to kiss her and pinning her to the wall with his body.

"Boss?" came a voice down a level on the stairs, breaking them from the little spell they were under.

Shane growled quietly in his chest. Not pleased with the interruption, but Vee was a little relieved. Their lips parted suddenly, the lack of contact there immediately making them both breathless.

Shane let her down gently from where he had lifted her on the wall.

"I'm here," he said, taking a step away from her and tearing his eyes from hers regretfully to see who was coming up the stairs.

"I brought some bricks," Markus said as he reached the top, gesturing with his full hands at the broken windows on either side of the hall. They had to make it seem like it was some sort of teenage vandalism or a burglary attempt.

"Mm..." Shane murmured in approval, still not fully in control. The proximity to Vee wasn't helping. His wolf didn't want to let anyone else, especially not another Were around her.

"I... I think I'll get out of the way," Vee said, still grappling with what had just happened a moment ago. She pushed herself from the wall and moved quickly toward her apartment door. Shane reached out a hand and grabbed hers as she tried to pass him. She looked up at him, eyes still mirroring his. "We'll talk another time," she whispered, assuring him. The sincerity in her eyes as she said the words was the only thing that allowed his fingers to loosen and drop from hers.

She walked quickly, but carefully through the glass to her apartment, stopping close to the stairs to offer a smile and whisper a "thank you" to Markus, before closing the door. She couldn't have the reaction she wanted to, what with all the Weres in and around the building, but she felt like screaming.

She very much could have died, again. And Shane… they kissed. They kissed and it was electric and powerful. It was the best kiss she had ever had in her entire life, not that she had had many. She tried to calm her heart as it beat wildly even recalling it. He was right out there; she could just pull him into her apartment and…

CHAPTER 24

There was a tap on the glass of her window.

Durran.

Her beating heart sank to her stomach at the sight of her. Why did she suddenly feel so guilty looking at her friend?

Vee opened the window and watched Durran crawl through it.

"Where were you?" Vee hissed, transitioning her guilt to irritation.

"I came, but Shane was already here," Durran told her, eyes looking at the ceiling as soft footsteps could be heard moving about on the roof.

"He did take care of it," Vee murmured, eyes following hers.

"I don't like the Sha being so close to you," Durran whispered, eyes turning red, as if she was burning holes through the building at the Sha on the roof above. Vee noted in that moment how strangely similar and different the Sha felt from other Weres. They buzzed like Weres, but it was like their frequency was more intense at all times, similar to a Were that was close to a change.

"As long as they stay there, and I stay here we're fine," Vee whispered back, trying so hard to believe it herself. She somehow knew that if one got close to her, they'd know something. They'd be able to tell she was different without even knowing her abilities.

They both stood for a moment, listening to the quiet commotion above them.

"You smell like him," Durran said, her voice not being able to hide the sadness she felt. Vee realized, in that moment, that Durran had been nearby the whole time. At least since Shane had arrived. She had seen Shane kill Downing.

Had she seen the kiss?

Did she know?

Why did it make Vee feel like she had betrayed her?

She didn't know what to say. There was no denying she smelled like Shane. They had been wrapped around each other, even if only for a minute before they were interrupted. Vee was silently grateful that Markus had come up the stairs when he did. It could have intensified quickly at the rate they were going, and the way they had just abandoned themselves to their emotions. All the Weres… and Durran, would have been there to listen to it. She shuddered at the thought.

"I think they have things in hand. I'll come by the shop tomorrow," Durran said, locking eyes with her for a brief moment, before moving back out the open window.

Vee stood still in the middle of her living room, not sure what to do with herself. She couldn't leave her apartment, and she certainly couldn't go back to sleep. Tomorrow was Friday, somehow that brought her the feeling as if things were full circle. Had this all just been over the course of a week? It felt like months had passed.

She sat on one of her futons in the darkened room, listening to the quiet movements and hushed con-versations outside. Shane and Markus weren't in her hallway anymore. They had migrated outside with the other pack members who had arrived. The Sha were coming down the fire escape at the back of the building. Things were wrapping up.

"Is Vee okay?" Tommy asked, as he rushed over to Shane who was standing on the front walkway of the apartment building.

"She is," Shane said, glancing at the windows of her apartment.

"I was listening to the police scanner on my way. Someone called in about a possible break in…" Tommy told him, a bit of urgency in his tone.

"Yes, we should go," Shane affirmed, looking away from her window and gesturing for the others to head back to their cars. "I'll ride with Markus," Shane told Tommy, who nodded and jogged back to his truck to get back to the house.

Shane made sure everyone was headed out before he and Markus made their way back to the car. The Sha would leave Vee alone for the night, but he wasn't so sure about tomorrow. Depending on what the Sha decided when he arrived back at the house, they could be there for a few more days. He knew she hated being guarded, but he knew now there were few things he feared more than her being in jeopardy.

Shane remained lost in thought for most of the ride. Markus also remained silent, but he fidgeted a little, finding the absolute lack of conversation uncomfortable. He was usually much more of a talker, being that he was a salesman by trade.

"Did you want me to go back after?" Markus decided to ask. Shane looked over at him, considering it for a moment. Vee would have enough on her plate with the police heading to the building. A random car coming to sit outside the building might be noticed and considered suspicious.

"No. She's safe for tonight," he said, giving him a half smile. Markus smiled back, but then his face faltered slightly, shifting his eyes back to the road.

"I'm sorry about earlier."

Shane sighed, looking back out the window. He wasn't upset about the interruption, now that his wolf was more safely tucked away, and he had a clearer mind. That wasn't the ideal place or time for him to show his affections to her. He knew this was too fast for her. It was too fast for him. He hadn't cared about anyone this way since his wife died, and it scared him a little how much different, how strong the feeling was.

"No, it is better that you did," Shane told him, running his hand through his hair. He would have to think about everything much more when he had time, but right now, he had to push away the thrill of her responding so eagerly to his touch.

They pulled up to the house, Min was waiting outside as Shane got out of the car.

"We don't have to deal with the lone wolves tonight, but I did send most of the others back to the ranch to deal with the remains," Min told him as soon as Shane got closer. While he strangely enjoyed the Sha being there for this short visit, having had a few brief bonding moments with a few of them, he would rather not have them poking the weight of their power over his territory any longer than necessary.

"Let's get it done tonight," Shane told him. Min nodded, walking with Shane into the house. Shane stopped briefly at the center hall, glancing at his destroyed dining room. The front window was shattered, broken pieces of the wood framing sticking out jaggedly. The dining room table was completely splintered, with the chandelier lying broken where the table once stood. Even the doorway into the kitchen was ripped apart. Nothing to be done about it now, but he hated the idea of having his home the site of a construction zone.

As he turned away from it, he saw Aho and Yona where waiting in the living room with Thomas and the four lone wolves. Ethan didn't restrain himself as he came forward to embrace his father. He knew Shane would come out victorious against Downing, but he had worried, nonetheless.

Once they parted, Min came to stand with the other two Sha.

"Aho has told me Shane Keenan, leader of the Westport Pack, is to make the final judgment on these four lone wolves; Idris Abdur, Jesse Schmitt, Ethan Keenan, and Philip Song," Min said, bringing the attention back to the task at hand. Shane looked over each of them. All of them were good men; if they hadn't been, they wouldn't have tried to save the woman Downing had been attacking. "For harming a human in another pack's territory, for creating a werewolf and abandoning them, your punishment is as follows," Min began, his words holding a strange sort of weight, as if he had said a spell. He gestured for Shane to continue.

"You are not to convene with other lone wolves or run with any packs that you do not hold blood relation to for four years," Shane said, his own words shockingly powerful as they left his lips. The four lone wolves shook a little as if the words had entered and bound to them. Shane had witnessed this power the Sha held, but he had never been a vehicle for it.

"Go now," Min told them, eyes bright as he looked them all over. They could not stay together, even now. They all had to leave the city immediately.

They all took a moment to shake each other's hands, Idris pulling Ethan into a tight hug and whispering, "See you in four years," making them all chuckle. This punishment could be far worse, and they all knew it. Once the other three departed, Ethan came back to his father.

"Thank you," he said, clapping his hand on Shane's shoulder.

"Come back on the next moon," Shane said, taking his adult son's face in his hands.

"We'll see… I didn't get to talk to Patrick this time around," Ethan said, giving a lopsided smile.

"Yes, he's going to be disappointed you're gone when he gets home."

They both just looked at each other for a moment, Shane pulling him in for one more hug before Ethan left, revving his motorcycle a bit and driving down the street. Shane turned his focus back to the living room, Yona was already tending to Thomas's arm, which had still been hanging limp and disfigured at his side.

"We will need to talk another time about your… Vee," Min told Shane, joining him in the hall with Aho at his side. Shane tensed a bit at that, eyes coming to rest on Aho's face. Aho's expression was peaceful, and his eyes twinkled a little as they locked on Shane's. It was as if Aho was telling him Vee was not in danger, not with them, at least, but it didn't help shake his worry. Not knowing why they could possibly have an interest in her would always be worrisome.

"I understand," Shane said, hoping the "other time" was far in the future.

Once Yona had managed to get Thomas's bones back in place, she touched his head lightly and smiled at him. It was as if she were treating a child, but it didn't come off as condescending.

"You'll be back to yourself in a day," she told him, turning to join the others. Thomas nodded a thank you to her.

"Goodbye, Shane Keenan," Min said with finality.

"Min, Aho, Yona," Shane said with a slight bow of his head before they left.

Once their car could no longer be heard, the whole house seemed to sigh in relief. The Weres came out of the woodwork, joining Shane in the front hall as he closed the door.

"Is Vee okay?" Margaret asked, seeming to echo the sentiment of everyone else. Shane looked around at all of them for a moment. Their faces were all genuinely concerned. Most of them had never even met Vee, even as the locksmith that would work on their houses, yet somehow, she had not only become important to him, but she was also important to all of them.

"She's fine," he assured them, failing to hide his smile now that it was the second time that question had been asked of him that night.

"I told you," Tommy said to Margaret, giving her narrowed eyes as he came forward, eating leftovers he must have found in the kitchen. "What about tomorrow?" he asked, turning his focus back on Shane.

"The Sha are gone, we could probably leave her alone for a day," Shane said, internally hoping he would be able to come up with an excuse to go talk to her. Patrick and Lori burst through the front door at that moment, having watched the Sha leave from Thomas's house across the street.

"I need to finish updating her to the twenty first century, so we're going there tomorrow," Patrick told his dad, having heard the last snippet of the conversation as they crossed the street.

"What?" Shane asked, confused.

"I started helping her get her inventory on the computer today. I'm finishing it tomorrow," Patrick told him, leaving no room for debate.

"And I already told her we'd see her tomorrow," Lori chimed in, grinning. Shane smiled and sighed, tiredly running his hands through his hair. Even if he didn't really want to give her space, craving her company, it seemed like his pack had certainly accepted her into the fold. How could he argue with that?

CHAPTER 25

Vee had barely slept. Not surprising, considering it had been past 3 a.m. when the police had finally left the apartment complex. She didn't particularly care for having to lie to them, but she couldn't very well tell them werewolves climbed up the building and broke out the windows. The unseen potential burglars were much more feasible for the humans to understand.

The remainder of her sleepless night had been fighting off dreams of Shane. He was everywhere in them. Holding her, kissing her, touching her. She could feel that deep emotion again in her dream. Why couldn't she place it?

Midi, the cat, had found her way to Vee's apartment at some point in the night as well, eagerly meowing at the door to be let in. Once she decided she wasn't going to be getting anymore sleep, she let the little cat wander in and sit with her until her alarm went off at 5 a.m. She was dragging exhaustedly, when she pulled up to the shop at seven, but was surprised to see Patrick and Lori waiting outside the door already. They had drinks and breakfast in hand, smiling as she got out of her car.

"I wasn't expecting you two today," she said warily, unlocking the door.

"I told you we would see you," Lori said, raising her chin proudly as she marched in. Vee smiled a little, locking the door behind them before she went to turn off the alarm. She unlocked the back room for them, before she attended to the flashing light of her voicemail.

The messages were from three people inquiring about pricing for various things. Thankfully no house calls. She couldn't imagine doing much more than in-house business for the day. In fact, she might take the rare Saturday off, just to mentally recover from everything. She wrote down the customer information to call later during normal hours; it was still far too early in the morning for anyone to pick up. After she set her things down, she wandered into the back room to see both teenagers, busily back where they left off the evening before. Lori set her pen on the clipboard she was holding and handed Vee the coffee she had brought for her.

"I think I got it right, based on how yours smelled yesterday," Lori said, her feelings hopeful, but unsure. Vee tentatively took a taste, not even considering that anyone would have purposefully smelled her travel mug of coffee. Somehow, she had gotten it just right.

"Not bad. New abilities are serving you well, I see," Vee told her, a twinkle in her eyes. Lori nodded proudly. Becoming a werewolf was, of course, not ideal, especially as a teenage girl, but she was clearly trying to find the silver linings. She was no longer "left out" of the important goings-on that her father and brother had always been part of, and she was discovering new things she could do all the time. "So, no Tommy today?" Vee decided to ask, finding it a little strange that they had been unaccompanied.

"My dad let me drive us this time. He tried to tell us you should get the day alone, but I promised you I'd finish this," Patrick told her, looking over at her from the screen. She raised her eyebrows, a little shocked that Shane tried to discourage them from coming and that they wanted to come anyway, despite there being no obligation.

"Interesting," was all she thought to say in response, trying to process that a little.

Her brain started down a little rabbit hole. Why the sudden change of heart from Shane? Did he decide the kiss was a mistake? Of course, he did. He had his pack, his family to worry about. He couldn't be getting involved with someone like her, and for that matter, she shouldn't be getting involved with him.

She started looking through her supplies to see if she had everything she needed for the orders before she called the customers back for a quote. Well, really it was a way to distract herself from her own thoughts. Focus on work. That was always her go to. Distract and ignore.

They all worked rather quietly for most of the morning, Vee getting out the antique locks that she planned to complete for the day from the back room, while Lori and Patrick brought her inventory into modern times. Once 9 a.m. rolled around, she felt like she could finally reach out to the customers who had called, and realized, after looking at her own notes from earlier, she did not have everything she needed to fulfill one of the orders. It was brass fixtures, all of which had been thrown out after Lori's change.

"Lori…" Vee said, having a thought and hoping desperately that she wasn't going to regret it. Lori wandered over, her curls bouncing as she took each step.

"Hm?"

"How would you feel if I left the shop open with you two while I ran to the hardware store?" Vee asked, each word difficult for her to say as they left her mouth. Lori's eyes lit up immediately.

"Just tell me how to do the register, and I will take care of everything," she said, absolute glee pouring out of her. Vee took her through how to ring someone up and pay it out. She did a basic once over in the shop, explaining pricing and descriptions.

"Please don't make me regret this," Vee said, looking Lori in the eyes as she slipped her messenger bag over her head.

"I'll keep an eye on her," Patrick hollered from the back.

"You won't regret it, I promise!" Lori said, eagerly waving as Vee walked out the door.

Vee, still very nervous, having left the shop in someone else's hands intentionally for the first time, to teenagers nonetheless, made her way to the hardware store. She tried to focus on what she needed. The list was long, but since she was here for one order, she decided she might as well put that dent in her saved money now, rather than have to find time for more trips.

As she walked through the store, making her way to the lock section, it took her past the window section. A now very familiar buzz hit her, stopping her in her tracks. She followed the feeling, weaving through the aisles of windowpanes, until she finally came upon him.

"What are you doing here?" she hissed from the end of the aisle, Shane directly in the center of it, looking at large picture windows. He looked over at her, equally shocked to see her standing there.

"I could ask you the same thing. Patrick and Lori are supposed to be with you," he said as she made her way down toward him.

"I left them in charge," she said, realizing how absurd it was as the words left her mouth. Shane burst out laughing after fully taking in what she said.

"You, what?"

"I had to get some supplies for a customer I lost… from Lori's thing…" she told him quietly, eyes shifting nervously. "I'm not happy about it, but they're doing a really good job helping me. I figured leaving them for an hour, early in the day, would be a good test."

"Test for what?" he asked, his laughter easing slightly, amusement still fluttering around him.

"I thought I might let them work for me a little this summer," Vee told him, the thought forming just as the words came from her mouth. Shane looked her over for a minute, his feelings mixed and confusing to her.

"You would do that for them?" he asked, crossing his arms across his chest.

"Everyone needs to start somewhere."

He found it interesting, if nothing else. She complained about having her life turned upside down by getting involved with them, but she wasn't completely shying away from them either. In fact, in this instance, she was welcoming them into her life. It wasn't perfect, but it was a better direction than letting her slip through his fingers, which is what he tortured himself with during his sleepless few hours the night before.

"You said we'd talk…" he murmured, letting the words come out before he could stop himself and changing the subject abruptly.

"Well, not now," Vee said, rather exasperated, looking around to see if anyone was nearby.

"Later?" he asked, trying to restrain the hope from his voice and from her.

"Sure…" she said, her fingers going to the strap of her bag nervously. "You never answered my question, you know."

"What question?" he asked, more as a reminder and less as a demand.

"What are *you* doing here?" she asked, this time a little smile dancing at her lips.

"Ah, Downing destroyed my kitchen and dining room, including the window. So, I'm trying to find a match for the living room. It's not really going so well," he told her, looking back at the windows displayed. She stepped a little closer to him, looking over them as well.

"You might have to replace both windows," she said, moving a little forward to read the energy efficiency sticker placed on one.

"That's what I'm starting to realize," he said with a sigh, but watching her now that she was in front of him, instead of the windows.

"These look nice, and they fit with the style of your house. I'm not really sure why people destroy the beauty of those old houses, making them all open and modern. Why buy an old house if you don't want it to look that way?" she asked, her voice a little sharp as she complained a bit at the end. "But if that's what you're going for…" she trailed off, realizing she may have been offending him and turning back to meet his eyes.

He smiled a little, having thought the same thing moments before she discovered him there. The windows in question had a more old-school look about them. Even a seemingly normal conversation about windows stirred something in him. She felt the same way about old houses and old things, like he did. Preserve, improve, but don't completely change it. He had always thought his feelings on the matter stemmed from being old himself.

"I feel the same way," he told her, noticing her worried expression. It melted a little with relief at his words. They both stood there for a moment, his words somehow having more meaning in that moment.

"I should probably get back to why I came here in the first place," she said, stepping back away from him.

He nodded, saying nothing as she turned and walked back down the aisle.

Vee got to the lock and key section and took in a deep breath to recalibrate herself to the task at hand. He was everywhere, invading her thoughts, popping up places she went. She couldn't escape him, but she wasn't sure she wanted to, which troubled her more. She got most of what she needed—there were a few things the store was out of as well—and made her way to the check out, not feeling the buzz or getting a glimpse of Shane. He must have left already. Relief and disappointment.

She made her way back to the shop, wondering if she would somehow see it burned to the ground when she pulled up. It was still intact, thankfully, when she passed it to park a little ways down from where she had before. As she entered again, there was Lori, talking to a customer about the antique locks she had on display.

"I'm trying to restore one of the houses in Hyde Park, but so many of the fixtures have been broken or stolen," the woman said, eyes happily gliding across the assortment. Her mane of hair was barely being held back by the large clip at the back of her head, and her eyes and face looked oddly familiar to Vee as she passed by.

"Restoration is one of Vee's specialties," Lori told her, looking up and grinning at Vee as she made her way to the back room with an arm full of supplies.

"How many of those do you have?" the customer asked, looking up at Lori with excitement.

"Let me check," she said, scribbling down the number Vee had placed just above the lock in question and moving back toward the inventory room. "She's wanting a bunch of these," Lori told Vee, handing the scribbled number over to Vee. She took it, heading to the shelf where she kept the finished restoration pieces and started to try and count by hand.

"What's the number?" Patrick asked, not looking up from the computer.

"Hm?" Vee murmured in response, trying not to lose count.

"What number did Lori write down?" he asked, spinning around in the office chair to look at her. Vee held out the note, not looking up from her counting. He snatched it from her, quickly typing it in the computer. "You have ten ready to go, but I think Lori said there were a few unfinished ones in that box over there," he told her, causing Vee to pause.

"How did you…?"

"It's done. Well, I'll have to update it with what you just bought, but I have it all in here now," he told her, his satisfied smile and the feeling of pride at his accomplishment was infectious. Vee couldn't help but smile right back at him. She came up behind him, looking at the detailed digital spreadsheet he had created for her. "You just have to search for the number, and as long as you update it regularly, you'll know exactly how much you have."

"You are amazing," she said in awe, tearing her eyes away from the screen to go talk to the woman in the showroom, but not before giving Patrick a quick side hug.

Vee went back out, now feeling, in the absence of Lori and Patrick's buzzing presence, the low throb and hum of a Witch. She didn't react as she came back over to the counter where the witch stood. She had helped Witches many times. In fact, they often purchased locks and keys, she assumed for various spells and rituals.

"I'm not sure how many you need, but I have ten like that one restored and ready," Vee told her. The Witch looked at her, a feeling of suspicion creeping into her as she looked over Vee, but her expression didn't hint at it.

"I'm missing six, but I have nine more that could use a cleanup," she told her, even her voice not letting on that she was definitely sensing something different about the locksmith before her.

"Let me write up a quote for you, and I'll get you the six today. Just bring me the others when you have time," Vee said, trying very hard to not let on the unease she felt at the Witch's feelings toward her. She quickly wrote up a quote sheet and went to the back for the completed locks.

Patrick's head snapped up to look at Vee as he smelled her increased fear.

"What's wrong?"

"Not now..." Vee whispered, counting out the six locks. She couldn't take any more preternaturals. She had enough of them on her plate already. She went back out, setting the pieces carefully on the counter by the register and ringing her up.

Vee glanced at the name on the card as she swiped it. Gwen Tallon.

"Thanks, Gwen," Vee said, smiling. Using someone's name in the preternatural world could be very foreboding, but it was the person who wielded the name back at the owner who had the power.

"I'll be back on Monday with the others. I am so happy I found you," Gwen said, lifting the bag off the counter after she paid. She seemed unfazed by Vee using her name. The way she said she was glad she *found* her, left Vee with the feeling that there was a double meaning to her words.

CHAPTER 26

After shaking the awful feeling the Witch gave Vee, the remainder of the day went fairly easily. Patrick and Lori didn't inquire about Vee's change in mood with the witch, which was a relief because she didn't need Shane having another reason to feel like he had to protect her. The interaction with Gwen Tallon could turn out to be nothing. If nothing else, she could have been suspicious of why a human had two Were teenagers working for her.

Lori did a great job helping any customers that came in, which gave Vee plenty of time to continue with restorations and other projects she wanted to work on. Patrick remained working on the computer, trying to connect the inventory to the tablet she used as a register. He had insisted that he could make it work so every time she sold a specific piece, the inventory would automatically update for her.

She had found it rather odd that Durran didn't make her usual appearance to take Vee to lunch, but she suspected that the presence of Lori and Patrick made her stay away. A little twinge of guilt bubbled in her because of it. She didn't want to push Durran away completely, but the past week had certainly shifted all their lives rather unexpectedly. She wasn't sure how much she trusted Durran at the moment, what with her reaction a few days ago and the appearance of that other Watcher at her customer's house.

It was nearing 5 p.m. and they were all dragging from lack of sleep. Vee knew she wasn't going to be getting much, if any, more business for the night, being that it was Friday evening, and they were at a point where driving would probably get dangerous if they waited much longer.

"Alright. I think we'll close for the night," she said, starting to put away her tools. Lori began turning off display lights, and Patrick put some boxes back in the inventory room before Vee even had to ask. It left her to simply do the end-of-day reconciliation and lock everything up. Probably the easiest closing of the shop she had ever had. She liked their company, and they were eager to help and learn. Even if she hated the idea of being involved on a regular basis with preternaturals, she had to admit that she wished someone had given her chances, despite her abilities, when she was this young. Someone who would have understood her.

"I could probably use both of your help a couple days a week over the summer, if you're open to the idea," she said as she was locking the back room, both of them waiting by the front door.

Their tired eyes lit up at her words, emotions filling with excitement.

"Really?" Lori asked, humming eagerly and grabbing onto Patrick's arm.

"Well, it won't be every day, but you've both been great these last few days. Plus, Patrick's going to have to help me figure out how to do payroll properly. We all know how much longer it would take for me to figure that one out," she said, making them both chuckle a little.

Lori ran up to Vee from across the room and hugged her, gratitude pouring through. "Thank you," Lori whispered as she held onto Vee. Her words were obviously not just about giving her a job, but heavy with what Vee had done for her the week prior. Vee squeezed her tight then released her, looking into her eyes and smiling.

"I would do it again in a heartbeat," she said truthfully.

With additional thank yous lasting for about ten minutes, she finally managed to shoo them out the door and watched as they drove off, hoping the excitement woke them up enough to make it home in the Friday night rush hour traffic. She set the alarm and locked up, heading to her car up the road.

She saw him leaning against her car before she felt him. Shane was watching her walk up the sidewalk.

"Twice in one day, Shane," she said stopping right in front of him and crossing her arms.

"Well, the first one was a coincidence," he said, shrugging slightly.

"Did you get your windows?"

"Tommy, Markus, and I installed them today," he confirmed, nodding. "You'll have to come by and see them sometime," he offered.

"I'm sure I will." As those words left her mouth, she felt a little embarrassed. She was presuming she'd be going back to his house. A presumption he certainly didn't mind at all.

"It's the first of many things that will have to be redone around there, unfortunately. I detest the idea of living in the house while construction is going on," he told her with a sigh, pretending not to hear the way her heart picked up a beat.

"Interesting, considering werewolves tend to be especially destructive," she said, raising her eyebrows playfully. He chuckled a little at that, nodding in agreement. She wasn't wrong; it just usually wasn't as bad as this, but as they looked into each other's eyes, their conversation easy and playful, both of them felt a bit more serious. Their chemistry was unmistakable, but they needed to talk about it. Something they both had been grappling with all day.

"Is this 'later' enough?" he asked, smirking a little as he tried to maintain the lighter mood. She narrowed her eyes at him and went to lean beside him against her car. Maybe she could think more clearly if she wasn't looking directly into his eyes.

"I suppose."

They were quiet for a moment, looking up at the sky that was starting to turn pink. Vee was struggling to know exactly what she wanted in this moment. She had been lonely for so long but had felt it was necessary for her survival. These feelings she was developing for him were new and exciting but could be short-lived. She had no way to know for sure. Why would she upend her whole life for something so risky? And just thinking about the insanity of the last week… was letting more people in her life worth it?

"I'm very used to being alone," she decided to say as a way of starting things.

"I've noticed," he said, taking in a breath.

Shane was having similar reservations. The last time he had surrendered himself to a person, he had lost her, and something of himself. He wasn't sure that he or the pack would be able to handle it if that happened again. If he let himself fall into his feelings for her the way he absolutely wanted to.

"That being said, I find you very easy to be around, which is rare for me." He could tell there was another side to those words. "You bring a lot with you, though," she said quietly.

"Yes, I do," he confirmed, trying not to feel defeated by her words. She was being honest, after all. These were legitimate concerns. They fell back into silence again as Shane tried to think of what to say to her, or rather, how to say it to her. A week was too fast for both of them. Even if he felt like he already knew her, in a way, and what he didn't know, he was incredibly eager to find out. He didn't like the idea of fate because he liked being in charge of his own destiny, but something about her made him feel like he was meant for her, and she for him.

"I don't want to promise I'll stay away completely, but I won't take over your life," he told her, turning to look at her face. Her eyes were downturned, watching her fingers as they fiddled with a buckle on her bag. She laughed at that, turning her emerald eyes to his.

"I find that somewhat hard to believe, Mister Keenan."

"I will try, but I make no promises," he told her, holding back the urge to lean over and kiss her smiling lips.

"I appreciate the effort, then," she said with a nod, equally trying to quell her own desires, as he was quite close, and she could feel the battle within him too.

"I did wonder about a few things," he said, glancing at his car, which was parked just behind hers, mostly as a distraction to keep himself in check. He had to uphold his word. If he couldn't do it after a minute, what good was it later?

"Hm?" she mumbled, turning her head to follow his gaze, mildly relieved that he broke the eye contact.

"Do you ever work with silver?" She raised her eyebrow, not fully understanding where his line of questioning was going. "Downing destroyed some of our… restraints, and I thought you might be able to fix them?"

"I *might* be able to. Silver is a rather soft metal," she told him, watching as he stood and walked to his car. From the passenger seat he pulled out a box of chains and shackles. Vee stood too, peering into the box to see the damage. There would be some soldering that she would need to do, but otherwise it seemed feasible. "Sure. I'll look at it tomorrow," she said, opening the back door to her car and gesturing for him to slip the box inside.

She found it very strange that she could feel a hint of something coming off those chains, like they were imbued with old powerful magic. It was a little surprising to her, having had no idea she could feel magic like that, but she supposed that's how she could tell the differences between preternaturals. She had just never been around an item that gave off its own vibration before.

"And one more odd question," he said once he closed the door, breaking her out of her confusion over her own abilities.

"You did say 'a few things' didn't you…" she mumbled, her face letting in the mild nervousness of not knowing his request.

"Can you tell that a child will turn before they go through the change?"

The way his voice wavered a little didn't even remotely amount to the wash of guilt she felt from him, now thinking again of Lori's change. How very different things could have been if they knew about her before it happened. Vee considered it for a moment. She hadn't really thought about such a thing before. She had noticed young children in the past that had a preternatural feel about them, but that was long before she fully grasped what each type was and what they meant, being that she was a small child at the time, herself.

"I don't know for sure, but I can try," she told him, realizing she was setting herself up to essentially meet every Were in the pack and their children. Shane couldn't hold back the reassurance he felt. The idea that his pack would, hopefully, never again be blind-sided by a young one changing, was comforting.

"Thank you," he said, sighing and letting some tension fall from his shoulders. He hated that he had to ask her, but ever since the thought popped into his head, he knew he needed to for his pack. Vee let herself feel his comfort, something she hadn't felt herself in quite a while. She found it fascinating how such a small thing that she did, could give him such an amazing feeling. She looked up at him, eyes still wary of the strange connection they had.

"Goodnight, Shane," she whispered, a faint smile on her lips.

"Goodnight, Vee," he said back, watching her move around to get into her car.

Durran sat atop the roof right above where Shane and Vee's little conversation had taken place. She had been watching all day, waiting for a moment when Vee was alone, but that moment had never come. Those little wolves had stayed all the way until the end, and then Shane was there, waiting.

She tried to find comfort in the fact that Vee had, while not outright rejecting Shane, put up a barrier. It would buy Durran some time to help Vee to see reason. That there was nothing good to come out of getting involved with Weres. She would have to repair what she had broken by letting her emotions get the better of her. Vee was a logical person, and Durran just needed to help her see that what she had been warning her about was the truth.

She watched as Vee drove away from her shop toward her home, leaving Shane standing on the side-walk, also watching her. She wanted to engage him, tell him he needed to stay away more than he had told Vee he intended to do. Her place was to watch and protect Vee, not his. But she knew starting a feud with this man would not lead to anything good.

How did Vee make her feel so irrational?

Cormac appeared, sitting beside her also looking down as Shane got in his own car and drove down the road. Thankfully, he turned to head back south to his neighborhood, but for a moment Durran had assumed the worst.

"Some Were drama going on with your human, Durran?" Cormac asked, turning to her once Shane's car was out of sight.

"A complication I hadn't been expecting," she said, turning her eyes to the darkening sky. He chuckled lightly.

"Yes, I'm a little surprised it didn't happen sooner, what with how often she seems to be working in that neighborhood," he said, looking down towards the bar scene that was starting to form a few blocks away. That took Durran aback. She turned to look at Cormac, sur-prise clear on her expression.

"What did you say?" Cormac looked back at her, assessing her expression.

"I had to learn about her to start my search," he explained, though his eyes flashed a little red as he spoke.

"I think you know enough, Cormac."

"You know, just as well as I, that beings fall into patterns, patterns that usually lead back to something," he said, shrugging a bit and turning away from her eyes which were now intensely glowing.

"What leads do you have?" Durran asked, trying not to snarl. Vee was *her* ward. Cormac didn't need to be getting any closer to her.

"That brother-in-law of hers has been doing some digging of his own. I've been trying to keep tabs on it. Seems like he hates her and is searching for a reason to completely cut her out of his wife's life. Once he has the information, I will have it, and I can go from there," he said, very matter of fact.

"You haven't been speaking with him?" Durran asked, horrified that he may have approached that dreadful man, and about Vee for that matter.

"No, no… I've been simply peeking over his shoulder while he pokes around."

"Frank has been trying to find a reason to cut her out, to isolate Vee from the only family she has, since Vee came back to the city. I doubt it will lead anywhere," Durran said, calming slightly, but her trust in Cormac was fading. It was one thing to look into Vee's past, to help find out what she was, it was quite another to be pushing his way into their lives. She could see, now, that he was a harbinger of bad luck, leading his previous wards down paths to ruin.

"Well, maybe I'll see something he didn't," he concluded, his voice smug and his face lighting up like a madman.

Regret.

Deep regret that shook her to her core was filling her. Why had she trusted him? Why had she always championed for him? He was set to be punished for hundreds of years because of the pain and death he brought upon his other wards, wards that would have changed the face of human history, had they been properly protected. She had unwittingly opened the door for him to do the same thing to Vee.

In that moment, she realized the werewolves were the least of her worries.

AUTHOR BIO

Chelsea Burton Dunn is a Kansas City native—the Missouri side, not the Kansas side. That matters to locals. Where is that you might ask? Right, smack-dab in the middle of the country. She has two beautiful children and is married to a superb partner, but let's not forget their two snuggly cats and eager-eater of a dog.

Having always been a little strange herself, she instantly fell in love with paranormal, supernatural, and fantasy books, movies, and tv shows as a child. Did everyone think it was a phase? Absolutely. Was it? Absolutely not. Being weird is a blessing, not a curse. She's always embraced that part of herself and those around her.

She started writing from a very early age, actually finishing a vampire novel in high school, but she had a bad experience with self-publishing and has since left that world she created behind, though she does boast a tattoo of a spade on her finger in its honor. She is a lover of music, having her other love and talent be for singing. She performed on main stage operas in the children's chorus from grade school to high school.

Chelsea loves to delve into the difficulties of life, love, and loss, while spicing it up with a little magic and monsters. As she liked to say when she was younger, "the monsters in my head need to come out to play every once in a while," so giving them life on the page seemed appropriate.

You can see more about Chelsea, her projects, and find her social medias by going to www.chelseaburtondunn.com

Sneak Peek at Moon Bound
Book 2 of the By Moonlight Series

It was rather cold, being March in Kansas City, but that didn't stop the individual outside the door of the locksmith shop from pounding on it relentlessly. Nor did the clearly labeled sign posted on the glass that read "Closed from 12 to 12:30 for Lunch." Vee glared out the glass door, lazily eating her sandwich and sipping her vending machine soda. She certainly wasn't in the mood for this; even knowing the person on the other side of the door was easily a great deal stronger and faster than she'd ever been.

To further her irritation, her sandwich fell apart as she took a bite, the kind of sandwich catastrophe that couldn't be fixed, so you had to either eat the individual ingredients separately or ditch the idea of eating it all together. With a more than frustrated sigh, she crumbled the paper it had been wrapped in and deposited it in the waste bin behind the counter.

Now that her lunch was ruined, she knew she might as well see what the hell the man banging on the glass, making it quiver as if it were to break, wanted. She walked slowly, leisurely to the door, pulling out the keys from her jean pocket and unlocking the deadbolt holding the door closed.

The tall, broad man yanked the door open and stormed through, forcing her to back up to make room for him. His large eyes, normally soft for such a burly looking man, burned with anger, like an animal on the hunt.

"Could you not pause from your precious sandwich long enough to do that fifteen minutes ago?" he asked, his voice booming and nearly shaking the glass of the doors and windows as much as his fist had.

"Can you not read?" she asked defiantly, pointing to the sign without breaking eye contact with the fuming man. He sucked in a breath through his teeth, closing his eyes and trying to center himself. He could not lose his temper with her.

"Damnit, Vee! What the hell is wrong with you? I came here because I was told to."

"I can tell. When you come in just to chat, you usually don't attempt to break down my door. Why don't you go run back and tell Shane I'm not in any mood for whatever it is he sent you here for? I'm not here for you all to just harass at any given time, Tommy. I'm tired of this endless stream of drama you all keep bringing me into," she hissed, her eyes narrowed and nostrils flared.

"That *we* keep bringing you into?" he practically growled at her, stepping closer so he towered over her. They were under the impression that she had gotten herself into this on her own. Helping someone in need didn't seem like a welcomed invitation to invade her life on a regular basis.

"Get out of my shop," she said, her voice firm and stance unwavering.

"I can't leave here. I'm following orders," Tommy said, a bit more calmly, obviously trying to be more rational despite the temper he had gathered from standing out in the bitter cold while she ate her lunch. Normally, Tommy was a much more easy-going person, but the bone-chilling winter air seemed to make him unreasonably grumpy.

"Call him, then," she practically spit, turning on her heel to go back behind the counter. It was times like these that she wished they didn't have a friendship. She hated yelling at him, but with this behavior, he deserved it.

He watched her for a moment as she turned off the message from the machine so calls could come back through and pulled out her tools for the lock she had been fixing before she stopped for lunch. She was completely ignoring his presence, and he rolled his eyes and began pulling out a rather small cell phone for such a large man, dialing the number to his boss.

"What?" came Shane's deep, graveled voice from the receiver.

"She wants me to leave," Tommy said, his eyes shifting to look at her again. She was still pretending he wasn't there.

"Well, that's not what I said for you to do. Did you explain why I sent you? Or did you barge in?"

Tommy winced, watching the smug smirk spread on Vee's lips. Tommy's pause was enough to tell Shane everything he needed to know about how that interaction went.

"Give her the phone," Shane growled as Tommy reluctantly handed the phone to Vee's small, outstretched hand.

"What, Shane?" she grumbled, wedging the ancient flip phone between her ear and her shoulder as she continued with the lock.

"I take it Tommy decided against using his words?"

"What else do you expect?"

"I sent him to stay with you and give you the news."

"News?" she asked, raising a questioning eyebrow he couldn't see. He sighed on the other side of the phone, and she heard the distinct sound of skin rubbing on skin. He was rubbing his forehead with frustration. It was a nervous habit of his.

"The Shawnee Leader is on his way for a meeting, and I haven't exactly been forthcoming about having you as an asset. I wanted you protected for the next few days until I'm sure we won't have any problems."

Vee rolled her eyes. The way he said asset, he might as well have said she was his property.

"I don't need protection. I'm sending Tommy back," she told him as she found the bent piece and unscrewed it carefully.

"You're not as strong as you think you are. You'll need Tommy if something goes wrong in the meeting," he said, his voice on edge with anger.

"I didn't sign any contract. I'm not your employee or anything else. Tommy goes back, and I don't hear from you unless you want a lock replaced or a safe installed. Got it?" But before he had time to answer, she snapped the phone shut and swiftly tossed it to the hulking man in her small shop. She had forgotten how satisfying it was to hang up on someone that way. Tommy caught it, surprised, which amused her, and stood there for a long moment. "What are you doing? Shoo," she said, waving her hands as if they would magically rid him from her sight.

"I can't believe you talked to him that way," his voice as surprised as his expression.

"Well, I did. Now go," she said pointing to the door and narrowing her eyes, daring him to protest. On any other day, she would have been fine with him sitting in her shop and chatting with her, but today, knowing he was on orders, she didn't want him within a hundred feet of it.

BOOK CLUB QUESTIONS

1. Who do you think Vee will end up with: Durran or Shane? Should she start a relationship with either of them? Why or why not?

2. Who was your favorite/least favorite character(s)? Why?

3. Do you think Vee and her sister will ever have a relationship again? Why or why not?

4. Should Eliza leave her husband because of the way he treats Vee? Why or why not?

5. Vee's powers as an empath can be viewed as an overlap with expectations that women cater to others' emotions. Since Vee is a tomboy who

doesn't engage with her own femininity very deeply, can we connect her rejection of her powers with her rejection of her own femininity? If so, in what ways? If not, why?

6. Do you think Midi the cat is more than just a normal cat? Why do you think this way?

7. Why do you think Durran chose a female form when Vee became her ward?

8. Do you think the author had this story take place in Kansas City, quite literally in the middle of the country, as a metaphor for Vee's own life, since she is stuck with the difficulties of being between worlds? Do you think it would be better set somewhere else? Where?

9. What do you think Vee is since she doesn't seem to be any known preternatural?